Benefit

Benefit

SIOBHAN PHILLIPS

Bellevue Literary Press
NEW YORK

First published in the United States in 2022
by Bellevue Literary Press, New York

For information, contact:
Bellevue Literary Press
90 Broad Street
Suite 2100
New York, NY 10004
www.blpress.org

This is a work of fiction. Characters, organizations, events, and places (even those that are actual) are either products of the author's imagination or are used fictitiously.

Library of Congress Cataloging-in-Publication Data
Names: Phillips, Siobhan, author.
Title: Benefit / Siobhan Phillips.
Description: First edition. | New York: Bellevue Literary Press, 2022.
Identifiers: LCCN 2021033503 | ISBN 9781942658993 (paperback) | ISBN 9781954276000 (epub)
Subjects: LCGFT: Novels.
Classification: LCC PS3616.H473 B46 2022 | DDC 813/.6--dc23
LC record available at https://lccn.loc.gov/2021033503

Bellevue Literary Press would like to thank all its generous donors—individuals and foundations—for their support.

 This project is supported in part by an award from the National Endowment for the Arts.

This publication is made possible by the New York State Council on the Arts with the support of the Office of the Governor and the New York State Legislature.

Book design and composition by Mulberry Tree Press, Inc.

Bellevue Literary Press is committed to ecological stewardship in our book production practices, working to reduce our impact on the natural environment.

♾ This book is printed on acid-free paper.

Manufactured in the United States of America.

First Edition

10 9 8 7 6 5 4 3 2 1

paperback ISBN: 978-1-942658-99-3
ebook ISBN: 978-1-954276-00-0

Benefit

1

I STOPPED WORKING IN AUGUST 2011, after I saw Mark Harriman at a symposium on war. I'd lost my teaching job three weeks prior. "A Decade of Global Conflict"—that was the symposium, part of a list of university events still deposited automatically into my email once a week. I recognized Mark's name under "distinguished speakers." He and I knew each other briefly, right after college, when we were both Weatherfield fellows. Before the global conflict. So that was more than a decade ago, I thought when I saw the announcement. Of course I knew it was. Still.

Losing the teaching job, I should clarify, wasn't what made me stop working. That post had always been temporary, stopgap, two introductory English classes a term at a small all-women's school north of Boston, renewed semester by semester as I stayed on in my Cambridge apartment applying for permanent positions. "It's fine," I said automatically to the assistant dean when he called. "It's fine." My mind accepted his regretful news with the speed at which one can seize on a bad outcome already much imagined. The dean felt terrible, he explained, especially given my exemplary performance, though he knew nothing about my performance except for the patchy comments on student evaluations. One I remembered: *She seems like she'll be a hard grader but she isn't.* "It's fine," I said again. I hung up on our mutual embarrassment as soon as I could. Losing the teaching job meant I worked more. I could spend all my time on a revise-and-resubmit I needed to finish, an essay about Henry James's friendships. The first version was theoretical—what was James's idea of human connection?; now I turned it historical, assembling sandy heaps of details into which I might pour additional effort. Lists of names. The one-bedroom I rented didn't have air-conditioning. I left the windows open to the dark when I was too tired to read anymore, then came to a sweaty consciousness around two or three without any sensation of rest except the knowledge of waking. Sometimes I fell back into sleep around four or five.

Losing the job did mean I had no source of income, and I couldn't logically renew my lease at the end of the month; I called my mother and asked if I could stay with her for a bit. "Are you all right?" she said. "Of course. Labor Day? That will be nice. And you're okay? It's no trouble. You're sure?" I wanted to get off that phone call, too. But my mother's baffled worry at the world has always accompanied her acceptance of it. And I would be all right: the security deposit, plus I could sell my car, which still worked, some of my furniture maybe— this is what I figured, almost instantly, while listening to the assistant dean. I would be all right. "I'm just working," I said to my mother. "I just need a place to work." I drove over to a strip mall in Allston, where a bored man in a coverall showed me the rectangle of aluminum and concrete into which I could place all the cheap books and printed-out articles that wouldn't fit into my mother's house back in Royce. Also my yard-sale desk, if I wanted, my card table, my milk crates of pans and stained mugs and mismatched bowls. In my twenties I seem to have eaten most meals out of bowls. "Climate-controlled," the man told me, and spit, though that couldn't have been true without a strange definition of *control*. I carted my things over in six trips.

This felt like working, too. I should have rented a van. I should have asked to borrow a larger car from someone—easier, quicker. I didn't have enough money, though, or the right friends, and I trusted whatever took the most time and effort. I assumed more was better, or would prove to have been better, at some future date. Further along than a decade, evidently. This faith had always been what I substituted for ambition; the Weatherfield Foundation identified "students of promise and ambition." I promised only to work. James, for example—James was my chosen specialty because his collected writings seemed to offer not only the most frustrations but also the fewest rewards. He produced many long books that grow progressively more difficult without ever becoming obviously experimental or solidly classic. James's writing would never be significant or easy. On this I had spent a decade. On this I could spend a lifetime.

Yet I think I knew my reliance on sheer effort wouldn't fool others that long. Rejection—jobs, the last job—didn't entirely surprise me. Acceptance surprised me. The Weatherfield, for example. There were twenty-four fellows each year granted some paid postgraduate time at Oxford or the Sorbonne, universities at which the fellowship's patron, a younger-son American heir to money from Weatherfield Sugar, spent some of his aimless Gilded Age adulthood not quite getting a degree. Most of the others chosen seemed not to have reached this point in their lives by striving to make sure that there was always more to do. Except Mark, maybe—Mark wasn't at all like me, but I recognized in him a familiar drive toward the uselessly difficult. I'm sure I took justification from it. Once, he mentioned that he had picked his events in swimming because they were the hardest—this was after he repeated a mocking comment from someone else about his status as a dumb jock, to which I responded that I thought he was a swimmer, and he laughed and said, "What are you implying?" and then, to my apologies, my protestations, "Don't worry. I'm kidding."

"Okay," I agreed, relieved. "I was trying to pay a compliment."

And he was only half kidding. "Swimming is hard, you know."

I nodded. "What is your thing? Is that the question? Your event?"

"Distance." He explained: "five hundred free, one thousand free, sixteen fifty free."

"And those are the hardest."

"Well, it's subjective, what's hardest." He reconsidered. "But yeah, the sixteen fifty—" He stopped, shrugged, looking down and away. "It doesn't matter."

I said, "It matters." I stopped there. You don't need to dissemble, I wanted to say. But to mention the tactic presumed too much. That would have to wait. Mark was tall and broad and muscular, with pale, mottled skin and rough reddish hair, too irregular in his features to be uncomplicatedly good-looking while offering a restful impression of steady physical competence. With this, though, came an almost sheepishness, diffidence shielding the intensity. Publicity and hearsay in our little group of American fellowship winners already knew that he held some sort of college athletic record along with a perfect undergraduate GPA; during social gatherings, he was often gently teased about his accomplishments, in the reassuring assumption that no teasing could rile him. Yet his serenity was watchful. His characteristic expression was that half shrug accompanied by a glance down and away—to avoid pretension, to let everyone off. "Yeah, well—" Others could relax, should relax; others should experiment or enjoy or be themselves. He had things to do. Since we left Oxford, Mark had completed the Marine Corps Officer Candidates School and been commissioned as an officer in the United States Marine Corps and served three tours in Iraq and one tour in Afghanistan.

I read the biography in the symposium program. I got to the event a little late. I didn't put to myself why I was going, the day before I left Cambridge with the last of my boxes packed—I didn't ask why because I'd never really decided to go. I slipped into the back of the small auditorium at the Mitchell Center, where wide carpeted tiers of seats looked down on a stage, a podium, a table and chairs for panelists. The room was full. I was the only one in jeans.

But a friendly older man in the back row, shifting to let me find a seat, didn't seem bothered by my presence. "Are you at the center?" he asked.

"No, I . . ." A pause. His question was kindness, I knew; at these sorts of events, it was welcome: say where you belonged. I didn't have a good answer to where I belonged or what I did or what I was—no longer a student, no longer or not yet a professor. I usually said "an academic," a convenient adjective turned noun that indicated something irrelevant, or something tied to a certain kind of institution. "I thought it was open to the public," I said.

"Of course," he said. "Very important."

I went back to the program. Up front someone making introductions explained how lucky we were to hear from a variety of experts, including those with "real on-the-ground experience. This symposium is about letting those different experiences talk to one another."

Everyone on stage nodded. Four men in suits. I didn't see Mark anywhere.

o O o

I don't want to give the impression that Mark and I talked much to each other back in our fellowship days. We were not friends. A kind of sorting happened with various supposedly selective groups of postgraduates, and the small size of the Weatherfield cohort did not exempt us, made divisions more important, rather. Small towns maintain good and bad neighborhoods as compact as a couple of blocks. I grew up in the not-good-enough part of Royce but didn't expect to recognize so firm a consensus, so quickly, about which Weatherfield fellows were, in fact, going to be distinguished, famous, powerful and which others would fade into a respectable professionalism. The third option was hardly to be entertained; at worst you could do something offbeat, like the fellow a few years older who moved to Berlin and became a sculptor. Mark was friends with Greta, who went to Dartmouth and studied chemistry; Caroline, from Brown, who had already spent a year working for an NGO in Senegal; Justin, who went to Yale and knew three or four languages and played the cello; Zac, Stanford, currently working at a biotech firm in Silicon Valley. Others of the successful group seemed slightly more independent—Heather, for example, who graduated from a state school and studied math. But Mark and Greta and Justin and Caroline and Zac—as far as I could tell—were the ones who met for pints in the evening and stopped by one another's rooms without invitation or reason and decided together where they would travel during term breaks. "Is Mark coming?" one of these friends might ask, in his absence from a required event where the full group of us milled about, and another might reply, "I'll text him," or "Yeah, he said he'd be late." They talked enough to know where they all were.

Meanwhile, Mark and I had, I think, a total of three conversations. The first was in the fifth or sixth week of Michaelmas term, when we both were assigned to a dinner with a wealthy donor who had graduated about four decades before. These meals happened once in a while, purpose unclear. A card arrived: The dress code was "smart." Smart was difficult for women. But I squashed my worry over the ambiguity with the thought of a free meal; living stipends, I found, drained quickly if they were all you had to live on, even though I didn't eat out much, nor did I often buy tickets to the Hall. Mostly I heated soup and assembled sandwiches in the kitchen at one end of my dorm floor: a sort of toaster oven, a sink, one burner, a fridge with defensively labeled cartons of expired milk. I took food back to my room as I continued my attempt to read everything already written about the topic of my weekly essay. My room was a 1970s-era bed-sit with thin orange carpet in a concrete block off one of the side streets, the kind of structure tourists edit out of their Oxford impressions. Sometimes, admittedly, I panicked that I was not experiencing enough; then I scheduled an hour to look at labels in the Ashmolean or spent five pounds on a chunk of the strangest-looking cheese I could find in the covered market. But I couldn't manage enough of those spasms of real life to make them amount to anything, nor did I know what they were supposed to amount to; I went back to my schedule of work, my notebook of page numbers and quotations.

At the dinner with Mark, however, in Mark's sure management of the alumnus, I could pretend for a little while that I was making memories to which I would later return with fondness and pride. The three of us met at a low-ceilinged restaurant with a fire and a piano and a few small rooms of round white-clothed tables. The menu included an elevated rarebit and a trout of noteworthy origin and an interpretation of toffee pudding. Outside, the evening dampness thickened into rain. I remember Mark arrived in a lined trench coat over his suit. The right outerwear was a step above the basics of "smart," the dark skirt into which I had squeezed my always unsatisfactory thighs. But Mark was consistently well dressed as well as trim, well dressed in a manner stylish for being absolutely free of originality. I suppose his attitude toward clothing somehow made it more rather than less plausible that he would end up in uniform. He talked with the older man about half blues and the Port Meadow; he confirmed the happy memories of what didn't change and sympathized with the regretful memories of what did. Mark already had plans for Bonfire Night. He put "sir" on the end of his replies until the other said, "No need for that 'sir,'" after which Mark sounded just as natural with a first name. I was not natural about anything. Following a brief question about my course of study, the alumnus only asked about a Shakespeare scholar he had studied with, a genius, "but he probably retired."

"Yes, he retired," I agreed.

"Really."

"Uh—I'll check."

"Oh, it doesn't matter."

I hated again my tendency to automatic assent, in conversation, when I was nervous—it felt like I was always nervous—and I resolved not to say anything I didn't know to be true. At coffee, when the older man decided to give me one last chance, looking over with an avuncular indulgence to ask about me, my future, had I ever "thought about public service"—I swallowed and began: "Well . . ." What would be the truth? "Probably not." On the walk home, I tried to apologize.

Mark looked at me sidelong, assessing, and didn't reassure

me too quickly. I appreciated that. "You think it went bad?" he asked.

"No, you did fine," I said. I also appreciated his blunt, not-quite-grammatical question. "He liked talking to you."

"He just liked talking." Mark thought for a moment more, his face intent; then his forehead smoothed and he half-shrugged, a decision: "I think we did okay."

I held on to the "we." The two of us shared his umbrella, walking too quickly and closely to get out of the rain; I could feel the uncertainty of my heels on slick cobblestones every few steps, and my elbow just grazing his.

"You all right?" he asked.

"Yes." I looked for something else to say. "That guy wants you to run for office."

Mark waited long enough to respond that I had time to realize this was the wrong topic. Then, more quietly: "Yeah, well." That look down and away. I kept silent for a half block more.

The rain went peevish. Mark squinted at his phone and steered us into the recessed gate of a college to read the screen under cover. "Where are you headed? You meeting everyone at the Turf?"

I was not meeting everyone. I did not know about these meetings, or about everyone, really. "I have to work."

"You do?"

"I have an essay."

"For real?" His voice sort of lilted when he was interested.

"Yes." He was waiting. "A real essay," I said, making a grimace.

Mark didn't match my mockery. He was serious. He said, "You're showing me up."

"What do you mean?"

He shook his head. "You're doing it."

"It's just work."

"Nah." He stared, figuring something out. I gave the sort of exhaling laugh that signals someone is looking too hard to see you. That didn't change his demeanor, either. "I got it," he said.

"What?"

"All that stuff about Henry James."

"Oh, God. At dinner? Please forget that. I don't know what I was saying."

He smiled. "You said a lot of it."

"I'm sorry."

"No, it's all good. You're like—" He stopped. "I got the name right?"

"James? Yes."

"I didn't take many literature classes."

"Yes, why would you." I knew something about his kind of interest: the wary respect for literature held by men—mostly men—who read a few novels and recognize a few poems, or who plan to read and recognize a few later, as an enrichment for their political theory or physics classes and their lifetime of medicine or law. But I already took irrelevance as a sort of fortification. I said, "It's fine."

"Well, I want to." He stopped smiling; he seemed almost aggressive. The conversation deflated. Then Mark rallied and squinted at me. "For real, though. You always work this much? I mean work this late?"

"If I have to—well, yeah. I always do. Often."

"Cool." He cut me off. "So we could work together sometime."

"Work together?"

"If you want, I mean."

"Yes! Or—yes. Whatever." I didn't know what I was agreeing to. That didn't seem to matter to my reaction.

"Right on. I'll email." Mark held up one hand.

brought a bottle of bourbon, made fun of the sweet potatoes, and added his tactics for getting through tutorials, hungover, without having read the book. "You just pick some line in the first paragraph and say you didn't quite understand and you really want someone else to explain and then someone else talks for the whole session while you nod like yeah, uh-huh, okay, writing this down—" Laughter at this, the kind that both disowns and endorses. Zac brought stuffing—the stuffing wasn't bad but wasn't right; the herbs were different. But caring about any of this was beneath us; Thanksgiving was stupid—what it remembered, what it lied about. Mark took a large plate and ate steadily and smiled at others' tales and didn't add any of his own. He had not, of course, emailed me about working together. He sat near Caroline, who collected money for the perfectly roasted turkey she'd ordered. Heather came with an extra tray of cookies and whipped cream for the inadequate number of pies. I made the sweet potatoes, from a recipe of my mother's I misremembered. Mark bought bakery rolls, his assignment, and a container of cranberry sauce that was unexpected and much lauded by everyone attending—that much tasted genuine.

I left early. I was trying more, by November, to do things that weren't work: I loaned a mug to the Kenyan chemist who lived a floor below me and was working on the total synthesis of a compound usually made by a marine sponge, and one afternoon I walked around the Deer Park. I took the bus to London to hear *La Traviata* and see an exhibition of Rembrandt etchings. I should know about opera, about art. I hadn't read the book on which the opera was based and worried about that too much to decide what I thought about the music, but at the Rembrandt show, I stared for a long time at a print of a bridge, wondering about its combination of absolute precision and some sort of ease. Over the winter break, I decided that I would use the money I saved from not flying home to buy a winter coat and a better suitcase—smaller; all I had was my mother's old, square, hard-backed Samsonite. These purchases made sense to me.

The second time Mark and I definitely exchanged words was, I think, January. I heard an intercom buzz one night when I was about to go to bed. I thought it was a mistake until it repeated, longer. Mark's voice on the other end had the controlled tone of someone remaining calm in a difficult situation, for everyone's sake: "Yeah, could you come down for a sec?" When I pulled jeans back on, got a cardigan over my T-shirt, pushed my bare feet into clogs, made my way to the street, I saw Greta was with him. She stood apart near the other narrow curb with her arms crossed and her head down, and when I got closer, I could see that she was crying, muttering under her breath, also drunk.

"I remembered you lived here," Mark said. "Would you walk her home with me?"

"Are you okay?"

"We're fine; she just needs to get home is all?"

It was the kind of question that seemed more authoritative than a statement. I said, "Right." We steered back to her dorm, awkward, mostly silent, and Mark asked for Greta's keys and opened her door. He waited outside. I gathered that I was supposed to go in and sit among the discarded clothing and empty diet soda cans in her room as she pulled off her sweater and bra and jeans and kicked her loafers in different directions and finally stomped into the adjoining bathroom to take a shower. "Are you sure . . ." I think I said.

But the shower calmed or sobered her or both, and she came back, glowing, in track pants and two tank tops layered on top of each other. She pulled a comb through her long hair and the thick floral haze of her shampoo suffused the room. "I feel gross." She looked hale and strong. Her eyes still hadn't met mine. She flipped her hair over. "All right, you don't have to babysit anymore, I'm going to bed, see, I have water, I have Tylenol, I'm fine, go tell Mark." Mark was leaning against the wall outside. When I said that she was okay he was already moving off, hands shoved into his pockets.

He said, "I'll walk you back."

"You don't have to."

"It's late," he said, automatically, before pausing to look at his watch. "Midnight." He put a hand to his forehead for one pained intake of breath.

"You okay?"

"Yeah." He tried to shake off his worry. We started again. "It's cool." Then after a bit: "Greta goes out a lot."

"She does?"

"Greta's a scientist." As if this were the logical response.

"She is."

"What's your program again? Right, literature. How did you decide?"

"It's what I've always done. I mean—I don't remember."

"Ah." He nodded. "Yeah. Okay."

"No, not like that. I wasn't single-minded. I just—I just kept going."

He waited. He didn't understand.

I said, "You don't like your program?"

He shook his head, a slow rhythm. Weary disappointment. "It's kicking my ass."

"Oh," I said. Then: "Sorry."

"I did history in college. It's the major for people who don't know what they want."

"But you did well." He couldn't answer that, so I said, "You have time. You don't have exams till next year."

"Collections," he pointed out.

"They don't count."

This was true. But Mark said, "Yeah, well—" and looked away, disappointed this time. He was walking too quickly, his hands still in his jeans pockets. "I go to these tutorials?" he said. "The others know what they think. They read their essays. They have it all worked out. You know what I mean?"

"Yes," I said.

"I'm like, really? When did you decide that?"

"Yes," I said.

"I can't tell if I'm not smart enough or it's something else."

"Yes," I said.

He stopped for a second to look at me. He had been expecting reassurance.

"I mean—"

"Nah, it's okay. You don't have to say anything."

We were walking again. The comment about dumb jocks was probably from Justin. I could hear Justin saying it with the openly ironic tone that gets away with what could be an insult. Plenty of other fellows were athletes, but most of them were from different sorts of schools—Mark and I had both gone to small private colleges that were not especially distinguished. Mostly, I assumed those who held firm opinions had already read everything, though I also knew that couldn't be true; mostly, I didn't understand how they decided to stop reading and make up their minds. Every new list of things I needed to know only got longer, as it went backward—for James I needed all of Emerson; for Emerson I needed all of Goethe. My only reassurance was if I stayed in school as a career I might have time to catch up. If I worked enough. "You still have time to work," I told Mark.

"Yeah," he said. "I do." He seemed genuinely more relaxed. We were at my door.

"Thanks," I told him. "I honestly didn't need you to walk me back."

That sounded churlish, but Mark wasn't listening: "What are you up to now?" he asked.

"Probably sleep?"

He shook his head. "Right. Sorry." Then he squinted and got out his phone. "Do I have your number, though?"

I gave it. It was the early days of cell phones, and in England they could be cheaper than landlines, so almost every student had one. I barely used mine. Mark had an easy relationship with technology. He enjoyed handling machines. It was like clothing—he knew how things worked, he knew the rules, and he knew what he could do with them.

"I'll text you," he said, and then, half skeptical at his own idea, as if just coming up with it, considering the proposal as he voiced it: "We could work together sometime." He was not considering my agreement.

I had my keys out. "Sure," I said, "that might be good."

In my room was the facedown copy of *Portrait of a Lady* I had abandoned to brush my teeth. I had almost made it to the end, where the main character sees a ghost.

And of course I don't mean to imply that Mark wasn't smart, though others, other fellows, seemed to have a different relationship to intelligence as well as to work. I remember, at one of the all-hands social gatherings that spring—birthday drinks in the college bar—when someone asked a question about an Aristotle lecture and someone else—Caroline?—replied in a bored, dismissive voice that yes, all the smart people were rediscovering virtue ethics, and then a third—Justin?—repeated "Smart people?" and everyone laughed. We were smart people because we were laughing at the idea. Some of us were. By that point in the year social routines seemed to be fraying; fewer replied to that one email thread with all of our names on it; Justin and Greta bickered over the rubble of a grocery store cake about her refusal to abandon an experiment in the lab and go out with him after. She was really getting somewhere, she said. She didn't want to drink more. Caroline told Justin to lay off. "Just don't be like Mark," Caroline said to Greta. Mark was sitting slightly apart, forking up bites; he was single-minded about eating. "The good soldier going to the optional lectures." Mark didn't reply. He had not, of course, texted me about working together. The original structure of that bar was built in the fourteenth century, maybe earlier; you had to duck through the entrance. Walls of creamy irregular plaster rose into rounded corners and slightly crooked beams. Justin thought it worth mentioning, when it came to virtue ethics, that the PPE degree was outdated, establishment, and colonialist. Was anyone going to defend it? Not Caroline. Caroline shook her head and held up her hands, laughing. Mark was not going to defend it, Justin continued, now that he had a collection prize. "Does everyone know"—Justin raised his voice a bit to the half dozen picking over sticky plates, to the others not from our party drinking in a different part of the room, to the student cleaning taps with a rag—"that Mark here won a collection prize?" Mark got up to throw away his plastic fork and told Justin to shut up. Justin said he should take pride. Mark got a beer. He liked to drink and eat in sequence, so he could concentrate on each in turn. Greta looked disgusted; Caroline laughed again. No one else added to the exchange. I left a few minutes later.

Onstage, someone was nodding. Someone else was describing the "decade following September 11, 2001" as "one of the most crucial the world has ever known." Renata, my adviser in graduate school, once underlined *crucial* on a draft; Renata immigrated to the United States and kept scrupulous track of the words people in this country regularly disrespected. "Crucial," she wrote next to my sentence, "really occurring at a crux?" I don't think I've used *crucial* since.

o O o

And then the second year was a turning point, of course. The rest of the Weatherfield mission, after identifying "promise and ambition," wanted to "provide these students with inspiration and enrichment for their own benefit and the betterment of society," and what it provided instead was maybe a year of delay before everybody needed to figure out once more what came next. Most already knew. Greta had deferred attendance at medical school. Zac and Mark and Caroline would go to law school. Justin would live in New York; he wrote reviews, already, for a weekly paper there. Grad school in general was a possibility, or other additional fellowships. Certain jobs also seemed possible—certain specific jobs. On 9/11 itself I was in Puerto Rico, in fact, at a three-day seminar sponsored by a management consultancy firm so that young graduates of outstanding potential could see what consultancy might be like. Weatherfields were invited as a matter of course, though those who mattered were supposed to refuse the invitation, with its embarrassingly obvious mixture of vetting and recruitment to the embarrassingly obvious quest of making money. I realized this only after I arrived, but at least I hated the conference, which over and over presented us with invented companies and asked us to determine how each might increase profits without compromising "core values." I assume these were also invented. At least I was inept at the assigned tasks. When I heard about the attack on the Twin Towers I felt, along with confusion and grief, a craven worry that the news meant we couldn't leave. We couldn't, for three more days. By that point Congress was voting to authorize military force against terrorists: open-ended, whatever it took.

We couldn't leave the country, of course—we could probably have left our hotel, but no one did; guests collected instead in the lobby, drifting like the schools of fish in a nearby aquarium, gathering up those who wandered near in their shock and uncertainty and moving on to the bar or buffet area before separating and dispersing and floating back again. Waiters brought out trays of lemonade and sparkling water and gave away all the glasses and then hovered without collecting empties. Everyone hovered. Rooms were equipped with televisions but many seemed to want to watch in public spaces. There was so little to watch, and that little was so much—the distant silent flash of the explosion, the fuzzy interviews with eyewitnesses on the street, the terrifying slow-motion clips of collapse, the statements of hastily assembled terrorism experts, security personnel, and transportation reporters. Each image and comment and scrap of conversation appeared over and over, so the real-time coverage was a loop of stunned surprise, reinforcing with firmer and firmer certainty a basic uncertainty: "We simply don't know what is going on." "A huge shock for everyone." "It's equally possible they know no more than we do."

We didn't leave; also, events were suspended. Events were over, mostly. We'd all been marshaled to a final party the previous night, when a group of blond women in navy suits who called themselves "support staff," along with a number of more efficient and less cheerful employees of the hotel, set up a small wooden platform on the beach. White lights fuzzed into a patch of darkness; badly amplified bass thumped over chatter: We all had to cap our weekend by eating and drinking and dancing a lot. Consultants worked hard and played hard; one somehow implied the other. But this was the only way to get dinner, so I waded out into the sand to eat beef and grilled vegetables off a large white plate. The food was not very good. It hadn't been all weekend, and its plenty added to the confusion of my despair. I had the urge to go through our daily "breakouts" and collect all the bite-size cubes of unripe tropical fruit on abandoned trays as we practiced the right jobs to cut after an imaginary merger. "We're interested in talking to you," a Putnam Marsh partner told us via video screen the first day as we ate some bland meat the buffet card labeled "jerk chicken," "because we know you will appreciate an atmosphere of real meritocracy." We were told to define our "core skills." The company's policy was "up or out." It was the same policy used by the U.S. military. I finished eating as quickly as possible and walked back up the path toward my room holding a glass with three ice cubes and too much whiskey. The liquor was pretty good, if you ordered it straight. I could get just a little tipsy in my room.

"Laura." Mark stood to one side of the path, under a rhododendron just outside my door.

"You scared me." The drink shook. I'd been trying not to think about Mark. I was surprised he'd come at all. And then I didn't see him; he must have skipped some group talks about global reach or active listening or leadership as responsibility. It was not like him to skip things.

"Sorry." He exhaled. A cigarette looked small in his hand.

"What are you doing?"

"You want one?"

"Yes." He fished out a pack. I asked, "Were you waiting for me?"

He ignored that. "I didn't think you'd go to the party," he said. He emphasized the last word, or maybe slurred it a little.

"I got some food." I leaned forward to a light in his cupped hands. It took a moment. I could smell his breath, tipsy and nicotined, and his fingers. I was aware of the proximity of his body, his warmth, his scent. "Thanks." I exhaled once. I tried not to smoke very often in those days because I couldn't afford to and it felt so good when I did. Now I never smoke, of course. "I got a drink."

He said, "Can I have some of that?"

I gave him the whiskey. I probably shouldn't have. His eyes already looked bright and jumpy. He didn't return the cup. It was plastic, molded to look like an old-fashioned glass. "Are you okay?" I asked.

"I'm good." He drank. He confirmed this, convincing himself: "I'm good."

"You want to come in?"

He didn't answer. He drank more. He said, "So you want this job, huh." His tone was a dare. It wasn't a tone that men used on women. Not usually.

I said, "You mean Putnam Marsh?"

"Yes."

"I wouldn't get it."

He made an expression I couldn't decode. Disgust was part of it. "I thought you did literature."

The last word—more disgust, or maybe that, too, was the sprawl of alcohol. I moved away from the aggression anyway. "What about you?" I asked, careful.

"Yeah. What about me." He threw the ice from my glass into the bushes. A quick jerk of the wrist. For a moment, I thought he was going to throw the glass, too. But he caught himself. I looked around almost by instinct—checking if someone else had seen or overheard. Mark said, "Sorry."

"Maybe you should come inside."

"Okay."

I ground out the cigarette and unlocked my door. The rooms were less spacious than one might expect, though mine had a little patio. Mark paced the length, as if assessing the dimensions, assessing how much of them he took up. A lot. I asked, "Do you want some water?"

"Do you have any more whiskey?"

"I can get some."

"Forget it." He turned his back to look out. "I've been thinking."

I waited.

"I don't want to go on with this bullshit."

"Which?" I was still waiting near the doorway.

"I think the most important thing is not to do anything you don't want."

"Okay."

"Right? You can't be honest otherwise."

"Well—"

"Pretending just makes everything worse." He looked out into the darkness.

I said, "Pretending about what?"

He didn't answer.

I said, "You don't have the job yet." I meant this to be comforting; it came out accusatory. This happened a lot, this switch.

He said, "I'm not really talking about a job?"

"The degree?"

He didn't answer. "I guess I sound like an asshole."

"No."

"When I left for England, everyone at home—my family, I mean—was like, 'Mark is in England.' That was the point. I didn't have to do anything else. And then I'm like, 'Here I am, what is the point? What am I doing?' And my mom is all, 'You've worked so hard to get this far.'" He made a scornful gesture that was more forceful than he probably meant and the blinds at the screen door danced a little. He pulled his fist back and looked at it.

I said, "Maybe you should have some water."

"Yeah, sure."

On the counter of the bathroom stood two liter bottles I hadn't dared move before now. I wasn't sure if I would be charged. I gave Mark one.

"Thanks," he said.

I said, "I don't really care about your degree."

He drank. "Yeah," he said. "Yeah, I know."

"I don't even know what your degree is about."

"Yeah." He reflected. "Me, neither."

PPE was philosophy, politics, and economics, the program for everyone in Britain who wanted to work in government or near it and for everyone from the United States who wanted to go to law school or run for office. It began just after World War I in the confusion and hope of what was thought to be a new world order, when Modern Greats opened up Oxford degrees to students without training in ancient Greek from elite schools and ensured that Oxford graduates continued to administer properly the conditions of contemporary life: war, revolution, depression, colonies. Justin was probably right about PPE.

Mark said, "Also my mom is awesome."

It made me smile, that word. But his tone still felt violent. I sat on the little chair in the corner with the balls of my feet on the floor and let the wicker knuckle into my thighs. "Tell me about what you want," I said. "Tell me what happened."

"Nothing happened," he said quickly. He'd spent the summer in Washington, in an internship, going to meetings, living with a roommate whose goals were to acquire cocaine and get invited to this party thrown every month by a political staffer

Mark hated, and then he went back for two weeks to his hometown in Ohio, where his father ran an auto-parts store and his mother—his mother didn't work except that she did the accounts for his father and a couple of other stores; so yeah, she worked, but she wasn't—anyway, I knew what he meant. He had two sisters—one of them was engaged to a good guy—and he had a little brother who was autistic and went to school every day, even in the summer, on a special bus. This wasn't what I'd asked, but I kept quiet. Mark had never said this much to me before. He sat on the floor, his knees near his shoulders, his forearms resting on his knees. As he talked, he unscrewed and rescrewed the cap of the water bottle quickly. His parents married for love, he said. He said this matter-of-factly, as he would say that they married in June. He was the first man in his family to have a college degree. He stopped. "What am I talking about?" he asked me.

"You're talking about not doing anything you don't want," I said.

He looked at me then. He leaned over and hit my knee with the water bottle, gently. It felt so intimate I almost shivered. He smiled. "Don't listen to me."

"Oh, never."

"Don't listen to me, but you know what I mean."

I was struck again by the sheer physical fact of his body—its size, its force. The confident way he deployed it. I thought about what would be the true thing to say. "No, not really."

"Not really?"

"I mean you haven't said yet what you mean."

He smiled then. "Right." The word evolving as it formed. Then: "Right on. See. That's how it is with you. This is why—" He stopped.

I waited. "What?"

He didn't answer, but his face suggested he'd made a decision. "You want something to drink?"

"Sure."

"I'm going to get something to drink."

"Okay."

"What should I bring you?"

"You choose."

"Okay. I'll be right back. And we can talk."

I agreed: "We can talk." He left.

Late afternoon on Tuesday after I could finally call my mother, I put on a bathing suit and walked out to the beach again. The weekend's schedule had not allowed any swimming. The water was warm, salty, so clear as to be unnerving. Mark had not returned with drinks, of course, the night before. I kicked out to the end of the area cordoned off for the safety of hotel guests and did a few laps back and forth. I floated. Then I came back in and tiptoed through the lobby toward my room. The television was still repeating that the attack had changed everything, and we flew home on Friday through enhanced security. But in a couple of weeks the Weatherfield fellows had returned to England and France, and at the end of the academic year, when results came in, I missed a distinction by three points; my paper on Henry James, the professor explained at our final meeting, substituted details for argument. I hadn't asked him for this explanation. He sounded regretful. Mark got a first in PPE.

In June, I moved back to the United States to start a doctorate and Mark enlisted. The weekend in Puerto Rico faded. Years after, if the question came up—"Where were you when . . ." —I could say, "A hotel, weirdly enough" and not think about Mark's high five before he left my room. When he walked out he was still fiddling with the cap on the water bottle. I didn't, in the end, have to pay for that, or maybe the consultancy firm paid, or maybe I should have paid and I got away with something.

Onstage at the Mitchell Center, a panelist was talking about the importance of building bridges between civilians and the military. He was explaining the center's directive to connect people and make visible the experience of war.

o O o

This was the last topic of the morning—a culmination of sorts. Earlier discussions had focused on terrorism, torture, and the law; then democracy, democratization, and sectarianism. Experts cautioned one another on the importance of economics and ideology, the specifics of geography and religion, the deep-rooted tendencies of extremism and secularism. Caution, specificity: These were the tones of the panels. The correct tones. I wasn't really listening. I tried to remind myself that it was right, the opposite of wrong; it was good that professors and strategists and veterans stand at podiums and point to slides and pass a microphone back and forth during the question and answer period: "What we can say now—" "The evidence suggests—" "I'll only add—" This is how we avoid mistakes, learning from experience. How someone does.

I think I'd followed the war about as well as most people over the decade prior. I think I knew about as well as most people how stupid it was, how futile, how incompetently handled, murderous, bigoted, how wrong. I knew these things in the vague way one knows things of great but not much personal relevance. During all this time I was reading what other people thought about literature; I was writing detailed and unnecessary summaries of these thoughts in careful essays; I was teaching classes, taking classes, submitting grades and essays, revising, resubmitting; I was getting married, getting a used car, getting divorced, extending my lease. When the largest protests happened I was probably in my library carrel, a place of dust and brown-painted metal so cold that I wore a hat and scarf as I typed. When the "surge" began, I was at the exact midpoint of writing my dissertation. I think I remember the arguments and justifications. Things were bad, they went, and a change of tactics was certainly necessary and a different strategy should be deployed, but the first thing, the most important thing, was to add more of everything, because more would, if not manage something right, prevent the worst of the wrong. I watched a news program in an airport bar, a barrage of numbers: over 100,000 civilians killed in Iraq, nearly 4,000 American troops, and over 28,000 soldiers wounded; in Afghanistan, over 500 troops killed, over 1,500 wounded, thousands of civilians, but no one even knew because the tracking was spotty. Over $125 billion spent by the United States in Afghanistan, $450 billion in Iraq, about $6,000 per second. I was on my way back from a conference at which I gave a paper to four others, all of them students waiting to give their own papers. I ordered ginger ale because I couldn't afford alcohol. Ginger ale was the soda I hated least. Numbers are impossible to assimilate after a certain point, impossible to credit. Everyone knows that. I opened my laptop next to the glass so I could continue to work. "We need to get beyond the facts and figures of our military actions," the panelist was saying at the war symposium, "to think about people."

He pushed up his glasses. His remarks were introductory, exhortative. "We owe it to the generation that fought these wars." *Generation* made everything less human, but the importance, this speaker urged us, was humanity. We owed human understanding, human attention. We ought not to remove ourselves in a false purity or false guilt. We are a democracy, he reminded us, with civilian control of the military, yet it was too easy for too many not to know anyone who had been through war. This is why the Mitchell Center was embarking on a longer initiative about leadership across military and civilian organizations. He sat down. The connection to leadership remained unclear to me, but another figure had come to the podium to agree on the contemporary problem of civilian ignorance: Such ignorance could lead to a faulty condescension toward soldiers, or maybe a faulty reverence, an unthinking support for more military action, or an unthinking opposition, a general horror of war, or a general ardor for it. I looked up from my program and realized that Mark was on this panel.

Actually, in that bar, in early 2008, I had opened my laptop to read a story about Mark. The story was written by one of the embedded journalists offering readers on-the-ground experience. This one followed a platoon in Anbar Province; Mark was in Fallujah, commanding a team that patrolled for high-level Al-Qaeda operatives. They swept streets and buildings in the green glow of their night-vision goggles. The embedded journalist had been out in these goggles. He spent a few sentences on the officer's background, the Weatherfield, swimming, his hometown. He was naturally interested in how a young man of such bright and infinite promise had chosen war. "I had to be part of this." That was the quotation from Mark. "I knew it was the most important thing. I knew this was what I had to do."

At the war symposium Mark looked exactly the same. Maybe slightly more relaxed than I remembered, more comfortable in the reserved power of his large, lean frame. It was as if the previous ten years hadn't happened, though of course if they hadn't happened he wouldn't have been on the stage of the

Mitchell Center in a symposium about war. He had worked so hard to get this far.

Actually, when I returned from the conference where I gave my uninteresting paper to four other uninterested students, Renata said I should take a break from work. "Read something else," she wrote on a chapter draft; "you're not thinking well right now." So I spent a few weeks seeking out more articles and books about the experience of war. Even at that point there were plenty; I could read right into the experience—the ugly, ad hoc density of sandbags and concrete and concertina wire; the pall of settled dust and old sweat; the smell of sewage tanks and burning rubber and gasoline and decomposing flesh; the texture of sandstorms and the patterns of tracer fire and the sound of a mortar attack. The feel of body armor in one-hundred-degree heat. I read about the tense watchfulness of a gunner in a convoy, the spikes and valleys of adrenaline in a team clearing buildings, the madcap valor of a grunt kicking trash piles for IEDs. I read about instant coffee lumpy from too much hot cocoa mixed in or MRE chocolate bars spread with MRE cheese product. I read about skulls in ditches and corpses in muddy culverts. I read about a quick-clotting compound that hardens into a fresh wound and sometimes prevents a person from bleeding out. I learned that a soldier in the street should avoid standing in one place for too long to prevent a possible sniper from lining up their shot. I read "hearts and minds" and "weed out the weak" and "head of the snake" and "clear-hold-build" and "human terrain teams" and other phrases I forgot to define; I read about speedballs and go pills, MRAPs and TICs and FOBs and COPs and other acronyms I forgot to decode. I gave all of this a lot of what you maybe could call human understanding, human attention. And then I stopped reading and went back to my dissertation.

Before I read, I thought it logical that humans would need the most extreme reasons to adopt as their work the task of violence against other humans, that the choice to kill should be the most viscerally difficult one we make. After the surge ended I submitted my dissertation and began application letters for jobs I would not get. After the surge ended Mark left the Marine Corps with a Bronze Star and started law school and then came here, to the Mitchell Center, where at the war symposium someone was laughing and handing the mike down the row of chairs onstage and it was his turn to answer something.

o O o

I meant to leave right away at the noon break. But I was trapped for a moment by a group talking over their reactions and unconcerned about the fact that they were blocking the route to an exit. When the clump of idlers eventually moved off and I picked up my bag again, quickly, I saw Mark notice me. He was several groups of conversation away, near the stage. Recognition passed over his face. He made a small "Excuse me" gesture to those around him. I pressed myself back into a folding seat as the others passed toward the aisle.

"Sorry," I said to them.

"Laura." Mark was there.

"Hi."

"I had no idea you'd be at this thing."

"I know. Me, neither!" I sounded inane. I didn't know what to say. In never deciding to come I had overlooked what might happen if I did.

"But it's great," Mark added in a hurry. "It's great to see you."

"You, too."

"I guess I knew you were here for your degree," he said. "I thought you'd finished, though."

"I have," I said. I left aside more explanation. I said, "It's my last day in town."

"Right on." He nodded. "And what's next?"

"Back to my mother's, for now."

He narrowed his eyes in concern. "Is she okay?"

"She's fine." I smiled. I think it was a smile. "And you? Where are you?"

"Here for a few months." He made a gesture at the wall, where the full name was stenciled: The Mitchell Center for International Peace. "A fellowship."

"Fellow again."

He laughed. "Yeah, well." He looked away.

"Congratulations."

"We should get together, though. Before you go. You have anything tonight? I have dinner with—" He tilted his head at the rest of the room, emptier now. "But after? A drink?"

"Sure."

"I'll call. Give me your number." Someone was already saying his name near the stage.

Mark's remarks at the symposium were brief. He was there to listen and learn as much as to offer any opinions, he said. What he did have to offer was just what everyone had mentioned already: the fact of experience. And if his experience had taught him anything relevant to this particular conversation, it was definitely the connection; there wasn't one thing of value he learned in the military, he said, that wasn't useful to him in civilian life, too. "And probably vice versa? Yeah, I would say vice versa. And I'm not just talking about courage. I'm talking about all of it. Decisions, empathy, people." He passed the mike back.

I waited until ten o'clock. At 10:30, I washed my face. At 10:45, I brushed my teeth again.

Mark called at just eleven. "Hey."

"Hello."

"Yeah," he said. "It got late." I could hear the rush and hollow of the street behind his voice. "Can you meet tomorrow?"

"Tomorrow I leave."

"Oh, right. Right."

"It's fine. I understand."

"Man, I wish—hang on." A muffled moment. Then quieter; he had paused somewhere, maybe.

"Where are you?"

"Walking. I still don't know my way around. We ate at some Italian place. It took forever." He laughed at what he had endured. "I was thinking tonight about that time you and I had dinner in Oxford."

"We had dinner?"

"With Tom."

"Oh. Right. That guy."

A moment as Mark thought. "Hey, why don't I stop by your place? I mean just for a minute." He was moving again; I could hear the change in his breath. "I'm north of the Square, I think. Wait. I'm on Kirkland. Is that far?"

"No, that's pretty close."

"I'll come to you."

I hadn't turned on the lamp again. Moon and streetlight streaked my living room, the slumped bags and the last boxes, now marshaled into a neat little barricade. The black marker across the top of each read "Books." I should have been more descriptive, but when I began, I didn't realize how many I would fill. "I think it's too late," I said.

A pause. "Yeah, you're right."

"I mean—" I almost reversed.

"Some other time." He was moving again; I heard traffic and his accelerated breath.

"Some other time."

And then with no chance of Mark coming over I paused for a moment and remembered what it was like to work at Oxford. I remembered the places and times of my work, all the rooms and hours Mark and I never met. Evenings at the college library, a space barely altered for a century or five, full of priceless volumes rotting through their bindings and leather chairs leaking grimy puffs of stuffing. Weekdays in the English subject library with its low ceilings and wide tables and squares of industrial carpet. Afternoons in a nook on the second floor of the Radcliffe Camera, listening to coughs and footsteps bouncing across the curve of the stone walls. Saturday morning at the Bodleian Upper Reading Room, with its high painted frieze of dead thinkers and streams of sunlight polishing the blond wood carrels. I would get there at the opening; I would put in my slips at the desk; I would unpack my notebook and a pen. I would pack them up in the evening and unzip my bag for the guard on the way out. I remembered getting up so early to take the Oxford Tube to the British Library for a day that I could watch the fruit vendors setting up stands of pears and apples and currants in the farmers' market next to the bus stop. I remembered staying up so late as I finished my master's exams that I opened my window to the little milk truck shuddering up my street, glass clinking faintly, like a medicine cabinet on wheels. On the phone at the end of a failed decade I remembered not what came of it but the work itself, happy, peaceful. You can remember something that never happened. That never could have happened, that you know now was wrong from the start. That was when I thought, I should stop working.

"It was great to see you today," Mark said. "I wish we had stayed in better touch."

"Well," I said, "you were at war."

"Right." He laughed. "I forgot."

"Really?"

"No. No, I did not forget."

"I didn't think so."

He was moving again. "Good luck with your trip."

"Move."

"Move. Good luck with that."

"Thanks. You, too. Good luck with everything."

I shut my phone and tried to sleep. The next morning I deleted the draft of an email I had written to Renata, asking her if she had heard of any temporary jobs. I tore up a hypothetical essay I had outlined in the margins of the symposium program after Mark stopped talking. It would begin with "The Moral Equivalent of War," a speech by Henry James's brother William from a hundred years ago that worries about a twentieth century so peaceful that men would lose the "absolute and permanent human goods" that came from combat; William recommended a kind of national service corps to promote those "martial virtues." Eight years later, when the Great War arrived, Henry was so adamant that the United States enter the Allied cause that he switched his citizenship from American to British and then served nominally as the head of a volunteer ambulance corps to transport injured soldiers in France. They were "gentleman volunteers"—young writers and scholars, often—and James thought their impeccable credentials a "positive added beauty," their work "unlimitedly inspiring to the keen spirit or the sympathetic soul." It was fit use for their "energies and resources." It would show "vivid and palpable social result."

I took the train to Royce. I told my mother I had lost my

job. I might be staying with her for longer than she expected. "Oh, that's too bad. Do you need anything? Are you okay? I worried about this. Are you all right?" I moved the file about Henry James and his friendships to the trash bin on my laptop and thought about Mark's casual mention of "Tom."

And then a few weeks later I got the email from Heather. It had been a while since I had read her formal, friendly email prose. It came back like a familiar perfume. She and I certainly needed to catch up, she wrote. She looked forward to that. She also wanted to discuss with me an assignment that arose in one of her projects recently and made her think of me. Of course I had so much to do already, Heather wrote, but was I interested nevertheless in some extra work?

2

I HADN'T TALKED TO HEATHER SINCE 2007. Before that we were friends. Were we friends now? If we were friends I'd have to tell her everything that had happened in the last three years, the last three weeks. I wanted to skip that part. The part where she tried to help. Also I wanted her help.

Our friendship always needed explanation. We were Weatherfield fellows together, at Oxford together, so naturally we became friends. But while we were at Oxford our friendship was strange because Heather is beautiful and I am not. And after that our friendship was strange also because Heather has money and I do not. I think these are the simplest explanations. They sound bad or wrong only because people avoid discussing directly things like beauty and money.

What I look like. My hair frizzes. My head is too big, even for my body, which is also too big. My fingers are knobby and my nails look ragged no matter how clean. Heather is tall and slim with very dark hair and big eyes and fingers that taper to pale pink almond shapes.

I knew that Heather and I were friends because she told me. I would not have known otherwise. Claiming friendship seemed presumptuous. Facebook changed this, of course. Heather and I met before Facebook. Now you have friends in your queue like you have dollars in your bank account. All those little pictures of people. I don't really check Facebook. I do check my bank account. Often. More since I lost my job.

Heather has so much of a job that she has extra jobs. She is on boards. She volunteers. She does things pro bono.

People avoid discussing directly things like beauty and money because they are impossible. They are not real. Also ruthlessly real. They are illusion, also inarguable.

I wrote back to Heather that it was very good to hear from her and that yes, I was interested in work.

Pro bono, for good, not for money.

She wrote with details. She was now on the board of the Weatherfield Foundation and helping with the centennial gala this December. She hoped I had already heard of the centennial gala. She hoped I was even planning to attend. The foundation wanted to produce a commemorative essay to distribute at the event, explaining the history of Ennis Weatherfield. Could I write this? It would entail some research. *Unfortunately, the deadline is fast approaching.* She apologized for the time line. She hoped I would say yes.

From the research. *Foundation* in the sense of charitable organization is a relatively recent usage. It dates only from the turn of the twentieth century. The Weatherfield Foundation is an early example. The first few decades of the twentieth century were a good time for foundations. In the first few decades of the twentieth century, a small number of people gave away a large amount of money.

The Weatherfield Foundation was prepared to pay a fair or even generous rate for this work, Heather said. *Given the time line.*

Heather told me we were friends when she did not invite me to her wedding. This was in 2002. *I am so sorry,* she wrote. *The guest list is not entirely under my control. I hope this will not affect our friendship.* Oh, I thought. Friendship.

To be clearer, in the first few decades of the twentieth century, a small number of people gave away a large amount of money because in the last few decades of the nineteenth century, a small number of people made an even larger amount of money.

The lack of a wedding invitation was not a problem, I wrote to Heather in 2002. I told her that she had saved me from buying a new dress. You know how much I love shopping for clothes, I wrote. Or rather, not shopping. Heather wrote back, *I am glad to have helped. But I hope you will buy yourself a new dress anyway.*

This was our pattern as friends. I was to say something ironic. Heather was to say something kind. Something that confirmed her kindness. Also indirectly her beauty.

Heather is very kind. The word has a mild formality that matches Heather's manner. A slight remove. At Oxford, she stood to one side of the elite group of fellows without a sense of exclusion. She did not fall short. She was doing something else. Something to do with beauty. And men? Or just math.

Math was her subject. Advanced and theoretical. No one could talk to her about it, really. She was beyond any of us.

Heather's wedding in 2002 was canceled. She canceled it, I think. She wrote to me only that while she regretted the confusion and pain this had caused, it was clear that Wesley was *not the right partner* for her. Heather does not say exactly how things happen and does not say directly what she likes or wants. She says what is the right thing for her.

Heather started work as a management consultant after our second year at Oxford. Before this I had the impression that she would stay for a doctorate. She took a job with Putnam Marsh. I didn't ask why. It was the right thing for her.

Management consulting as a field also began in the early part of the twentieth century.

Heather's manner of speaking assumes one can and should approach emotion often and with placidity. She uses a lot of those words and phrases that populate the overlapping edges of the clinical and the economic. Words and phrases quoted in magazine articles about self-development and self-promotion. *Work-life balance. Actualized. Paradigm shift. Personal growth.* Heather uses these words precisely, so precisely that they do not seem clichéd. They seem useful. They seem to allow a person to talk frankly about emotion and feelings without becoming emotional or feeling much. *The best way to cultivate authenticity is to honor your intuition.*

Of course the *why* of a job at Putnam Marsh is probably money.

I wrote back to say I was interested in the Weatherfield job. Heather was so glad. We would talk it over. Catch up. I should come to the city. I should stay over. *Old times.*

Heather is adopted, she told me once. Her parents adopted her when they thought they could not have children. Eighteen months after adopting her they conceived a biological son. *It's a common pattern.*

Old times. I used to travel to New York about twice a term. More. These were the years after Heather canceled her wedding. I was in graduate school and she was working at Putnam Marsh. I would ride the train down and stay overnight. Heather's apartment on the Upper West Side has lofty windows looking west over the park and the river. I would get there while Heather was still at work. I would take the key from the doorman. I slept on a daybed in the narrow space Heather called her office. I knew where the sheets were kept. When Heather got in we would open wine and order dinner and talk. The next morning I would pretend I needed to find a source in the New York Public Library or see a museum exhibition relevant to my scholarship. I wanted only to wake up in Heather's home and make coffee in the beautiful machine that whispered and hissed in her kitchen before I rode back to Cambridge in silence.

This was our pattern as friends. In some ways Heather was my closest female friend. In some ways we weren't close at all. I wondered if Heather was close to anyone.

We lost touch sometime after she left Putnam Marsh to work as the chief financial officer of a new company. A start-up. Something about small personal loans and Web 2.0. It was very personal, and it was big business. I thought of Heather in the fall of 2008, when the worldwide economy collapsed because a lot of people with not much money had been granted loans they could not repay.

No, that's not right. The worldwide economy collapsed because a few people invested in the value of those loans. These investments were called "securities."

Securitization is an even more recent usage than *foundation*.

The word *foundation* means the funds kept for support of an institution in perpetuity; the word *securitization* means turning debt into a tool for investment.

Investment is older than *securitization* and has changed less than *foundation*. But it has changed, a bit; one used to invest one thing with something else, and now one can just invest in a thing. Or one can be invested in a thing. That, too.

Foundations depend on investment. Almost the entire budget of the Weatherfield Foundation comes from investment income. And contributions, of course. Investment and generosity, impossible to distinguish.

Heather was generous. She invited me to New York often. She invited me more than I accepted. I was careful of that. I loved being there. When my husband left me in early 2006, I wrote Heather an email saying so in a few sentences and she called me right away. I let it go to voice mail twice. On the third time I picked up. *It's not healthy for you to be alone right now*, she said. I am alone right now, I said. That's the whole point. *I think you should get on the train.* I don't think I should run away from my problems. *It's not running away. It's a change of perspective.* I looked in the mirror. I had $812 of my ex-husband's purchases on my credit card and my monthly income was $1,284. I looked at my tired skin and puffy neck. I remembered my mother's tone when I told her. The *Really?* The *Oh no.* She would never suggest I get on a train. I said to Heather, I'm sorry I'm being difficult. *Women especially apologize too much*, Heather said. *Whenever you have the impulse to say sorry, you should train yourself to say thank you.* Thank you for the fact that I am a terrible person. We laughed. *Oh, Laura. I'm glad to hear that you've kept your sense of humor.* The next morning I wadded a change of underwear and a second sweater in my backpack next to my laptop and rode down to New York.

I thought of Heather in 2008 but I did not get in touch. I was not the one to get in touch. Heather was. That was the pattern of our friendship.

I think the first thing you should focus on, Heather said to me when I arrived at her apartment after my husband left, *is repairing your self-worth.* I wanted to forget my self altogether. In New York, I could walk for a long time on straight avenues without getting lost or thinking about where I was. I could watch the late light quiver into a golden bruise over the river at the west end of a street. I could stop considering if I was in the wrong life or a bad life but instead feel I was in no life at all.

From the research. Ennis Weatherfield, when he died, was worth six million dollars. Those six million dollars became the principal endowment of the Weatherfield Foundation.

The foundation was worth about $100 million in 2007. The foundation lost twenty million dollars in 2008. The foundation recovered eight million dollars in 2009. The foundation is now worth about $110 million.

It would be easy for me to say that the pattern of our friendship was about power. I don't want to say that. I want to say the pattern was about beauty.

Self-worth may be a little too abstract for me right now, I told Heather. She waved her hand. She had ordered Thai food for delivery. She always ordered for delivery. The kitchen in her apartment was full of unsmudged stainless steel. Heather had no time for cooking. She got home late and took off her suit and hose and heels and small gold hoop earrings and changed into drawstring cotton pants and a woven wool cardigan in deep green that hung asymmetrically and fastened near the top with a single square button. Heather's loungewear looked as polished as the outfits she wore to work. In fact she often worked in the evening after changing clothes. *Affirmation*, she explained. *No one can make you feel inferior without your consent. Eleanor Roosevelt. Do you want to split an order of the spring rolls? I should warn you they are really greasy.* I wanted an order of spring rolls to myself. I didn't say that. I said, Let me pay for dinner. She said, *Don't be silly.*

But our friendship and its patterns was not a subject I could afford to think much about. Why Heather might invest in me. What she might gain from it.

I trusted her.

Heather is probably the smartest person I know. She was born in a town in Oklahoma with fifteen thousand people and sixty-three churches. The town had two elementary schools and three ranches. It had one bookstore that sold gift baskets and plants as well as books, two of those fast-food restaurants at which orders are brought out to cars on roller skates. She was the first woman to win a Weatherfield fellowship from her state. In high school, she taught herself AP calculus in three months. None of the teachers there could really help her, she said. Eleventh grade. That spring, she was prom queen. She had a 1530 on the SATs, but her high school guidance counselor didn't mention any colleges more than one hundred miles away. *He didn't know any better. I probably wouldn't have wanted to travel that far anyway.* She attended the state university honors program on full scholarship. She dated a football player and joined a sorority and took advanced algebraic topology. Advanced algebraic topology was an independent study. No one else understood it. At graduation, her professor for the independent study confessed his love for her. Oh my God, I said. I can't imagine. *It was very sweet.* Did he harass you? *Harass me?* You know what I mean. *He was married.* As if that matters. *He was just confused. He didn't know what he was saying. Bless his heart.* At Oxford, she studied, I think, four-dimensional manifolds.

Sometimes I wanted Heather to bless my heart. Mostly I feared that she would.

My not thinking about our friendship could be cowardice as easily as courage. *I read somewhere,* Heather told me, *that every decision comes from a place of love or a place of fear.* The idea being that love is better? *Of course.* But the two are hard to tell apart. I didn't say that last bit.

Heather and I did not talk much about other Weatherfield fellows. I did not know much about Heather's other friendships—past or present. I knew mostly about her relationships with men.

The dissertation I wrote in my twenties included a long study of *The Golden Bowl. The Golden Bowl* is a novel by Henry James. Here is the plot. A rich American father has a rich American daughter. They go to Europe to buy art. The rich American daughter meets and falls in love with an impoverished Italian prince. This prince needs money from the rich American father and daughter. He marries the daughter. But unfortunately, she has a beautiful American friend who used to know the impoverished Italian prince. The beautiful American friend marries the rich American father. Then the beautiful American friend and the no longer impoverished Italian prince begin an affair. The rich American daughter discovers this affair. She does not tell her friend or her father what she knows. That would wreck everything. Instead, she makes sure her father and friend return to America to run their American museum. The rich American daughter stays in Europe with her prince. At the end, everyone is happy. This is a happy book.

The bowl of the title is a symbol. In the book, the golden bowl has a crack in it. It is a clumsy symbol is the general consensus. Everyone thinks it's too obvious. Then everyone argues over exactly what it means.

Heather's relationships with men: numerous but not frivolous. They were always deliberate, even if sometimes casual. She did not do one-night stands or flings. She went on dates; she dated, sometimes several people at one time. *Sean and I are going to brunch. Matt is taking me to a jazz concert this weekend.* I told her, I don't know anyone else who actually dates. *Dating helps you meet people.* As if that's a good thing. *Dating helps you discover yourself.* As if that's a good— *Laura, you're terrible.* Heather was smiling. I know I am, I said. Don't mind me. Keep doing everything exactly as it should be done.

I think you need to be very beautiful to do everything exactly as it should be done. Also, you need to have money.

Heather's beauty is refined. She makes clear how perfection is a matter of small adjustments. Heather makes appointments to get her eyebrows shaped. This doesn't seem vain. Responsible, maybe. Heather is like one of the quizzes in women's magazines about financial health. These quizzes tell you how much you would save if you made coffee at home rather than buying it at a shop. You, too, could do this. It's just about rounding up.

Once when Heather was in middle school, she came to a question on a math test that asked her about the hundredths place of 275. She wondered whether to write 2 or zero. She wrote zero and the teacher marked it wrong. She told me this story. Heather never earned less than an A in any class she took. Our second year at Oxford, she sat for a sample LSAT without preparing and got a 180. She recommended I do the same. *I think it's helpful to know your baseline for these standard-ized tests. Just get the number.*

But I did not feel judged by Heather. I did not feel that she would bless my heart, even, or find me sweet. This could be love or cowardice. Both.

My basic question about management consultants used to be this. Why one company needed to hire some other company to tell the first company what it already knew. *Because you can't advise yourself*, Heather said. *You need an outside eye. Like asking a friend how an outfit looks.* You look great. You always look great. *You're very kind.* So do you! No, I don't. You must be a lousy consultant. *I am a very good consultant.* I know you are.

Strategy was her specialty at Putnam Marsh. Strategy is an objective and facts-based focus on making the right decisions.

Heather and I began to be friends, I think, one night in late November of our second year at Oxford. I knew her before that, of course. But we didn't speak. That evening, I was at a pub near the Parks Road that was loud and big and moldy but popular for meetings because convenient. I was there with an Australian from my Bloomsbury tutorial. I saw Heather as I was coming out of the women's bathroom. The ladies' toilet: a carpeted stall with a pull chain on the tank and a puddle of gray soap in the well of the sink. Heather stood in the narrow hallway outside the door. *Laura*, she said. She gestured me over. Her voice was low. *I'm so glad you're here. Do you mind if I trouble you for a sanitary pad?*

I only had a tampon. It was slightly squished from resting in the bottom of the pens and pencils pouch of my backpack. Heather looked taken aback but accepted the wrapped cylinder and smiled again. *Thank you*, she said. *I definitely owe you one.* She closed the door behind her.

Then a few days later, she wrote me a note. I guessed that lovely handwriting was hers even before I saw the name. *I realized when I saw you the other evening that we haven't had a chance to get to know each other. I wonder if you would like to have coffee this weekend.* We met at Blackwell's, the ancient bookshop that had given in to fashion and installed a coffee counter on the second floor. We bought frothy lattes in big white mugs. We sat in an upper window looking through a smeared square out to the street. Everyone hates the coffee here, I told Heather. *Really?* I explained how Americans were supposed to know that espresso drinks at Blackwell's were too large and too weak and not hot enough. Heather smiled. *I find them comforting.* Yes, I do, too, I admitted. Heather smiled again. *If I bought a cookie*, she asked, *would you eat half?* I said that I would. I thought there was no way that Heather wanted a chance to get to know each other.

I told myself instead, later, that she wanted one of two things that talking with me could offer. A clarification of feeling, for one. Putting it into neat and explicable terms. How was I doing? Heather wanted to know, and I said I was fine, and Heather nodded her head slowly, as if my reply had been profound agreement. It was such an uncertain time, she said. She was feeling the stress of all the uncertainty. I nodded back. I wasn't sure what she meant. She meant the attacks. The difficulty of being so far away from home with the world like this. She told me that the latest scientific findings suggested that the human body processes emotional strain and physical strain in the same way. I said that made sense.

These things were not in fact what Heather was feeling. I discovered that later. It didn't matter. Heather broke the cookie into small pieces and pushed the plate over. I chewed as she talked. I said, I'm eating all of this. *Please. Go ahead.*

Heather assured me that she would go home over break. She went home every break to see her family. Could your parents come here? I asked. She shook her head no. Her parents didn't really travel. Especially now. Her father refused to get on a plane. *He says he's gotten this far with his feet planted firmly on the ground.* Isn't that a metaphor? I asked. *I don't think he believes in metaphors. He works in finance.* Does that mean he works for a bank? *Actually he sells insurance.*

From the research. The foundation began with Ennis's money, but it was Hugh Weatherfield, Ennis's father, who made it. He took Weatherfield Sugar from a small family operation in the 1850s to a corporation shipping more than a million pounds of sugar a day a few decades later. This made it a mid-size firm, among sugar manufacturers.

Heather did not grow up with a lot of money. I think her family was comfortable and I'm sure she had school clothes and an allowance and weeks at summer camp. But she was not accustomed at a young age to the kind of money she earned later. The kind of *resources*. It seemed however that she always knew how to have such resources. And it seems to me sometimes that such knowledge is money's prerequisite rather than its result. How to tip. How to engage a personal shopper. How to order when no one is sure who will pay and how to flatter an angel investor when no one is sure what they like. How to give. How to spend. How to be beautiful.

Beautiful is one of Henry James's favorite words. He uses it to describe people and objects but also to describe actions and manners. "It would be too beautiful if you *would!*" This is a Jamesian sentence. Beauty is a grace and magnanimity of gesture. "Her beautiful generosity." "She had been beautifully hoping." These are Jamesian phrases.

Also all of James's books are about money. Most anyway. Money drives plots. Money floods virtues. Integrity, for example, is "subject . . . to infinite endorsement." Confession is a debt. In *The Golden Bowl*, after the rich American daughter discovers her husband's betrayal, this is how James describes his willingness to admit it: "So far as seeing that she was 'paid' went, he might have been holding out the money-bag for her to come and take it."

But no one does admit anything in *The Golden Bowl*. Not really. No one takes the "money-bag." Everyone has enough money already.

To discuss the Weatherfield job, Heather and I met for lunch at La Maison—a French place in midtown, near the offices of Putnam Marsh. We had eaten there together before. Small, artful open-faced sandwiches called tartines cost nine dollars. On the menu each price appeared as just a number. No decimal or dollar sign. The values floated gracefully around the page. Heather sat at a window table wearing a nubbly beige shift and pale beige pumps. Also a scarf. I wore a cotton shirt and jeans and clogs. She stood up to hug me. Her bracelets clicked down her arm. We exclaimed at the same time how good it was to see each other. We laughed at ourselves. *I've already ordered some sparkling water*, she said. I remembered the feeling of Heather, hugging her. Her fragility. Her symmetry. Her slim, light bones against one's chest. We looked at each other at arm's length.

It is quite literally good to see someone as beautiful as Heather is.

After our meeting at the ladies' toilet in late 2001 and our conversation at Blackwell's a week later, we saw each other regularly during those dark and anxious months of winter into spring. We met for a coffee or a cocktail. Heather liked cocktails, also wine; she did not care for beer, she told me, or whiskey, or even cider. When she went out with men, she sometimes had to drink a cider. When she went out with me, she could run a finger down a menu of improbably named fruit and vodka mixtures and choose one she hadn't tried before and admire its appearance when it came and sip it a few times and leave it unfinished. Heather sitting upright in high-heeled patent-leather boots. *Patent is so practical in the rain.* She carried a checked vinyl shoulder bag that snapped shut and a clear umbrella that folded into a small pouch.

Heather proposed our meetings via notes in the pigeon post, the mail system at Oxford that moved scraps of paper between cubbyholes in different colleges. Heather enjoyed lettering real notes. We went to expensive cafés with few seats or aggressively designed hotel bars with geometric lighting. Heather saw no reason not to patronize the fancy establishments, the ones catering to tourists or businesspeople rather than to students.

On her notes she wrote everything except for her signature in capital letters. The loops in her *p*s and *b*s not squat and round, but slim uplifted ovals. I returned my agreement with a messier than usual scrawl. A torn corner of spiral notebook. This was also the pattern of our friendship.

Mostly the pattern was that I coaxed her to tell me things about men and she enjoyed it. The second of the two things I think that talking with me could offer. She told me about the Indian law student from Wadham. *Unfortunately I think he's something of a playboy.* The Canadian philosophy tutor who said *precisely* all the time. *I don't think we're compatible except in bed.* A disorganized British physicist who lived on Cowley Road. Mostly, the men were older, though she went out with a gangly and overconfident undergraduate from Germany who pursued her for several weeks. *He's trying his best.* Her most constant reaction to all seemed a fond tolerance for their inadequacies. When she talked about sleeping with them she most often seemed to do so out of pity.

I had something like a boyfriend in college, a political science major with whom I had sex a few times on the top bunk of a dorm room before he started avoiding me and I could also pretend with relief that we never knew each other. I had several long email correspondences with boys I would never have approached in real life. Yet with Heather, my lack of experience seemed to mean that I could ask the questions too embarrassing for others. For her. He refused to go down on you? What happened then? And: He said that? You're kidding. What were you supposed to do? And: What, with the condom wrapper? And he just lay there? Heather blushed with pleasure. She sipped her drink. *Laura, you're terrible.* Smiling.

I'm so sorry I haven't been in touch, I said in La Maison when we stopped hugging and sat down to our sparkling water.

Oh that's my fault, Heather said. She settled her napkin and bracelets. The last few years had been difficult. *I was foolish enough to let my support system fall away.* Was I her support system, then? Was I supposed to be?

From the research. In the late nineteenth century, Hugh Weatherfield's business success came to the attention of Henry Havemeyer, a sugar magnate who had grown up in the firm of Havemeyers & Elder. Havemeyer was nicknamed "the Sugar King." Hugh Weatherfield had a choice. He could sell his company to the Sugar King or succumb to a price war in which Weatherfield Sugar eventually had to be sold anyway.

I repeated the word *difficult*. You mean the crash? I asked. *The financial crisis*, she said. Right, the financial crisis.

Heather seemed to like Putnam Marsh when she was working there. She liked the feeling of always moving to the next thing. *It's encouraging. I don't want to limit myself.* She liked the chance to advance, the *atmosphere of growth*.

Even when Heather and I were in touch we never really talked by phone or email. Our conversations were too inconsequential to make a phone call, to send an email. We talked when we were together. When we were together inconsequence settled into a kind of ease. At least that is what I felt. Heather in those grad school years: *Why don't you come down?* I shouldn't. *You sure? Of course. I'll tell the doorman. I'll try to get away by around nine.* Heather letting herself in at 9:30. *I'm so glad you're already here.* Heather emerging from her room in a silk tunic over dark leggings. Heather opening a bottle of white wine. *Should we order some Lebanese food? Would you prefer sushi?* She told me her feelings about a yoga class. *I'm really convinced by the more holistic approach.* She told me her feelings about diet. *I've discovered that dairy is poison for my skin.* I liked hearing these considerations. I filed them away. Those years, I grimly rode the elliptical for twenty minutes a day at the university gym and packed peanut butter sandwiches to eat in the bathroom before the second discussion section I taught for extra cash. She told me her feelings about travel. *I probably should take a few shorter trips but really we're hoping to coordinate two weeks next year so that we can go to Thailand.*

We was Brandon, a medical student who left for a residency, and then Rob, an investment banker whose cat caused allergies, and then Neil, who worked at what I think was a hedge fund— Neil lasted; Heather began to talk about *shared values.* He was the right fit for her. *Though Wesley should have cured me of dating bankers.* I say what I think was a hedge fund because I did not and do not know the distinctions among capital and equity and management and trading, and the website for Neil's company didn't explain what it did. On a dark background, it displayed in white script a quotation about creativity and new ideas.

I think Heather appreciated the "up or out" of Putnam Marsh because it provided a way to be exactly as ambitious as she wanted to be without the worry of being a woman admitting ambition. Though Heather would admit ambition. She would recommend ambition. She could call it *personal development.* Maybe *self-optimization.*

I never stayed long when I visited Heather. *Stay as long as you want.* I always left after one night, maybe two. *Did you find the towels? Should we order some food?*

At La Maison, Heather had also ordered a popover for us to share. *They're so good here.* I agreed; they were. *So tell me everything. What's going on with you? Where are you working?*

I am still not sure how Heather regarded my career. I think she indulged the supposition that my smaller income meant a greater integrity. I think she assumed something similar about my looks. *Integrity* may be the wrong word. I think she regarded my career as akin to a religion she didn't understand but would of course respect and would profit somehow from exposing herself to. She would be enriched in some way.

Heather is about self-optimization, also self-forgiveness.

Actually I'm not working right now, I said.

Encyclopedia entries on Havemeyer, the Sugar King, generally can't conceal their admiration for his grasp of money. He got rich by enlarging his company. He got rich by cutting prices, underselling competition, acquiring other interests. He forced other companies into bankruptcy and targeted refineries that had overextended. He expanded, centralized, invested. After a certain point everything always yields to what's larger. That is money. *An atmosphere of growth.*

It was surprisingly easy to tell Heather I didn't have a job. *I'm so sorry,* she said. She frowned at me across the table. Her expression was kind. *I know what it feels like.* I didn't answer that.

In 1887 Havemeyer officially created the Sugar Trust. The Sugar Trust was a monopoly. It bought most of the sugar companies in the United States; it increased profits and consolidated production. It erased the names of some of the companies. It kept others. The sugar was the same.

Are you looking to change fields? Heather asked. *To do something new?*

The drive of money is toward sameness. Growth begets sameness? That can't be right. Growth begets change.

I didn't answer and a server approached. Heather ran her finger down the menu. *The avocado with sprouts is excellent. I've read that anything sprouted is much more nutrient-rich.* I said that made sense.

But what about you? I said when our orders were in. Where are you working?

When Hugh Weatherfield died he split his money between his two sons. Ennis was the younger. It was money from the Sugar Trust that gave Ennis a worth of six million dollars. It was money from the Sugar Trust that created the Weatherfield Foundation. It was money from the Sugar Trust that paid Heather and me. And Mark and the others. Or rather, it was money that money made. Money does not care where it came from.

It's been an eventful few years.

Do you ever think about being adopted? I asked Heather
once. It was when we were talking about having kids. We were
talking in general terms. *I suppose I think about medical informa-*
tion, Heather said. But other than that? I asked. *No. I don't think*
it has had much effect on my life. Other than the big effect, I said.
Heather was silent. I said, I don't meant to pry. *Oh, you didn't.*

To start with, Heather explained, *Empowerance is no more.*
Empowerance is the start-up? I asked. *Was,* Heather said. I told
her I was sorry. *Oh, don't be. The moment wasn't right. Success*
and failure are often about timing. Yes. *It was a positive experience.*
It really clarified my goals. That sounds good, I said. Clarity.

In the winter of 2007 when Heather told me about her new
job we stood in the dark on the roof of her apartment building.
It was a cold night. Heather was wearing a deep red sweater that
looked soft and earnest against her dark hair. We were meant
to be at an all-women's Valentine's Day party thrown by one of
her work colleagues. *We all thought it would be healthy,* Heather
told me in her invitation, *to counterprogram the holiday.* Heather
then pointed out that the counterprogramming was scheduled
for three days before Valentine's so everyone could spend the
actual holiday with their husbands and boyfriends. *So there's*
that. But you should come down and join us. I think you would
really appreciate this group of people. When I arrived in New
York, though, with my backpack and resolve, Heather said she
had an honest question for me. *Please feel free to say no.* Would
I mind if she cancelled? Oh my God that would be great, I said.
I'm not exactly feeling well enough for a social gathering at the
moment, she explained. Yes, wonderful, I said. I mean, not wonderful that you feel— She smiled at me. *You could have just told*
me if you didn't want to go. I didn't want to stop you from going.

Well I thought it would be a nice opportunity for you. We bring out each other's worst instincts, I said. She shook her head. *No, our best. Have you eaten?*

I put down my bag in her office. I had been working on the same dissertation chapter for over five months now. Renata was ignoring my emails. She often ignored my emails. *It's such a clear night,* Heather said. *Let's go up on the roof and look at the city.*

We took a bottle of red wine and two glasses. I looked out at rows of windows of indifferent light. Each one was some other life. Wind cut across the tops of the buildings and sirens rose and fell somewhere in a canyon of avenue. I felt what I always felt about New York: a sensation of deep exhaustion and enormous force that would always feed on each other.

The real origin of money, of course, the furthest ancestral progenitor, is work.

Sometimes I wonder if it isn't beauty.

I've decided to leave Putnam Marsh, Heather told me. She explained the new company. *It's the next step. The right step for me.* Congratulations, I said. I raised my glass. She clinked. *Thanks.* She didn't drink. What is the job, exactly? I asked. She didn't answer. I said, Would it mean more math?

More math was a joke. Sort of. The joke began at Oxford, one spring evening when we were drinking tall gin and tonics outdoors. That far north, spring evenings don't seem to end. The light fades only in a long aristocratic exhalation. Heather and I had just finished our degrees and we were celebrating by sitting mostly quietly together. I felt daringly content. I said, Tell me what you like about math. Heather laughed. *What I like about math. What a question.* I didn't mean it to be funny. *Let me think. Do you want my real answer?* I definitely wanted her real answer. She said, *What I like about math is that numbers are beautiful.* Numbers are beautiful?

And also I'm good at it. Math. But don't tell anyone I said that.

Why shouldn't I tell anyone you said that? I asked. Because it's true? She looked at me. Okay, I won't tell anyone you said that. *Thank you,* Heather said. She stirred her gin and tonic. *Have you seen the cartoon? I'll show it to you. The biologists want to be chemists and chemists want to be physicists and physicists want to be mathematicians and mathematicians don't want to be anybody.*

Wow, I said. *Exactly,* she said. I knew that Heather was starting with Putnam Marsh in a few weeks. That was the first time I wondered about ambition, about women's ambition, about Heather's. We settled into quiet again.

But after that I would ask whenever she mentioned a work project. The feasibility study for restructuring a regional bank in the Midwest. The possible merger of two pharmaceutical firms. I have just one question, I would say. Does this mean more math? She would laugh. Sometimes she would answer. *Yes, I suppose this one has a lot of math.*

On the roof she did not laugh. *No,* Heather told me.

Heather's father was a financial consultant before he was indicted for securities fraud. He was never convicted. Of course he was innocent. *It's just a risk of the business,* Heather told me. *This is why every doctor has malpractice insurance. The truth is what doesn't kill us makes us stronger.* Heather's father found a new job at an insurance agency, which was *only too happy to hire someone so overqualified.* And her father loved the work. *It's all for the best,* she said. *Our family really bonded.*

The wind was coming up colder. I took a sip of wine. I tried to think of something light or scandalous I could say. Well then, I asked her, would it mean more money?

Heather pushed back her hair with one hand. In the other, she held her wineglass by its rim. *Yes, more money,* she said. She looked thinner than ever, more beautiful. Soft blue veins were visible through the skin of her temples. I felt a rush of love that left in its wake a terrifying film of loneliness.

Are you all right? I asked her. Are you okay?

When Hugh Weatherfield sold his company to Havemeyer he was issued shares in the Sugar Trust. He was therefore bound to hope for its success. The success of the trust was his enrichment. The word *trust* means a measure of confidence in something, a measure of care for anything, and a legal combination of profit-seeking entities designed to reduce competition.

Heather and I never talked about Mark. Why would we. She looked at me through her blowing hair. *Neil and I broke up.* I waited for more. I'm sorry, I said finally. That did not seem to be right. Was it your decision? She didn't answer that, either. *Have you ever terminated a pregnancy?* she asked.

Heather and I did sometimes talk about children. I told her I didn't want them. I'd be a terrible mother, I said. *You'd be a wonderful mother*, Heather replied. I'd be a poor mother, I said, correcting myself. And poor is terrible. Trust me. Heather said, *Money? That can change.*

I moved over to her on the roof. Oh, Heather. She said, *Ten days ago. Just after my final interview for the new job. I'm so sorry. It just wouldn't work, with the timing—* She stopped. *I'm fine. I'm a very healthy person.* I said, You're the healthiest person I know.

Prejudice would tell you women are not good with numbers. But a person with a uterus is always counting. How long it has been since your last period and how long till your next and how many days till it stops. I remember reading Freud's analysis of money. Money as shit, Freud says, moneygrubbing as anality, moneygrubbing perverting the healthy practice of a little boy who should give away his excrement to the father. I remember wondering about menstruation. All the dense material women give away every month. To no one. To the world. All the matted dark value that goes under the name of blood.

I thought I would be a mother by now, Heather said. *I honestly thought I would be married by now.* I put one arm around her. I could feel her bones in the red sweater.

It was my decision, she said. *To break up. It was my decision and I'm the one who feels awful.*

I waited. *I do want children*, she said. I said I knew she did. I wasn't sure that was true. I said of course she did. She said, *Thank you.* I wonder if she meant *I'm sorry.*

The Sugar Trust's real name was the Sugar Refineries Company. After the Sherman Antitrust Act, it was reorganized as a corporation, the American Sugar Refining Company. A Supreme Court case ruled that the company's domination of the refining industry could not be dismantled by the federal government. Havemeyer next extended his control to the National Sugar Refining Company. Monopoly became oligopoly.

I said, You have to do what is right for you.

She looked down at her glass. *The first was in college. I was dating a boy I didn't care about and neither he nor I was at the right stage of life to be a parent.* Of course, I said. She pulled her hair out of her mouth again. *And then, at Oxford—* She stopped again. *Please don't tell anyone this.*

Who would I tell?

The Sugar Trust had been organized as a trust rather than a corporation in part because of the secrecy afforded by a trust arrangement.

Do you ever think about the other Weatherfield fellows? she said.

The Golden Bowl is set up so a series of lies is good policy. So a series of lies is the right thing to do.

Not really, I said. *That's probably for the best,* she said. *Do you remember that weird weekend we all went to? Putnam Marsh? That terrible weekend. You thought it was terrible?* I was just bad at it. *I'm sure you weren't.* You were very good at it. *Yes I was.*

She paused. *I guess we all didn't go. Only some. You and me, a few others.* I said, Mark. Heather didn't answer.

The 2008 crash was possible because a series of deregulations allowed massive fraud in the financial industry. Institutions certified something as secure that was not.

I always felt that the others looked down on Putnam Marsh a little, Heather said after a pause. *Like why would you go into this field that's about business? They all thought it was just making money.* Right, I said. *Certainly I didn't think I would take the job when I went to that weekend. But then things changed.* Right, I said again. *I thought, you know, you only ever take care of yourself. That's it. You only ever can take care of yourself.* She looked at me. *Do you know what I mean?*

In 2007, the words for growth and forgiveness and change and optimization did not yet include *self-care*. Not often. Heather wasn't talking about self-care anyway.

I said I knew what she meant.

Heather continued. *None of the others would have gotten the job. Maybe Caroline. Maybe Zac.* I agreed: He was good at math. *Yes. But the others? They wouldn't.* I wouldn't, I said. Heather shook her head. *That's not what I meant. With you, it was more that you wanted something else.* I said, Who knows what I wanted.

My dissertation focused on characters in Henry James at the periphery of the narrative. The most important example is a character in *The Golden Bowl* called Fanny Assingham. She is not part of the central quartet, the rich American father and the rich American daughter and the impoverished Italian prince and the beautiful American friend. Fanny Assingham has little money and no children. She therefore can do nothing herself. She stands on the sidelines and talks about what other people are doing.

Heather folded her arms. She put down her wine. *Mark would not have gotten it,* she repeated. No, I said.

Actually Freud did talk a bit about blood. It was at the very start of his career. Before he had settled on the key theories of psychoanalysis. He was treating a patient who had terrible nosebleeds and heavy periods. This patient was active in the women's movement. Freud thought her symptoms were caused by sexual abuse from her father when she was a girl.

Are you cold? Heather asked me up on the roof. I'm okay, I said. But you? You look cold. We should go down. *I'm cold,* she said. *But I don't want to go down yet. Don't repeat any of this,* she said. I said, Of course I won't. Heather said, *I trust you.*

I said, I trust you too.

After Heather's father was fired for financial malpractice and before he was hired as an insurance agent, he spent several months holding Bible Study for friends and family in his wall-to-wall-carpeted living room. I have seen pictures of these meetings. Heather showed me. Her father stood in front of the beige stone fireplace and preached on the week's text. Then one Sunday he stood up in his pew and explained to the congregation that he had been called to tell them how the pastor was leading all of them away from the true and verifiable teaching of

Christ. He asked those who wished to follow the path of righteousness and walk humbly with their God to come with him out of this unholy space and into a new church with himself as its head. Then he turned and walked slowly down the central aisle, holding his Bible aloft. Heather and her mother and her brother were the only ones who followed. The next week her father started his insurance job.

Let's go downstairs, I said, and I'll make dinner. *You don't have to cook.* It will be easy. *Oh, there's nothing in the kitchen.* I'll find something. *No, let me order us dinner at least.* We went downstairs and Heather phoned for salads from a Mexican restaurant. We drank more wine. I left the next morning.

So tell me about the clarity, I said at La Maison.

Havemeyer, the Sugar King, was especially friendly with the chairman of the House Ways and Means Committee, who was persuaded to eliminate the sugar tariff in 1890. This vastly enriched the trust; also it led to the annexation of Hawaii and the Panic of 1893. Unemployment rose to over 25 percent in New York, over 40 percent in Detroit. Havemeyer refused to answer questions from Congress about his political donations. He was accused of contempt of court and found not guilty.

I'm back at Putnam Marsh, Heather told me. *But I'm spearheading a new initiative.*

What's the initiative? I asked. *Women's empowerment,* Heather told me. I watched her sip her sparkling water across the table. I wondered what would happen if I asked, Does this mean more math? I didn't risk it.

At the height of his power, Havemeyer himself decided, every day by ten o'clock, the national price of refined sugar. At the height of its operations, the American Sugar Refining Company controlled 98 percent of the country's sugar production.

And my work on the Weatherfield board, Heather said, *which is especially rewarding. I'm learning as much as I can there.*

In 2008 the United States government decided a few financial institutions that had issued fraudulent securities were "too big to fail" and spent hundreds of billions of dollars to make sure they did not. At the time, the total cost of this action was over two thousand dollars for every resident of the United States.

Heather said, *One of the things I've clarified is that I'd like to move permanently into the nonprofit sector.*

I've never really understood the nonprofit sector, I said. I was eating the last of my sandwich. I used a bit of crust to sop up the sauce. Heather had most of her lunch left. *It's fairly complicated,* Heather told me. She tore in half the piece of popover still on her plate. *Tax code, regulatory apparatus.* I mean I never understood the basic premise. Isn't there also profit? I mean, don't you need money before you give it away?

Among those "too-big-to-fail" institutions in 2008 was Citibank, which opened in 1812 as the City Bank of New York and later counted Havemeyer as one of its directors. By then it was the National City Bank of New York. The National City Bank of New York was perhaps the most important of the financial institutions that around the turn of the twentieth century consolidated New York's position as a center of finance by ensuring U.S. control over Caribbean sugar production. Its president resigned after an investigation of the bank's role in the 1929 stock market crash. In 2008, Citibank got $45 billion from the U.S. government.

Heather said, *Nonprofits can be mission-driven in a way that other corporations can't afford to be.* I nodded. Can't afford to be. I said, So you would work for the Weatherfield Foundation?

After the 2008 financial crisis I briefly wondered if I should ever put my money in any bank again.

Right now it's volunteer, Heather said carefully. *But the board is thinking about a capital campaign. We will eventually need a new financial officer.* That could be you, I said. Heather smiled. *Well . . .*

The American Sugar Refining Company was one of the twelve corporations that made up the original Dow Jones Industrial Average. In the financial crisis of 2008, the Dow Jones lost over seven hundred points in a single day.

I decided to risk it. I said, Would that mean more math?

Viewed another way, Fanny Assingham is not peripheral to *The Golden Bowl.* It is she who introduces the impoverished Italian prince and the rich American daughter. It is she who sets the whole narrative in motion. *At some point,* Renata wrote at the end of one of my dissertation chapter drafts, *you may wish to consider whether your description implies a stronger indictment of narrative structure.* But I didn't want to indict anything. Certainly nothing I was working on.

More math. Heather laughed. *I don't know. It's so good to see you, Laura. I've missed talking to you.*

Me too. Talking to you.

I'm so glad you can be part of all this.

In 1909, the American Sugar Refining Company paid two million dollars to settle a civil suit over unpaid customs duties after the company was convicted of fraud. A spring concealed in the scale at the Brooklyn docks had for years been reducing the recorded weight of raw sugar.

Of course I continued to put my money in banks after the 2008 crisis. What choice was there. At least that's how I thought about it. I had so little money anyway.

A congressional investigation, after Havemeyer's death, dragged out its inquiry for over a decade and eventually concluded that the American Sugar Refining Company could for the most part continue its investments and activities without any violation of antitrust laws.

I said to Heather, I'm not sure yet what I'm part of. The benefit, Heather explained. A renewed focus on past and future. *The centennial comes at the perfect time for the foundation*, she said. For you, too, I said. She smiled. *And for you!*

Emotional connection, in *The Golden Bowl*, has "the same deep intimacy as the commercial, the financial association founded, far down, on a community of interest." There is nothing ironic or regretful in this statement of fact. James was interested in interest. It was his job to make things interesting. He is a great novelist. *The Golden Bowl* is his last great book.

I think this could be a great opportunity, Heather told me, *to leverage your skills in a new direction.*

I had so little money anyway, but being poor does not help. The Weatherfield Foundation goes on, and the money continues to grow, and I go on having taken it.

But is it a new direction really. I didn't say that. I said, I'm grateful to you.

Heather smiled. *Oh, I'm grateful to you!* We smiled at each other. *Basically, what I've learned in the last few years is that everything that looks like a setback is a chance for growth.* I said, I'm not sure about growth. *Growth is just living.*

Heather no longer practices her religion. She seems never to have consciously lost any faith or repudiated any institution. She seems simply to have moved somewhere else in time. I asked her about it once. She went to Christian Fellowship in college, but she didn't like the people. *I just didn't click with any of them.* She went to a church at Oxford for a few months before stopping. *The worship style here is really different.* But do you still believe? I asked. Have you changed your beliefs? *I think my belief is always evolving,* she replied. *Yet the core belief hasn't changed.* I stopped myself from asking the next question. I said, I don't mean to pry. *Oh, you didn't.*

Soon after Weatherfield sold his company to the Sugar Trust, Andrew Carnegie wrote the famous essay called "Wealth," which argued that the proof of wealth is giving wealth away. When the piece was published in London, its title was changed to "The Gospel of Wealth."

How about personal life, though? I said as I ate Heather's portion of popover. Are you seeing anyone?

Havemeyer the Sugar King gave away money, of course, but mostly he bought art—beautiful things, beautiful paintings. His daughter founded a museum.

Oh gosh, yes, we barely talked about that, Heather said. *You'll laugh if I tell you.* I said I wouldn't.

Too big to fail was supposed to be resignedly pragmatic. A shrug. *Too big to fail.* We would like to let them fail but we cannot. But I thought I heard in it something like naïveté. An almost childlike immaturity. A child looking up at parents. The big things cannot fail. The foundations must remain.

I'm seeing Wesley, Heather said. *Wesley? I know. We met each other again at a fund-raiser. He just got divorced.* I said, Wow. That's great. *We'll see,* Heather said, smiling. *I should have been cured by now of dating bankers.*

The conclusion of *The Golden Bowl* is supposed to be about the rich American daughter's separation from her rich American father. This is the substance of her growth. She must turn from her father to her husband. She must turn from the man who gave her money to the man who married her for it.

The waiter approached. Heather confirmed to him our inability to eat any more. He left the check in a small leather folder. *Are you staying over?* Heather asked. *I hope you can stay over. You're always welcome.* I thanked her. I told her I couldn't, though. I said something about my mother. Heather nodded.

"It's *always* terrible for women," says the rich American daughter at one point in *The Golden Bowl*. But she is not talking about herself. She is talking about the beautiful American friend. Her no longer impoverished Italian prince dismisses her statement. It's terrible for everyone. As for the American friend? "She's making her life."

Heather took out the check and reached for her bag. Let me pay half, I said. *Don't be silly,* Heather replied.

In 1915, four years after the Weatherfield Foundation was established, a national commission reported that "as regards the 'foundations' . . . their ultimate possibilities are so grave a menace, not only as regards their own activities and influence but also the benumbing effect which they have on private citizens and public bodies, that if they could be clearly differentiated from other forms of voluntary altruistic effort, it would be desirable to recommend their abolition."

Is the foundation paying? I asked. *I'm paying,* Heather said. Okay then, I said. Thank you. I really mean it.

Today there are over seventy thousand foundations in the United States that give away over forty billion dollars a year.

I'm just so glad that this brought us back together, Heather said.

We got up to go. Heather unfolded her sunglasses. *And you should talk to Justin right away.* Justin? Heather made a gesture. *Oh, I forgot to tell you. He agreed to write the essay at first. Then it fell through. That's why the deadline is so rushed now. You understand.* I said, I do. *He may have found some information you could use, something that would save you time. Anyway, you should check with him.*

Okay.

And about your fee, Heather said. *How much do you charge for things like this?* I thought for a second. I should have had an answer. I didn't. I don't really know, I said. Whatever you think is right.

cracking cement floor, and everything in it filthy with sugared dirt. Covered in a worn, deep coating of brown-black sucrose residue punctured with hardened pools and drips and splatters. The smell overwhelmed. How could it smell this strongly still? A thick pall of fungusy caramel rot. The smell seemed to suck all other oxygen from the space. The air felt like a sponge of candied gangrene.

"What do you think?"

"Colleen Brock," she told me firmly when we met, shaking my hand. A publicist employed by the Weatherfield Foundation. Of course, the Weatherfield Foundation was not Weatherfield Sugar, Heather had told me. But the historical link was worth considering. In the parking lot of the abandoned Weatherfield factory, Colleen punched numbers into a box and fished out a key. She opened one of the padlocked metal doors and propped open a view of the dark insides. She wore heels and a pantsuit and several overlapping necklaces. She gave me a folder printed with her company logo, a business card slipped into a slit on one of the pockets. She was as efficient in the task of impressing me as she was in the job of assessing the space. She could do both as a matter of course. She walked from nowhere to nowhere in the vast room with great purpose. She seemed most interested in narrating to me the real estate values of the surrounding neighborhood. "The whole Brooklyn industrial waterfront," she explained loudly, "so hot right now." I nodded. I had noticed that, I said; on my walk from the subway, interspersed with the blocks of fissuring parking lots and torn wire fences, large billboards advertised condominiums about to be constructed. "I imagine there are big plans for this space, too," Colleen said. She sounded almost wistful, as if she would like to be part of those big plans instead of the more minor ones she was charged and already bored with. Her heels scritched on the grit of the cement floor. "I think developers have their eye on it. I would imagine this will be completely transformed by spring." She looked around in admiration.

I made a noncommittal sound in the back of my throat. I had no reason to be there, but Colleen seemed used to handling the various random people who wanted to convince themselves they were part of the planning in any project. I did not bother explaining that I was not one of them. Heather had forwarded the first email to me and then cc'd me on the next. "Looping in Laura, who is handling a historical essay for the gala." An administrative assistant coordinated our schedules.

"Some sort of photo record maybe." Colleen squinted. She was talking to herself. In my folder was the same article I'd been FedExed overnight last Wednesday, a grainy brochure from a Brooklyn tourist board telling me the Weatherfield factory is one of the distinctive and cherished buildings in the area, operational for over a hundred years, from the late nineteenth century until the year of my college graduation, by which point the majority of production had moved south, a pink sign outside the crumbling structure left to help recall with pride the era during which Brooklyn was the center of American sugar refining. I realized, when I looked at those pictures, that I didn't know anything about sugar refining. I knew nothing about sugar apart from the fact that it made money. I had checked out a new stack of books from the library and picked one to read on the train on my way to the Weatherfield factory.

I read for the whole ninety minutes. I read on the first subway ride. I read while waiting for my transfer. I read on the second subway ride.

It's simple, the story of sugar, simple in the way long, complicated stories can be. Complications rewriting the basic idea. The basic idea is that in the five or so centuries of its cultivation, sugar has done more harm to the world and its people than perhaps any other crop. From the time Columbus planted cane on the island he called Hispaniola, from the time Europeans realized that vast sums of money could be made from this plant if non-Europeans could be brutalized and forced into the deadly work of tending it, from the time when so many people of what came to be called the "sugar islands" had died that European planters began buying and selling African people to do the dangerous, merciless labor in inhuman conditions, from the time when cane fields rustled across parts of Barbados, Louisiana, Brazil, Angola, Florida, Australia, Cuba, from the time when English people began to grow accustomed to the substance that would succor working-class men and women with the anticipation of sweet tea-tinged hot water or jam-smeared bread as they labored in factories at life-sapping intensity and length, working to get more of what allowed them to work more, from the time when governments began to organize foreign policy around the production of sweetness and the control of its price, from the time when cane planting began to destroy forests and erode soils and hack out life-giving vegetation, from these times forward, the legacy is consistent and continuous.

Oh, and I also read a bit about how sugar is made.

The process is tremendous, really; it's the kind of thing that would not seem worth the effort were it to be described as mere possibility and then seems inevitable, irreversible, because it has already been done. First the cutting and crushing of cane, to extract juice that can be boiled and crystallized, then the further processing, raw sugar dissolved into warm sludge, spun in a centrifuge machine to separate the darker syrup from the lighter crystal, dissolved into syrup to be filtered and perhaps refiltered after a "sweetening off," run through a different filter, boiled in a mammoth vacuum pan until the crystals are the right size, centrifuged again, dried—then packed into bags and boxes, at last, or maybe crushed to make even finer varieties and then packed into bags and boxes. All of the cutting, crushing, heating, spinning, filtering, boiling, drying—all of it takes time and immense machinery and vast amounts of energy. All of it ends in a uniform white substance without any identifiable feature but the most basic and universal flavor humans recognize. It seems a lesson in futility, or perversity, or tenacity; it seems a lesson in something. The publicist looked at me and when I exhaled to speak I could feel my stomach shriveling up into my lungs.

"Sorry," I said. "The smell."

She nodded. She didn't seem to be affected by the smell. "Right. It's a factor. Have you seen enough here?"

I nodded.

"While I appreciate the drive for authenticity, I think ultimately that this space will require too much modification to make for a viable event site." She was already speaking in the sentences of her memo.

"Right."

She made a note on her clipboard. "Also, the brief I have from the board is more about the future of the foundation. Not the past."

She looked at me as if I would contradict her. I didn't. We squinted, emerging into what seemed like the violent clarity of the sky.

Thursday, September 29, 2011
Today I thought about the premise of writing a diary, which seems likely to be a literal waste of time. The premise is that something coherent and valuable can be learned from a record of what I have done. Or make it generic. Something coherent

and valuable can be learned from a record of what someone has done. A diary implies a story to be found or a useful sequence of elucidation to be traced. Today I wondered about whether that could ever be true as more than an expedient instance of self-deception.

Today I wondered if a bit of self-deception might be necessary ground for anything worthwhile, and if so, how to know, how one should figure out its proper calibrations in each particular case.

Make it personal. How I should figure it out.

Today I also requested from the library three more books about sugar.

Friday, September 30, 2011

Today I walked almost ten miles, down from the campus to the river and back. The river hugs the parkway, so the route leads to more nature and more traffic, both, the rush and rattle of trucks and the wind in the trees. I turned at Main Street and waited at the long light to cross six lanes of Post Road and found the half-maintained trail skirting the small playground with a derelict set of swings—cracked plastic seats, rusted chains—before the row of warehouses and scrub brush and the culvert. I didn't realize I was walking to exhaust myself until I was heading back, exhausted. I am back at my mother's house now and blank enough to sleep.

Sunday, October 2, 2011

Today I got an email from Justin with an apology.

Justin and I had arranged to see each other Monday night, after my meeting at the factory. Justin chose the bar, of course. It had a pool table at the back and two shelves running along the four sides of the room. Hardcover books stood on these shelves in arrangements of two or three, leaning into one another like diagrams in old-fashioned calisthenics pamphlets. When I arrived at eight, Justin was already there. He seemed to have been there for a while; he was talking with a group near the front of the room. I thought I might back slowly out onto the sidewalk and then keep backing all the way, if necessary, over the Brooklyn Bridge to Grand Central Station. But Justin saw me and pressed my upper arm and told me he'd get rid of these folks, that he'd be back, one sec—he was still laughing gently at someone else's joke.

Justin has always been the type to touch a lot, to leave his hand in the small of your back or scrunch your shoulder; at Oxford, I assumed this habit came from living among white people who could not admit an ever so slight discomfort in the presence of a handsome, six-foot-tall black man, but on Monday, watching, I wondered whether it was some more basic assurance he felt in his own physical person, some desire to extend the feeling or even to share it. I sat at the bar and ordered a glass of red wine, which never came, and looked at my phone and stole glances at him and considered the fact that I could not even conjure the feeling of being so assured. He had just the fingers of both hands in the tight front pockets of his jeans and he leaned into the conversation with the half-interested, half-scornful pose of his sustained shrug. He tossed his head back. Now a glance at me, eyebrows raised—*I'll be there soon.*

Justin works as a writer and lives in Brooklyn, like everyone who doesn't live somewhere else, though I think he grew up in Washington; his father was a judge or maybe worked in government. I don't think Justin ever completed an Oxford degree. He began in PPE, but then switched after a term to a graduate program in social anthropology and then switched again in our second year to something else—I don't know what. His failure to finish a degree only cemented the impression of his success. He left for a job at *The Washington Post*, right away, then left six months later to write for a new online magazine in New York that closed within a year, then served for a while as something like a "senior writer" for *Wired*, and then had a different title, "contributing editor," at *The Mix*. And somewhere close to a year ago, he accepted the freelance assignment from the Weatherfield Foundation that was passed on to me when he decided it was too negligible or boring or paid too little; somewhere within that time, he may have acquired information it would be useful for me to consult. This was the only reason we were meeting. "Cool," Justin's email to me read. "Let me know when you are in Bk." "Jesus," he said when he finally ambled over, "I thought they would never leave. Okay. Yeah. We'll get a table."

I abandoned my glass of red wine and paid for two of the old-fashioneds Justin wanted. Justin wore a row of silver rings in one ear and a gray Henley shirt that consisted of some material that looked more fashionable for basically sharing the constitution of pajamas. Justin talked quickly, rushing toward the end of a paragraph and the bottom of his glass, almost surprised at how quickly he got to both, and then on to another round, fast. He was greedy for words and words were always there for him. I think I asked some questions. Somehow I knew he had sold a book for a large advance. A nonfiction book. People, he told me, who work in or with traditions that don't match their own heritage. He sketched a chapter on the unnoticed Polish man who played bass on a bunch of reggae records and one on the Mexican poet who spent years perfecting prizewinning haiku. He was interested, he said, in the personal impulses behind what could be called "cultural appropriation"; he put air quotes around that. "I mean, when it's not about power. Not just about power. Is it all power? Okay, yes, it is. That's basically the book." I said it sounded interesting. He said, "Come on, *interesting* is a bullshit word." I said that didn't mean I was bull-shitting. We mused briefly about what the opposite of bullshit might be. He got up to fetch more drinks.

I like conversations like these, the kind that seduce you into supposing that what sounds like honesty should be taken for approval, as if people like Justin don't talk this way to every-one. Justin returned with two new glasses. My questions were hardly necessary anymore. He didn't want the book to be inter-esting, he said. "I mean, I want to write a bestseller. Don't get me wrong. Definitely want that. I just don't want to be one of those assholes who's writing a bestseller, you know?"

"Okay."

"Nonfiction is so fucked anyway. I mean the whole category. If I had any integrity, I wouldn't be writing this. No, I mean it. It's fine. You've got to know what you're selling. I'll tell you, though, when to take me out back and shoot me. . . ." He paused to sip. "When I do one of those books, that's like a year of doing something. Or not doing something. You've read these? You've seen them? Like twelve months without electricity and how it changed me. Or whatever it is. Twelve months of reading books about twelve months of doing something. My pitch. My year of years. Jesus. Get a life. Which is the whole point? A life. Of these books? Supposedly?" He drank. He leaned even farther in. Hunched, again, this impossibly graceful, awkward pose. His hair fell forward. "You're living in Connecticut? You like it? I lived there for two years when I was in middle school. Yeah, it was cool—no, seriously, I hated it. I don't think I could live anywhere but New York. As an adult. Which is really sad. New Yorkers are such pathetic fuckers about the city. They think the fact they can't live anywhere but New York is proof they're super cosmopolitan. Anywhere but certain *neighborhoods.* I'm like, Ah, no? Not exactly? That is the definition of provincial? Let me ask you something. The Weatherfield people. They hate me, right? They think I'm a fucking deadbeat?"

"The board? I don't know. Do you care?"

"Good question. Yeah. I don't. Heather. Heather hates me. You're friends with Heather?"

"She doesn't hate you," I said.

"I never got Heather."

"What's to get?"

"Listen to you."

I blushed. "I didn't mean it that way."

"It's cool. I'm probably just suspicious of people who are nice. Heather, I mean. What are you hiding? I think the nice people are secretly, like, super misanthropic. Right? Come on. It's true."

I said, "I think I should be flattered."

"Ha. I'll tell you something about Heather, though. Did you know she was invited to sit for All Souls at Oxford? Seriously. That woman is *smart*. Yeah. Don't ask me how I know this shit. People tell me things. I swear. I don't even try. Anyway. You want another drink? I have to go to this birthday party, birthday drinks. Some guy I used to work with. He wrote that big story about Kanye last year? You read it? No? It was okay. I mean, it was pretty good, I guess. A white guy writing about Kanye. You do you. Right? Who else are you in touch with from our year? Jay? Watch yourself around Jay. He's like, 'I'm giving you motherfuckers nothing to dredge up.' He is squeaky-clean. But maybe it's just me. Everyone knows to keep their mouths shut around me. I'll tell you something about Jay, though. He failed the bar the first time. In Massachusetts. Yeah, yeah. I'm serious. Don't ask me how I know this. But I mean, what are you doing even taking the fucking bar exam?"

He scoffed. "Who else? This is fun. Zac out there in Silicon Valley, innovating, disrupting. Play money. Right. You're a professor? Of course you're a professor. Big surprise. You like it? Greta is also a professor, but she didn't really seem the type. No, she's a doctor. Maybe she's a doctor professor. Huh. You know what I mean, right? She didn't seem the type. I thought she'd be, you know, curing cancer. Who else?"

"Caroline."

"Oh, right, we all want to be Caroline. Caroline really is saving the world."

"I guess."

"And Lindsay's at some think tank. I think I quoted her in a story once."

At Oxford, Justin hadn't shown much interest in Lindsay, a thin white girl from Alabama with long brownish gray hair she always wore in a braided bun. She was too openly conservative. Or too southern. The post at a think tank came later. I said, "I'm not in touch with Lindsay. I'm not really in touch with anybody."

"Me, neither. Another round? You know who was obsessed with Heather."

"You?"

"Me, no. Mark. He thought she had that small-town goodness. It's a thing. You're in touch with Mark?"

"Mark? No. Why would I be?" I took a gulp of my old-fashioned. I could feel for a moment the small, cool breath of the ice.

"Okay, okay. Don't get all offended."

"I'm not offended." The buzz of the room around us had gotten louder. Someone shouted with excitement in the back, near the pool table.

"You look offended. There's no way I can write the Weatherfield thing. My book deadline is the end of the year." He held up his glass. "Seriously, one more? The timing—I've totally fucked myself even without other assignments."

"I shouldn't have any more."

"All right, I'll tell you, I wouldn't do this even if I had the time. It's a shitty assignment. Weatherfield, I mean. He was rich. He died. End of story. A piece like this, you need some personal interest. Hold the reader's little hand. Oh, wait. Shit."

"What?"

He looked at me, past me. "I just realized I should be writing a different book." He shook off the thought. "I mean, I already knew that. It's what my agent says. I should write a memoir. You know? Memoirs sell. You remember Tamara, like a year younger than us? She was a fellow." To my confusion, he added, "I mean, you definitely knew her." I hadn't. "Anyway, she's writing a memoir. I think she got cancer or something. We can't all be so lucky."

"No."

"Anyway, Ennis was a drunk who killed himself in a car accident before he was forty. No one cares. Why should they? You've read the stuff."

"The foundation records."

"There's nothing there."

"Actually, it was his wife."

"His wife?"

"Florence. Florence was the one who gave the money away. After Ennis died."

"Does that matter? Is she interesting?"

"Probably not."

"Ennis. What kind of a name is that?"

I said, "Irish."

"Irish." He stopped talking momentarily, as if the word proved his point. I didn't remember his point. I nodded. I had drunk too much. I wanted to ask him something about Mark.

I said the foundation should perhaps include something of the Weatherfield history, even if no one cares.

"Really. Why?"

I think I said, "By way of acknowledgment."

Justin shook his head no. "I get it, you have a Ph.D. You know what the fuck's going on. But those people don't care. The Weatherfield people. I'm serious. They read, like, the fucking *New York Times* op-ed page and they think it's intellectual. They just want an excuse to charge five hundred bucks to go to a party."

"It's a benefit."

"To whose benefit? Oxford? Never again. God, it took me like a decade to realize how much I fucking hated that place."

"You did?"

"I mean, it was like Stockholm syndrome. With a whole fucking culture. Jesus, the English. Get over yourselves. The empire is done. You're a small island in a bad climate. Learn to install a showerhead, for fuck's sake. Seriously. You remember those showers? It was like a watering can hooked up to a transistor radio. Like up to here on me. How is this supposed to work? I was like, 'You're not *all* four feet tall.' Right?"

I said I thought he liked it there. At Oxford, Justin smoked European cigarettes and went to a few events with a woman graduate student who was a minor member of the British aristocracy. He pointed out racism rightly and constantly, but when undergraduates protested a bop with an "Out of Africa" theme he seemed to find their sensitivity amusing. "Yeah, where's that going to end?" He joined his college's rowing team and became vice president of the Middle Common Room, then quit the team when he missed too many morning practices and the MCR after the Christmas bash, when officers were allowed to take home the extra wine. Meanwhile, he learned the rules of cricket well enough to talk back to commentary in pubs. He rented little Peugeots on weekends to travel with friends to places like Lyme Regis. He told stories of his mistakes with left-side-of-the-road driving.

I said to him, "I guess Oxford was kind of a waste of your time."

"Ha." He looked at me again. "Good way to put it. Waste of time. We'll go with that." He shook his head with admiration. "You're going back tonight? You want to share a car? No, I can't. I'm late. Okay, text me when you come back to New York. And when I'm in Connecticut . . . Ha. Not happening. Though I bet it's peaceful and shit there? Maybe I should live in Connecticut. Maybe I would write a fucking memoir if I lived in Connecticut. Maybe I would blow my brains out. Why are you there anyway? Okay, I get it, long story. Next time. I have to go."

On the train home, I should have read more about sugar, but instead, on my phone, I found one of Justin's recent essays in *The Mix*. I don't think I'd read anything he had written before then. The story was excellent. It profiled a young black woman from the Bronx with a heart-stopping singing voice who got a scholarship and was planning to attend college but was indicted at nineteen as an accessory to a drug deal while she was trying to help her mother move out of an abusive home. In between paragraphs of her narration, Justin explained how Medicaid works and why housing policy is so rotten and why poor kids can't go to private colleges even if they get scholarships. The writing was measured and precise. I cried a little at the third and final section. The comments below the story were full of admiration: "This is the most amazing thing I have read in a long time. This is a call to action."

Justin's email today, his email of apology: "Sorry I forgot to

give you that stuff I found. I'll put it in the mail by the end of
the week, I promise."

"Sure," I wrote back. "No problem."

Tuesday, October 4, 2011

Today I read some descriptions of cutting cane. A description
from less than a hundred years ago and a description from less
than fifty years ago and a description from less than fifteen years
ago and much of it seemed to match descriptions from several
centuries ago. The work is relentless. Cane fields are swelter-
ing, the soil radiating heat, the plants smothering any breeze.
Cutters move through with their sharp, heavy blades. One fist
grasps a stalk's tough base and the other swings the knife; then
two more strokes chop off leaves and several more, finally, divide
the stalk into portions. Assemble a pile and carry it to the truck
or carriage or railcar. Then again. Cutters stoop and rise and
stoop. Ripe cane left in the fields too long turns acidic, and cut
cane left too long dries out, so the work is intense, quick—but
also exacting, and careful, to avoid injury. Injuries are common.
The machete slips and slashes a finger, a tendon. And cane can
pierce skin, pierce an eye. The green plant, also, ignites a rash
on human skin. In Puerto Rico in the fifties, I read, the words
for working the cane fields were the words for doing battle and
defending oneself. In El Salvador in the nineties, sugar workers
started in the cane fields as young as eight.

Wednesday, October 5, 2011

Today I meditated. I have been reading about meditation, a
little, among books about sugar. I should have started with
Marcus Aurelius or the Buddha, but instead I started with
Meditation in No Time at All. I got this at the library, too. I
wonder if Heather has read this or would like it. Probably not

earnest enough for Heather. I liked the jaunty double meaning, though; also the typical self-help prose: breezy but taking a while to offer simple instructions. The simple instructions were to sit, breathing, without any thoughts at all, or rather, with plenty of thoughts I note without pleasure or regret and let pass. Clouds in a sky: This is what the book says. One's mind is the sky; one's thoughts are the clouds; one's consciousness is a sun that can observe thoughts come and go without agitation. I'm supposed to do this for ten minutes a day, then work up to fifteen, twenty, forty. Very shortly, I'm supposed to be sitting, blissful, for hours at a time. Today I tried. But it turns out my thoughts are not like clouds in the sky. They do not drift. They gnaw. My thoughts are rats in a field of sugar. Rats, I read, are one of the few animals that not only survive but even prosper when fields are cleared for cane. The crop drives out most wildlife, since it exhausts most land on which it grows. But rats prosper. In some places they are as little native to cane fields as the cane itself; they came with the colonizers and their plants, their plans; they grow fat and vicious on stuff that shouldn't have been cultivated in the first place.

THURSDAY, OCTOBER 6, 2011
Today I got an email from Renata. She wants to know what I am working on.

FRIDAY, OCTOBER 7, 2011
Today I exchanged text messages with Justin.

It took about ten minutes in full. I noted the time because it passed quickly, and usually I am too nervous, when texting, for time to pass quickly. I got a smartphone only last spring, when it seemed like taking a stand not to have one, and mine is the cheap kind sold only in optimistic colors, so I look like a low-income striver rather than someone with principles about thrift or fair labor or technological overreach. I don't use the phone much, except for maps. Texting makes me nervous because I'm not sure of the proper rhythm for beginning or ending a conversation. I remember one chat with a colleague, back when I was teaching, that started when she needed the time of a meeting, then veered into lunch preferences, and concluded when she at last typed something like "I should probably get back to grading" and I typed "OK." Later, she commented on how abrupt I was. "No time for pleasantries with Laura!" This she said in front of several others in a crowded hallway. I smiled and apologized. I am in fact good at pleasantries, I thought; just tell me you want pleasantries! Justin did not seem to want pleasantries. A line appeared on my phone screen around 4:00 p.m.: *I can't find that folder,* and I wrote back, "Who is this?" and he replied, *Justin.*

I wrote, "What folder?"

Weatherfield

I wrote, "Oh, it's okay. Don't worry about it."

I'll find it I just haven't yet. He texts very quickly. *Do you think Royce wants a weird black guy to come speak during Black History Month?* And then *I'm changing the subject* and then *My book agent thinks I should get a speaking agent lol* and then *And do more talks* and then *Something like TED; get on tv* and then *Apparently long-form has already jumped the shark; who knew* and then *Oh wait I guess we all did.* The phrases came one after another. Finally, I typed, "You would come here to give a talk?"

That's the plan

Maybe

I have a couple of pieces that could be talks

But not really

They're pieces

I hate the word pieces
Do you want to give talks?
I don't know
Not really the question
Good for the career
I guess it IS really the question
The answer is no
What about your book? Don't you need to finish your book?
Yeah
It's almost done
Writing is easy
Oh.
Ha, no
Writing is hard
It sucks
Why do you think I avoid it
I read the article you wrote.
Which one?
About the musician. It was excellent.
It was cheese
Not even
Cheese product
It made me cry.
You see
Do you not like it?
Fine
It's fine
Bad editing
It's never about the writing
What is never about the writing?
You know
I mean

Sometimes
The writing is never about what you're writing about
It's about, like, this bullshit idea of what writing is
This doesn't make sense
I think I understand.
Great I don't
I'm kind of high right now
Okay.
Not really
Just a little
It's the same in academics.
What is
Getting high
Research is never really about the research.
Okay
The expression is "research is me-search."
Did you just say that
That's corny as hell
I'm quoting.
Okay
Better
What is your research thing
I never asked
I wrote a dissertation about Henry James.
He was gay right
Jk
Yes, probably.
So what does it mean is there more to figure out about Henry
James
I mean what are you trying to figure out
What is the research

Characterization and indirection in James's theory of the novel.

What does that mean

It's the title of my dissertation.

It sounds like it

You're not really trying to figure out anything.

Really

I mean I wasn't.

I probably should have been.

It was a waste.

Jesus that's dark

Not really.

Not really

You are stone cold

What does that mean?

It means stone cold

It means teach me your ways

My ways?

Your strategies

I'm trying to meditate.

You're joking

I haven't figured it out yet.

Ha okay that's awesome

I can still talk to you

You know meditating is a white people thing

Not really. Not originally.

True

Well you've given me a lot to think about

I can't talk anymore

Okay.

I have to go meet someone

He wants me to write about him

I won't
Anyway about the talk
I think it's too late for next year
But I should probably do it
I hate these questions
They're good questions to have.
Yeah
I'm an asshole for complaining
No.
You're doing good work.
What Henry James story should I read
What have you read already?
Nothing
I'm an idiot
Give me something short
The Beast in the Jungle.
What's it about
Nothing.
You're really selling it
It's about figuring out too late that you've hidden your deep-
est desires from yourself.
Whoa
Did you write about that one
No.
One you wrote about
I wrote about long ones.
Shocker
Try Daisy Miller.
Sounds dumb
About?
I'll quote.
Oh god

It's about how far "eccentricities were generic, national, and how far they were personal."

What's the answer

I don't know.

Lol

I've got to go

Go meditate

Or something

Bye

I didn't even have to type a closing. It was a very satisfying conversation.

Justin seems to have perfected a life philosophy directly contrary to stoicism or Zen, a confidence built on insecurity—relentless questioning, relentless movement, relentlessly undermining himself and everything else. On this he has built assurance, integrity, purpose.

Saturday, October 8, 2011

Today I read about rebellion and revolution. For centuries, the work of sugar depended on people enslaved in Africa and packed into westward boats run by sound New England shipping concerns that could pretend not to profit from human chattel (I remember the term *triangular trade* from school units in maybe the fourth or fifth grade, and I remember liking the rhythm and alliteration of those two *t*s, and one leg of the triangle was made up of human beings). Then after abolition, the work of sugar depended on those transported from their homes in India or China or Japan to islands where they knew few words and no people. Or Puerto Rican families living in crowded two-room houses and underpaid in scrip only good at the company store. Black men in the Jim Crow South who were bused to the fields after promises of good jobs and told they owed the company already for the cost of the journey and food and thus had to labor for free, patrolled by men wielding billy clubs. Haitians in Cuba before the Revolution, sleeping in shacks at the edge of the sugarcane rows and sneaking water from the spigots that irrigated crops. Jamaicans in the cane of Florida after World War II, housed in concrete barracks near the cane fields, brought to the country on H-2 visas that sugar companies lobbied the government to issue yearly, strange immigration footnotes permitting people to enter the country not as citizens or visitors but as labor contracted to a company they could not challenge or anger for fear of being sent home and losing a season's wages. Growers compensated workers on an "incentive" system—by the row, the expected time set without arbitration by the foremen, and foremen guiding their estimates by what management told them, or simply shorting hours on a cutter's time card. In the 1990s, a long civil case fought for back pay from sugar companies in the United States that had cheated workers. In the 1940s, a sugar company was indicted for conspiring to commit slavery. In the 1930s, New Deal inspectors reported on cane cutters who were anemic and near starving. But what was wanted was not a government file or indictment or a circuit ruling. What was wanted was flame. In the thirties, striking sugar workers in Puerto Rico burned dozens of cane fields. In 1791, San Domingo was the most profitable colony in the world because of sugar and slavery, and when the revolution came "the whole horizon was a wall of fire." In 1831, in Jamaica, a Baptist preacher told enslaved sugar workers not to return after the Christmas holiday so that they might peacefully demand wages and freedom, and when British troops arrived with guns and dogs, massacring the rebels after a promise of amnesty, Jamaicans set aflame fields and stores and houses. In 1811, scores of enslaved people in southeastern Louisiana walked off sugar plantations and headed toward New

Orleans, collecting others as they went, marching to drums and music; and before a militia of white planters met them near Cannes Brûlée and killed dozens, taking the rest captive, impaling heads of the slain on spikes at plantation gates—before that, the rebels set fire to a long swath of crops and buildings. This "German Coast Uprising" does not appear in many history textbooks. What is wanted is not a textbook. When I read about Cannes Brûlée, I thought of crème brûlée and an official Weatherfield dinner for new fellows when this delicate dessert was served. Usually, cooks make the crisp caramel top with a blowtorch. That time it came etched with a small, graceful swirl scorched into the sweetness like a brand. The metaphor is so easy as to seem cheap, as to seem suspicious. I closed the book. I looked up more books. I closed the computer.

In my mother's kitchen I found a bottle of Plantation molasses; the bottle has an actual picture of a plantation on the front of it: blue sky, clouds, a big house. The background is yellow and patterned and the font for the brand name is an old-fashioned serif. Molasses is the only item the Plantation brand makes. Molasses was, for a time, cheaper than white sugar, since it consists of white sugar's remains, the brown glop on the bottom of the vat or the pan; now molasses is more expensive because it seems traditional. Molasses has flavor, character, history. The label of Plantation molasses is proud of this. Plantations were something like the first corporations, in fact. Taylorism, Fordism, the alienation of factory work: It's all there in sugar production. The brutality, the endurance of brutality, is there. "Some foam at the top is normal," the Plantation label reads. Of sugar varieties, molasses has the most nutritional content—a little iron, a little potassium, a few other nutrients. Molasses has been used for animal feed and to make rum. It can also clean rust from old iron. Molasses is good for cleaning guns.

MONDAY, OCTOBER 10, 2011
Today is Columbus Day. Today I tried once more to meditate. I might be getting better. I can't tell. Progress is hard to determine; progress is antithetical. I'm not making anything happen. The opposite.

TUESDAY, OCTOBER 11, 2011
Today I deleted the email from Renata.

WEDNESDAY, OCTOBER 12, 2011
Today I texted with Justin again. *Found that file,* he wrote.
　　About the Weatherfields?
　　Ha-ha, file
　　Makes it sound like I'm organized
　　I'm not
　　Thanks for finding it.
　　It's not much
　　There's a library with some stuff
　　I mean maybe it has some stuff
　　Great.
　　Don't think I did any work for this
　　Never.
　　I was at this writer's conference
　　God listen to me
　　Anyway someone told me
　　Actually I think it was a professor
　　One of your kind
　　Not really.
　　I'll send it
　　Give me your email address
　　(He had my email address. I sent it again.)
　　How is the work going

I'm not sure.
Mine is going pretty well
Good.
The last little bit
Since we talked
Who knows
This might burn off
What might burn off?
Hatred
All the best writing comes from hatred
Ha.
Not even joking
Trust me
Does self-hatred count?
Sure
It doesn't seem to help me.
Give it time
Speaking of hatred
I talked to Heather
Oh.
She's not mad
Of course not.
She's all come to the gala
Will you?
No.
Why would I
I don't know
Maybe
Depends who else goes
I guess
Now that Heather likes me
That's why you'll go?

Everything is personal
I don't think so.
Trust me
People don't seem to matter.
. . .
?
Sorry. I was typing something.
And?
I don't know how to put it.
It's about history.
Nothing is personal.
Are you going to the gala
No.
You'll go
Are you writing this essay
Yes.
You shouldn't
I need the money.
Well okay then
I need the work.
Take the money
Always
    I went to the Weatherfield plant. The one in Brooklyn.
There are a few old sugar refineries around there I think.
Weatherfield plant
As in factory.
I mean it's in Brooklyn
I didn't know that
It's abandoned now.
Yeah Brooklyn used to be something real
I'm not sure that's the word.
Now it's not

Don't you live there?
Yeah
I do
I'm sure right now will seem real later.
Good point
Nothing more. This exchange was less satisfying. After it finished I cleaned my mother's house. I spent hours. I did the vacuuming and mopping and scrubbing and then the stuff that never gets done—the dust on the top of the window frame, the grime at the crease where the kitchen countertops hit the wall. I told myself I was trying to be useful to her, but that wasn't the reason. I didn't know the reason.

Thursday, October 13, 2011
Today I read over all the notes I have taken so far.

Friday, October 14, 2011
Today I went back to reading about sugar refineries. I looked at pictures. Refineries appear at once so crude and so chemical, it's hard to remember the product to emerge is something humans will eat. Will crave. Unprocessed sugar arrives in mountains of brownish gray sand or large dull sacks on the back of a rusty barge. A dirty loader bucket funnels it in. The heating and cooling and spinning and dissolving and drying begin. Belts and gears shriek and groan. Vats hum. Workers quietly feed and tend. Sugar is everywhere, in different and transmuting forms, in sliding heaps and clouds of steam and streams of liquid and planes of crystals. The factory is loud, but mostly it is hot. The hottest part climbs to 130, maybe 140 degrees. Workers' sweat tastes sweet long past when a shift is over, and normal temperatures feel frigid all their lives. In old age, even, years after they have stopped putting on insulated suits to stand for half a day in the kiln department,

former refinery workers wear wool sweaters in July and shiver through sunny afternoons. The tremors last, too, the knotted muscles. Some get cancer—lung, kidney—from breathing and handling acid and lime. Some have burns. These factories are always going up in flames. The last and one of the worst sugar fires was in 2008, in Georgia; fourteen workers were killed and investigators found the disaster to be "entirely preventable"— but to eliminate sugar fires would mean eliminating the stuff itself. Sugar dust is always waiting for a chance to combust. Fine particles of sucrose are skittish as gunpowder. The Weatherfield factory caught fire three times; the last time, in 1893, three workers were killed. These fires, too, were probably preventable. The Weatherfield family, when they ran things, did not seem to have been much interested in prevention of anything. In the 1870s, workers were fainting with particular frequency and foremen requested a reduction in shifts on the hottest days, but Hugh Weatherfield refused. At the height of Brooklyn sugar refining, workers were mostly Polish and Italian immigrants; in 1918 the draft forced factories to hire hundreds of women, with wages accordingly cut and production expectations at the same level. After the next war the plant was unionized—the longshoremen's union; everyone who worked near the docks qualified—and pay improved, so if you worked the night shift, you got a bump, and if you died on the floor, your survivors got a fixed sum. In the eighties it was twenty thousand dollars. There are stories of those with cancer hauling themselves to work to die on the floor. Those were the best years. Already the union's power was eroding. Strikes increased. Strikes got longer, more bitter. Workers picketed through Brooklyn winters and threw eggs as scabs trudged across the line and trucks filled with sacks of sugar continued to leave the lots. When unemployment ran out, when strike funds ran out, the union agreed to contracts

waxed paper, creased envelope-neat on four sides, and oranges, the humiliating scent of which stuck to my fingers all afternoon, and cookies, and water in a dented silver thermos. She unfolded maps of New York or Hartford or Boston and then tried to refold them after she had traced with one finger where we would go. She read guidebooks and wall placards. We would come home with dirty tinfoil in the bottom of a canvas bag and a crumpled uncertainty in our chests about whether the excursion had been properly done. Whether we had learned something.

The cookies are made of molasses. Today I learned something. I learned about the black woman in nineteenth-century Massachusetts who invented them; she was married to a Revolutionary War veteran, once enslaved, who ran a tavern. She sold her cookies to sailors who needed provisions laced with rum and sugar for long journeys. I read about this. I also read a little about the white women in eighteenth-century England who refused to buy rum and sugar as a protest against slavery. Leaflets exhorted; china sugar bowls were inscribed with antislavery messages. Some of these rhymed. Sugar was a natural arena for women's political action because women were thought to have a natural proclivity for sweet things. This campaign against sugar was not inconsiderable. Hundreds of thousands of people in England, at one point, promised to give it up.

Monday, October 17, 2011

Today I realized I am getting worse at meditation. I thought I was getting better, but I am getting worse. Acceptance, I have made no progress on acceptance—I do not see the purpose, or perhaps I do not see the need. I don't want to accept more. I want to know more. Or *is* that acceptance, the latter desire? It feels like the opposite. Yet it would accept in that it would take more in. Take everything in. Today I thought about the drive to take more in—shameful, somehow, in its disorganized craving, its yearning for facts without purpose or plan or intention to turn learning into action or even, really, understanding; it isn't research, this avidity; it couldn't be. Research would come to something. It might be work, or what I referred to once when I used the word *work*. But work, too, would produce, and this is all consume—the stack of books, on my desk, to be consumed, the list of facts, next to a stained mug and a plate strewn with crumbs. Today I ate several more cookies.

TUESDAY, OCTOBER 18, 2011

Today I found out that in the last week or so Justin has written an essay for the Weatherfield Foundation centennial gala. Someone from the foundation emailed me to say they had received the piece, which provides a beautiful reminder of the individual experience of the fellowship. The foundation is now looking to find other fellows who may be interested in reflecting on their time in Oxford or Paris. The foundation is particularly keen to include a wide range of meaningful voices. If I have any suggestions they would, of course, be welcome.

WEDNESDAY, OCTOBER 19, 2011

Today I texted Justin to say I heard he had written an essay about the Weatherfield.
  Yeah
  I would like to read it.
  Don't bother
  If you don't want to share it I understand. But I'd like to.
  Sure I will email
  Please do. Not like those archival papers that you keep promising to send and never send.
  Shit I forgot

I know.

What is your email

(He had my email address. I sent it again.)

Ok I'm sending it now

The essay or the archival papers?

Yes

The essay

Tell me what you think

Especially if you think it's terrible

Hang on.

Jk if you think it's terrible never speak to me again

Jk if you think it's terrible save me from myself

Hang on.

The message came in. I read his essay standing up, in the kitchen of my mother's house. Absentmindedly, almost automatically, I ate several molasses cookies as I did. When I had finished I picked up my phone again.

I think it's very good.

Yes?

Yes.

Really?

Really.

Thanks

Glad you like it

You don't have to say that.

Okay I won't

Got to go

Sure.

The essay describes how Justin became a writer. It narrates the late nights at Oxford during which, bored and disgusted with his schoolwork, lonely and alienated from his companions, he began to write about his own experience for the first time on something that was not an application or assignment or questionnaire. He bought an electric kettle and drank large cups of PG Tips tea as he filled a notebook in longhand. In the morning he bought papers and magazines from an Irish newsagent who, when Justin asked what he should read, what he should buy, what he should write about, scowled back and said, "It's up to yourself." The essay describes how bad those first compositions were, and how hard he worked on them; it is funny and wry and moving, with precise descriptive passages.

Thursday, October 20, 2011
Today I wrote a brief message to say no, I do not have any good suggestions about individual experience and/or meaningful voices.

Friday, October 21, 2011
Today I stopped trying to meditate.

Monday, October 24, 2011
Today I received a next-day air envelope from Justin with a sheaf of photocopied sheets that describe a collection of miscellaneous correspondence in the Dawes Library in Philadelphia. Circled on the sheet are four boxes that include "Weatherfield" in their list. The Dawes Library and its collection are named for Edmund Dawes, whose sister seems to have known Ennis Weatherfield, or maybe Florence. I had forgotten about Ennis and Florence in my reading about sugar. Also Renata wrote to me again today, or rather forwarded something to me, an announcement for a conference on Henry James's heroines. Before I deleted the email I reflected that Florence could have been a Henry James heroine. I mean, historically speaking, the dates, the places.

TUESDAY, OCTOBER 25, 2011

Today I did some grocery shopping for my mother. I try to shop for us most weeks; my small bit of money can provide a small bit of food at least, along with some utility payments. I stood in the baking aisle and looked at the various kinds of sugar I could buy. I had no idea which I should purchase, if it even mattered. It probably didn't. A special display on the other end of the store was stuffed with bags of Halloween candy. I didn't buy any of that, either. I should have. Kids will come to the house expecting something sweet and we don't have anything. I've finished the cookies, even. I'll just leave the porch light off and pretend no one is here.

THURSDAY, OCTOBER 27, 2011

Today, and yesterday, and some of Tuesday, I sat in the Royce library, at the computer with all the databases, and tried once again to learn about Florence Weatherfield. I had almost nothing on Florence. Have almost nothing. A few facts and documents and mentions from her early life, before Ennis died, then nothing after the establishment of the foundation. It is as if she gave away the sugar inheritance and then spent the rest of her life without leaving anything to know.

FRIDAY, OCTOBER 28, 2011

Today was my birthday.

SATURDAY, OCTOBER 29, 2011

Today I stopped writing down what I did today.

4

METHODS CLASSES

*Census records from 1880 were organized by home address, with
residents listed next to rectangles of information—first "color," the
options for which were "white, black, mulatto, Chinese, and Indian,"
then "sex," the options for which were "male" and "female," then
"age at last birthday" and relationship "to the head of the family,
whether wife, son, daughter, servant, boarder, or other." Columns
followed for "civil condition," which meant single, married, widowed, or divorced, then "occupation," "health"—the census taker
might have checked "blind," "deaf and dumb," "idiotic," "insane," or
"maimed, crippled, bedridden, or otherwise disabled"—and "education," including space to mark "cannot read" and "cannot write,"
before columns for place of birth and place of parents' birth. Florence
Poovey lived with her father, Clarence Poovey, at 49 Irving Place,
New York City, along with a grandmother and two servants, W
for race, F for gender, thirteen for age, a daughter, single, at school,
also healthy, also literate, also born in New York, to parents from
Massachusetts. Ennis and Florence married twenty-one years later,
when he was twenty-eight and she thirty-four, and Ennis died seven
years after that, when he was thirty-five and she forty-one.*

When I imagined Greta's home I still pictured her lavish, haphazard dorm room at Oxford, but Greta, of course, no longer lived like a student. She owned a house—big, old, high-ceilinged, mansard-roofed, with a dining room in the center that seemed like the natural spot to do everything as well as the most uncomfortable spot to do anything. She led me there the first evening, to unload flyers and folders from the pockets of her several bags; a dark table on a darker rug had already acquired a stack of mail, of books, a soft lump of outerwear, or was it underwear, a few magazines. The wallpaper was a faded striped pattern of pale green, lavender, and deep red. "It's awful," Greta said, looking it over happily, agreeing with something I hadn't uttered. "But we don't really have the time or energy? We already ripped out and redid all the bathrooms, and that was enough to drive me even more nuts than I already am. Then the guest room. I told Judith, no more for six months. So yay for antique stuff. If it is antique. Probably not." She swooped into two exaggeratedly naïve voices, as if she were puppet-mastering a skit of quizzical idiots: "*Would you prefer your home decoration to be hideously unattractive or historically inaccurate? Actually, I would prefer my home decoration to be both, if possible? Okay, sure, for you we can make that work!* Oh, thank you, I'm immensely grateful."

The voices I remembered. Suddenly remembered. How little Greta had changed. Before I arrived I doubt I could have called to mind her tones and gestures, but from the time I saw her again nearly everything she said and did made me think, Of course, this is Greta. Amused at the circumstances amid which she always happened to find herself. She showed me her home, for example, in a state of hapless incomprehension, as if it were something bequeathed to her that she was cheerfully tolerating for a while, rather than something she and her partner had toured, chosen, signed multiple contracts to acquire, paid many thousands of dollars to own, painted and changed and improved in various ways. Greta said, "You know how these places are. Zero closets. Floors slanting. All the damn windows a different size." We moved to one of the damn windows, looked out. "The yard is good. We were looking for a yard. You've got a dog and a kid, you've got to have a yard. I mean, where else are they going to poop and break their arms and eat poisonous weeds? You tell me."

"I suppose nowhere," I said.

"Nowhere. Exactly."

She was a little bit thicker now, and the skin around her eyes looked older—but the wider curves and deeper lines only settled her more firmly into herself. When she came into the overflowing entryway, herself overflowing—carrying those bags and holding her child by the hand—she was able to knock the door closed behind her with one foot and fling out an arm that was—astonishingly—free to draw me in for a half hug without stopping her progress. "Laura! You found the key and I'm only half an hour late. Ronnie, this is Laura; we knew each other before you were born. Can you believe it? Before you were born. I existed!" She still wore her long blond hair piled on top of her head in a plastic clip; she had added rectangular glasses, bright red, and shiny clogs; her clothing, it seemed, had shifted from the vaguely athletic at all times style she practiced at Oxford—leggings, tops that zipped, color-block patterns— to similar shapes with looser layers and more sophisticated fabrics: a long silk affair between a dress and a shirt, a sleeveless jacket over that, a scarf, a necklace.

But she was unwrapping herself and her packages; she was leading me around; she was talking. We ended in the kitchen, at the back of the house, narrow but high-ceilinged, with silver appliances and the same wide wooden floorboards, warmly restored, that ran through the rest of the rooms. Some of Greta's things became an unruly pile next to the several different bins near the back door, one heaped with empty glass bottles, one full of paper, one closed over a liner. Heaps appeared everywhere, in fact, though it wasn't a small room—plastic bubbles of hot dog and hamburger buns puffed from the bread box; piles of grapes and bananas spilled out of a basket of oranges; boxes of cereal were squeezed into the space between cupboard and ceiling; a dishcloth tower softly tilted above the refrigerator. Bowls hugged each other inside the large bowl of a mixer, which rested on a stack of three cookbooks. One wall was darkened with blackboard paint and bore the word *Crispy?* in white chalk above various scribbles in orange and blue. Other surfaces, too, were covered in scribbles—these on paper, taped or magneted: the refrigerator, the wall above the sink, the strip of paint between cupboard and door, the front of the dishwasher. "Ronnie is quite the artist right now," Greta said, rolling her eyes at me.

"They're very nice."

"Oh yeah. Masterpieces."

With me she performed sarcasm but every interaction between her and her child was 100 percent earnest, the placid patience of good parenting. "Do you need a snack? Check in with your stomach. How does it feel?" Veronica, a delicate child with blond curls and purple sneakers, had no interest in a snack. Or in me. She retreated to a playroom. "She'll eat if she's hungry," Greta said. "But you . . ." I could not be trusted to eat if I was hungry. "Something to nibble on—there's some cheese in here somewhere." She pulled things out of the refrigerator, a wide, double-doored steel model with the freezer on the bottom. The kitchen was full of expensive equipment covered in household rubble. Her movements were quick. Her arms were full. Nothing fell. "These crackers are decent."

"Can I help?"

"You can drink some wine. Yes? Do you like wine?" She was looking already. She had a collection, apparently, on a dark wooden bottle rack in the nook behind the refrigerator, hidden by a jumble of aprons and tote bags. "This one—Judith hates this one, but if you start before she gets here she isn't allowed to complain. Or at least her complaining will be useless." The voices again: "Somehow this bottle is already conveniently open? *Why yes, indeed it is.*"

Greta was chopping onions. Greta was a professor. She had been premed, truly premed, she assured me; you could not *be* more premed than she had been. When she was a kid, she told everyone she wanted to be a doctor. "Operated on dolls, loved blood. Standard little premed ghoul. I thought I was set. *And then.* Have you heard this before? When did we last talk? It's been how many years?" Greta bashed a clove of garlic with the flat of a knife, then flicked aside the skin and turned her blade perpendicular to mince the flesh. She scraped the results into a pan. Her story continued: When she was back in the States after Oxford and heading to med school, she felt "actually sort of bored at the prospect? Like"—voices—"*um, I find saving people's lives to be insufficiently interesting, as a life plan?* Yes, I understand; that's definitely a reasonable position. *Actually, I think I'd like to throw over everything I am trained to do?* Oh, sure, why not. No," she continued, in her normal register again, "it wasn't that I needed more excitement. I just needed something more than . . . bodies. Ha! And then I took a seminar, on a whim . . . medical anthropology. Like"—voices—"*what is this? You mean to tell me medicine isn't everywhere the same?* Actually, get this, people in different times and places have differed. *They have?*

And of course I was a goner," she finished in her normal tone. She was scraping with a wooden spoon, speaking normally but still gesturing. "I mean, once you start thinking about culture, people's *experience*—" Greta waved her spoon over her head. She stirred while spinning the spice rack that squatted nearby; she palmed a few bottles, lined them up on the counter, and opened the first one-handed. "So that was that. For a while, I thought maybe an MD/Ph.D. But once I did my field work, eh, I couldn't be bothered with anything else. Including, like, the methods classes? Ugh. I think I loved the field work so much because I never really knew what I was doing." She paused to use her left hand for a bite of cheese and cracker. "Maybe that should be present tense. I never really *know* what I am doing." She shrugged, grinned.

"It seems to be working," I said. She was an assistant professor in the anthropology department at Haverford. I had seen her faculty page. It was where I had found her email address.

"Yep." She squatted to pull out a pot. "Let's keep it going, keep it going. Plus no one knows what anthropology is anyway, past the colonialist bullshit."

"I see." I had sent a tentative message to that email address, a message I hated for its roundabout cringe: I needed a place to stay near Philly for one, maybe two nights? I didn't want to impose, and I know we hadn't spoken in many years . . .

Greta fetched a noisy bowl from a low cabinet. "I was so glad you wrote," she continued. She was shelling shrimp; their limp gray bodies glistened, helpless, in a bowl on the counter; she threaded away dark bits of vein with a knife she'd plucked from a messy drawer. Her fingers were long, the nails bitten down, with a variety of flat silver rings on six fingers. "Actually, if I'm honest"—she looked at me over her glasses, puffing her cheeks, as if I'd just demanded her honesty and she was only reluctantly giving in—"the Weatherfield was probably the beginning of my tottering off the med school path." Voices: *"Here, why don't you spend the most vulnerable years of your emotional and sexual life in a gloomy town of a former imperial power that thinks it's a good idea to have pornography in daily papers?* Thanks, sounds like a recipe for a healthy development. *Well you're most welcome I'm sure.* I'm sure you know what I mean," she added in her normal tone.

"Um—yes. I guess."

"A freaking nightmare." She looked up. "I can't curse, because of the kid. Though I always forget." She rinsed her hands. "The kid is very quiet. She's okay in there?"

"She's lining up dolls on the floor in rows."

"For execution?"

"It does look kind of ominous."

"Not uncommon, I've got to say. Carry on, weirdo. Not you. Her. You don't have children, Laura? Right? And you eat seafood. Yes? No shellfish allergy? Am I about to kill you with this?"

"I don't have children. I eat everything. My mother's a cook." I don't know why I added the last sentence.

"Aha." She stopped stirring to look at me. "I never knew that about you." She said this as if she knew many other things about me. "Judith is the cook in *this* family. But she only gets a chance every now and then, when she's not working. Residency. It's a shitty life. She's a far better person than I am, though. She can take it."

"Oh," I said. "I mean, no, I'm sure she's not a better person."

"Don't worry, it's true. You'll meet her and you'll see."

The wine. The smell of warm oil, garlic, and basil. The whir of the fan over the stove. I had let myself in, following instructions, after making my way via train and bus through what had always seemed to me an unappealingly *worn* city, Philly, a place without New York's energetic showmanship or Boston's haughty tradition, a place with neither illusions nor hopes about what was cracked and dirty and useless, and when I got there the house seemed messy and cold, full of forgotten arrangements, odd colors, neglected corners, mismatched and wrongly sized furniture—until Greta arrived, and began cooking and talking, at which point the house seemed alive and right, part of a city secure and familiar enough not to preen or strive. Greta clicked on the burner beneath a pot of water. "I just sort of improvise. Whatever works, right?"

"Whatever works."

"So freeing! But wait, I'm talking too much. You must tell me about whatever it is that brings you to our fair city of brotherly love. And our ugly house of sisterly love. You said the Weatherfield."

"Um . . ." I didn't know where to begin.

I need to relax.

WHERE YOU LEARN

The annual reports of Bryn Mawr College list degrees conferred, after a statistical summary of the student body and a report on the college's needs, plans, and gifts ("generous contributions amounting to $3,425, which have enabled the Trustees to complete the swimming pool"), and before a description of the various curricula ("Dr. Warren lectured five times weekly . . . covering the vertebrate portion . . . In April and May, Dr. Morgan gave the part of the course on the development of the chick . . .")—including the student's name and place of origin, along with the school each was "prepared by" and the "group" in which they studied; also included are lists of "addresses delivered" at the school: "Northern Greenland," "Women in Buddhism," "Some Anomalies of Self-Consciousness,"

"Education." Florence Mary Poovey of New York City was pre-pared for college by *"Miss Mark's School, and by private study"*; her *"group"* was *"Latin and English,"* not an unusual or otherwise distinctive field. She graduated in 1889, three years before Ennis Weatherfield enrolled at Harvard College, which he left soon after, four years before he enrolled at Oxford, where he spent parts of three terms, and six years before he studied briefly at the Sorbonne.

When the front door opened, I had only just convinced Greta to let me help and was collecting forks and knives from their jumble. Greta cocked her head at the sound of the lock. Exaggerated surprise: "Whaaat? Judith is never this early." A slam. "This is all you, Laura. You should feel honored. Sweet-heart? You there?"

"I'm here."

Judith was small and buxom, with olive skin and dark eyes and curly hair; she was wearing large wooden earrings, sur-prisingly tight jeans, heeled boots. Her handshake (with me) was firm; her kiss (with Greta) seemed firm, also her voice, the accent of which I couldn't classify. "Shall I make a salad?" she asked. She paused amid the chaos of the kitchen, frowning in concentration rather than disapproval.

"Salad is ready for takeoff," Greta told her. "I need you to put the dog out. Where is the dog? Where is the kid? Where is my mind?" She was tonging pasta into wide white bowls. "How was your day?"

"My day was extensive," Judith said. "Exhausting. Good." She cocked her head. "Motorcycle accident."

"Aaaah. Don't tell me. I'll get too excited. Would you call Ronnie? I think she's upstairs with her books. Ronnie!" Greta did the calling herself. The table, cleared of piles, was set for four. Candles. Pasta bowls. Salad plates. An elliptical trencher of polished wood held dressed greens. Wine was poured into three glasses. Water with ice in four. Veronica climbed onto her booster seat. Greta put on music, in the background, a Pandora station of old-time country music too soft for me to make out the rhymes. "Jesus, I'm hungry," she said when she sat down. "Sorry, sorry. *Jeez,* I'm hungry. *Jeez,* I'm tired. Eat, everyone. What did I forget? Salt?"

"Nothing," Judith said. "Milk."

"Oh, the fucking milk," Greta said, getting up again and moving toward the refrigerator. "Sorry, I know. Language. It's a long story, Laura—" This was addressed to me, as if I had asked. "No, I guess not, just a boring one." She came back with a small mug of milk that she set near her daughter, who seemed not to notice or care, and who was twirling her pasta with much attention and two hands. "My mother went through this *thing* recently in which she got all excited about milk. Worried Ronnie's bones were cracking or rotting or warping or whatever because we didn't make her drink cow pus every day. Not even Judith's medical credentials seemed to convince her."

"That is not quite fair," Judith said mildly. "I don't object to milk. And your mother merely raised the idea. She did not argue about it."

"Oh, she would, if she thought she could get away with it." Greta sat down again, sighing at the burden of a mother who did not argue. She turned to me. "My parents are so overjoyed at a grandchild, they won't really criticize anything about our parenting. We could raise Ronnie as a nudist and they would basically swallow their tongues and hope she was coming for Christmas. A nudist is a person who doesn't wear clothing," she said to her daughter, who had looked up from her bowl, in wonder, "for philosophical reasons. Actually, I'm not sure it's for philosophical reasons. Maybe it's for health reasons. Maybe they're happier that way. Which could be philosophical?" She turned back to Judith and me.

"No." Judith did not elaborate. She held her knife and fork in the European way. She cut a shrimp into four small bites and pierced one of them, inspecting.

"So now we throw away milk every evening is the bottom line," Greta said. "We're teaching our daughter that waste is a necessary by-product of maternal guilt."

Judith was ready to be done with the subject. "Laura, what is your work about? I don't think I have been told. And I may not understand. Greta is the intellectual."

"I'm here to look at some material in a library in Philly—" I said.

"Ennis *Weatherfield*." Greta jumped in. She was chewing with gusto. She swallowed. "At that place downtown—Dawes? Laura's writing something for the gala I mentioned. Oh, God— do you have to go to the gala, Laura?"

"No."

"What a relief, right?" Greta said. "I'm one of those people who's like, 'Let me pay you not to invite me somewhere. Here, take my money, don't make me come to a fancy dinner.' Pass the salad?"

Judith passed Greta the salad. "This is about the man who created your fellowship?" she asked me. "That was his name?"

"Ennis Weatherfield," I said. "But he didn't create the fellowship."

"He didn't?" Judith asked.

"All I remember about Ennis—" Greta began. The conversation was surprisingly chaotic for a table at which the three-year-old was silent. Greta was now eating salad with her thumb and forefinger, a leaf at a time. "All I remember about Ennis is that he was too dumb to graduate from Oxford and the Sorbonne and so decided to pay for others to do it instead."

"That's not exactly true," I said.

"It's not?" Judith asked.

"It's totally true," Greta replied. She explained to those of us at the table: "I *would* probably go to the gala, I mean, let's say I could afford to buy a ticket, which I can't, but I would probably go *if* I knew who else was going. If I knew I wouldn't get stuck with some blowhard explaining his stock portfolio."

Judith turned to her. "You always charm the blowhards with the stock portfolios," she said patiently. "You always find them amusing."

Greta smiled at this reminder. "This is fact," she said to me. "This is one hundred percent fact."

I tried to smile back at Greta. In the small silence, I said to Judith, "It's true that Ennis did not graduate."

Judith furrowed her eyebrows over the wineglass, confused. Greta was grinding now at the handle of a cheese grater, bringing her face down to Veronica's to explain the word *blowhard*: "Someone who talks a lot and brags about himself and doesn't listen to other people." Veronica nodded in satisfaction, assimilating this. "Do you want some salad?" Veronica shook her head. She was cautious and grave. "Did you like your pasta?" A nod yes. "Do you want more?" A shake no. Greta looked up then, alert, as if remembering something. "However, I am definitely *not* the intellectual."

"Please," Judith said.

"Please *what?*"

Judith frowned at her. Greta frowned back, harder. They remained frowning at each other for a moment. The love was palpable.

"Whatever you say . . ." Greta almost sang her response.

"Whatever *I* say?"

"What*ever* you say . . ."

I concentrated on my food. The best part of Greta's work, she'd told me, were the friends she made doing it. I nodded at this pronouncement. I didn't know if she was supposed to refer to the subjects of her social-scientific research as *friends*—I didn't know if she wasn't, either; I was honestly unsure. Greta studied attitudes to medical care for pregnancy and early parenthood among low-income mothers in the United States; the friends were the women in Oakland and now Philadelphia housing projects and homeless shelters who answered her questions on where and how they delivered their children and why and if they trusted hospitals and doctors and nurses—"They *don't*, not much, surprise, surprise." Her specialty was happenstance, as Greta told it, another stroke of luck; she was drafted in graduate school to be part of a team gathering qualitative data on another topic altogether, and since she was starting to think about having a child herself, she "asked people about it and thought, Well *this* is certainly fascinating." Greta had not finished her first book, which was based on her dissertation; Stanford had extended the contract twice. "This year. That's what I've told my chair." She rolled her eyes. "Don't worry. Everyone *wants* to give me tenure. Otherwise, they'll have to admit they made a mistake!" She chuckled.

I said, "Of course." I told her I wasn't worried.

I looked down at the pearlescent glint from a fragment of shrimp shell in my dinner bowl. I said to Greta, "How can you *not* be an intellectual, if you're a professor?"

"A good point." Judith nodded.

"But." Greta held up one finger, ready to offer the clinching argument: "I've hated school my whole life."

"I doubt that," Judith said. "I doubt that very much."

"Seriously!" Greta waved her hands in front of us for emphasis. "School was fine, fun, whatever. I was smart and I was on teams and in plays and, you know, I was perky and blond. But when I was a kid I dreamed about reaching the age when I wouldn't *have* to go every day. I was counting down the years. And now I have to go every day for the rest of my life!" She laughed, then turned her fork toward her chest and made stabbing motions.

"Oh, stop it," Judith said at the same time Veronica asked, "You hated school?"

Greta really appreciated the liberal arts focus of Haverford, she'd told me earlier as she moved over the stove. "And you went to Royce, right?" She appreciated the way a liberal arts school encouraged students to explore, to do their thing. "I mean they're probably going to end up somewhere *totally different* from what they expected! Look at me! That's what I try to tell them. They come in all, 'Hello, I am an overprogrammed robot whose only goal was a college good enough for my parents,' and I'm all, 'Maybe don't think about your parents for a minute, just give it a try, see what it does for you,' and they are like, 'It has escaped my comprehension that this is even an option.'"

"It might not be an option."

"For the kids I'm talking about, it's definitely an option." She waved a hand. "I'm telling you, it starts young. We have Ronnie in a really good day care, you know, experience, active play, arts. But you should hear these parents. They've got their kids' lives mapped out till college graduation at least. I'm sure you run into this all the time." She shook her hands over the sink. At birth, Greta explained to me, Veronica was diagnosed with a heart murmur, "but it turned out to be innocent! That's the official name. Innocent heart murmur. Nice, huh? I'm almost sad she'll probably grow out of it." I murmured something about how awful that must have been. "Yeah, a few weeks of worry. But this stuff is so common. That's what you realize. You tell one person, you hear five stories. Right?"

"Right," I said.

Over the dinner table, Judith put a hand out to her daughter. "Your mother went to a school very different from yours," she explained. "Your school is a good school. And if something happens at your school that is not good, you tell us and we will make it better."

"Yes, definitely." Greta nodded. She put her fork down and calmed her voice again. "Speaking of which, I want to hear more about what you did *today*. Was it yarn?"

Veronica considered carefully as everyone watched her. "We did magnifying glasses," she said finally. "We learned magnifying." She picked up her glass. She took a drink of water. She put her glass down. She picked up the mug. She took a drink of milk. She told her mother, "School is where you learn."

"Yes, sweetheart. Exactly." Agreement all around. Greta scraped up the last of the salad.

"How about you, Laura?" Judith said. She was kindly bringing me back into the conversation. "Are you also a professor who hated school?"

I was still trying to frame a sentence about the creation of the fellowship and the consequences of Ennis Weatherfield's failing to get a degree. "Ah, I'm not exactly—" I stopped. "I didn't hate school, no," I said.

"That is a relief."

I said, "I don't think I was aware that hating was a possibility."

Judith raised one eyebrow—not suspicious, curious. But Veronica asked if she could go color. She had checked with her stomach and her stomach felt full, and her mothers said, "Yes, of course" in unison, and for a moment we all watched her small body as it trotted out of the dining room and climbed up the wide wooden stairs to a room where she would make some more art.

"Laura brought chocolates," Greta told Judith. "Really good chocolates." Then she turned to me. "I can't remember. When we were in Oxford, had I even come *out?*"

I need to know my options.

HELPING PEOPLE

The printed marriage license begins with a statement swearing "no legal impediment exists as to the right of the applicants to enter into the marriage state" and then lists questions "from the groom" and "from the bride," full name and "color" and residence and age and occupation and place of birth, names and birthplaces of parents, finally blanks for "number of marriage," "former wife or wives/ husband or husbands living or dead," and two questions, one asking if the applicant is "a divorced person" and one asking "when and where" the "divorce or divorces were granted." Neither Ennis Weatherfield nor Florence Poovey had an occupation. Neither had a former spouse. Neither was a divorced person. The register holds both names in its careful record-keeping script on August 7, 1901, after which a brief paragraph appeared in a few New York papers: "married yesterday at the home of her father, accompanied by their families."

I fetched a sponge from the kitchen. Judith had gone upstairs to her notes. Veronica was still coloring, somewhere out of sight. "Let me take care of the cleanup," I said to Greta. "Honestly, I'd like to. You can relax for a sec."

"Nah, I'd rather talk to you. Hear about your life."

"There's nothing to hear."

"I know *that's* not true."

"Believe me." I swiveled the sponge around to catch a splash of milk. "How long have you and Judith been together, by the way?"

"How long. Good question. A long time. We got together in my first year of grad school. We got married in 2007—thank you, Massachusetts. Judith's parents live there. Not that Pennsylvania gives a shit about our *lovely* wedding." She rolled her eyes. "You're married?"

I shook my head.

"I didn't think so! I can tell."

"How?"

"Here, I'll take those napkins. Will you eat here tomorrow?"

"I don't want to impose."

"Listen to you! You can't impose. We are preimposed. And we'll use these napkins again. Don't be horrified."

"I'm not horrified." I cupped my hand under the sponge. "I *was* married." I blew out the candles.

"You're divorced?" Greta paused. "What!"

"I am." She could not tell this, apparently. "That's me, divorced."

"Oh my God," Greta said. "What happened?"

I kept my voice neutral. "He left."

"Fuck."

"Well." I moved to the sink. After divorce was certain, I remember, I focused on making sure it cost as little as possible—since I sought, and found, copious first-person stories online of how expensive a divorce could be, and since I realized quickly I would be in charge of arrangements, even though Isaac was the one who ended the marriage. I wrote him several long emails detailing how we could cut down on fees and charges, and he replied with one- or two-sentence notes: "Whatever you want is fine." But none of this is what I want, I wanted to say,

none at all; I'm not thinking about what I want and I never
have; *that's the whole point.* The never thinking was my defense.
Also my indictment, I only realized later. No one can live with
someone like that. I would have been too late with the thought
even at the time of our last conversations. Isaac had already quit
the graduate program, one of many choices he made that never
occurred to me even as possibilities. We signed divorce papers
at a distance and his parents mailed me a check for our legal
costs in a card from the Metropolitan Museum of Art's gift
shop. "It wasn't that big of a deal," I said to Greta.

"Oh, wow. No, it's a very big deal."

"Well." I dried my hands on my jeans. "I was there."

Greta shook her head. "It's my night for bath time," she told
me in something of the same somber tone. "Come with? Do you
mind? I want to hear everything."

She didn't wait for an answer. Up a beautiful curved wooden
staircase. Into a spacious tiled bathroom with a claw-footed tub.
"Ronnie!" Greta called. "Ronnie!" Shouting even as she went to
find her child. I waited. It seemed inconceivable that one person, one very small person, could require so many things in a
bathroom. There was a molded lavender potty, plus another
special seat that fit on top of the toilet, plus a shelf of soaps
and lotions and creams and a basket of washcloths and several
towels smothering on a single hook—in addition to all the toys.
Standing naked on the bath mat, Veronica carefully undid the
fastener on a string bag of plastic shapes and dropped them into
the filling tub, one by one, as if each were a delicate, soluble
ingredient in a potion she had to prepare. The letter *I.* The letter *B.* The letter *V.* "That's the one for your name," I offered,
and Veronica looked at me, holding the *V* in two hands, and
nodded. She reached in and found a *P.* "Yes, that one, too!" She
must have Greta's last name. Greta moved back and forth from

a closet in another room, humming, taking certain articles of clothing away and bringing other, different articles of clothing in, folding things.

"You ready to get in, chicklet?" she asked. "Is it time for bubbles?"

It was time for bubbles. Greta sat on the edge of the tub. The room began to warm into a fruity humidity. I hovered in the doorway, leaning. I could see a curl forming at Greta's forehead, against her pink temple. "But did you like being married, though?" she asked me, one eye on Veronica, who gave small plastic people boat rides through foam. "Apart from the terrible guy you got. If that makes sense."

"It does. He wasn't terrible. I'm not sure." Our trip to the courthouse felt daring and sensible, rebellious in its romanticism and its practicality, both—weren't we in love? (We were. For a while Isaac and I enjoyed the triumph of confirming how in love we were; after we went to bed, one Thursday evening of a Cambridge November, we stayed there for three days, talking and eating sandwiches and having sex—though by the time we got married we had sex rarely, since Isaac stayed up late to watch movies and television on his laptop before skipping classes and I went to bed early and got to the library by nine to hit my word count; soon we saw each other only in the late, deflated part of the day, when each of us had failed to get something done.) And wasn't it only reasonable, our decision to make love official? (It was. For a while Isaac and I enjoyed the piquancy of our actuarial defense, when colleagues expressed surprise—"*Already?*"; we had figures about tax breaks, health-care costs, rent savings, a shrugging mention of the supposition that two could live as cheaply as one—*look how I am exploiting the very requirement to be exploited!*—though by the time we got married, I realized two can live as cheaply as one only if two are of one mind; the effort of pretending we were seemed to bow and sag our life more than any debt would have done.) I said to Greta, "I should have been ashamed of the whole idea."

"Nah." No hesitation.

"The idea of marriage, I mean."

"The idea of marriage! What a hoot. Really. Yeah, what about *that?*" Greta posed the question to herself, with voices: "*What is this thing called marriage? Who has created it?* Um, it's just an idea! It can be changed? Look at us!"

I blushed. "I know. That's what—I think—" Greta was so positive. I thought how meanings of that word, *positive*, over-lapped. I watched Veronica carefully pilot her toys around the edge of her tub. Each boat got equal time. "I'm not as strong as you."

Greta wrung out a washcloth. "That's not true. Five-minute warning, Ronnie." Over her daughter's head, Greta looked at me. "Was there anything that set it off? The split? C-h-e-a-t-i-n-g?" Her eyes widened.

I nodded.

"Oh, wow. And you couldn't get over it?"

"Wasn't really an option. Are you saying . . ."

"A year ago." She gave a little shrug. "Me, of course. It was stupid and fun."

I was supposed to say something. "What happened?"

"Afterward? Oh, things work out. You work things out." Greta trailed a hand in the bathwater and flicked a few drops. "You knock shit down and then build it slowly back up. Sorry. I shouldn't curse. Ronnie, you didn't hear that."

Ronnie was not listening. She piled bubbles on her arms, her shoulders. She was dressing herself in water and air. I felt an undertow of exhaustion now that was hard to fight. Since the guest room was being repapered, I would be sleeping in Greta's study, on the top floor—"It's kind of a junk room right now. But comfortable. I promise!" I assured her I didn't need much. I wanted now to be up there alone under an old comforter among the Ikea shelves of outdated textbooks with my nose in the weird animal scent of my own hair.

"That sounds tough," I said.

"It wrecked a few friendships." Greta looked pleased. "But the two of *us* are fine. Judith and I are both so *logical* about everything. Or illogical, maybe. Illogical in the same ways." She laughed.

Veronica rinsed away her bubbles with water poured from a plastic cup. I should have said something wise about my experience with infidelity. How the fact of it seemed to matter very much, and then not at all, and then very much again. How the pure creaturely pain, the manic hurt in one's fingers and wrist bones and earlobes and thighs that comes from picturing someone who once slept naked against your skin pressed against someone else's, how that feeling decomposed, in time, before turning into something more enduring and much worse. "I can tell," I said. "You and Judith seem like a great couple."

"Oh, yeah. We're ridiculous." The bath was draining. She toweled off her daughter. I thought of something else, something I hadn't remembered in a long time. The first moment I suspected my marriage would fail was not the realization of infidelity or the irrevocable decisions following infidelity but an evening soon after Isaac and I had signed things at city hall. An end-of-term gathering—not quite a party. I borrowed the Costco card of a girl I knew and paid cash for three large wheels of Brie, six loaves of French bread, a few jars of olives, two mesh sacks of clementines, and four thickly wrapped blocks of dark chocolate; then I went to Trader Joe's for two cases of six-dollar wine and we asked over everyone we knew. Our apartment was almost instantly too small; almost instantly, it smelled of sweat and cheese and the bad breath that comes of drinking cheap alcohol, and every conversation seemed to be complaints about school, gossip about school: I excused myself to check on things that didn't need checking and then found there was nothing to do but return to another group and the same topics. Why were we doing this, again? Why was I spending money and time this way? Isaac loved it; he stayed on the balcony, a half circle of four or five others around him, an extra bottle at his ankles, and I could hear laughter, chatter, agreement, protest, ideas. Then he looked up and caught my eye and smiled as if to confirm our pleasure and I thought, I'm not sure I like people.

Now I watched Veronica in the mirror, wrapped in a towel and her mother's arms. Greta said, "Teeth, Veronironi."

"I'm going to have to wish you good night," I said to them both. "I'm really tired. Thank you for such a lovely dinner. And evening."

"You do look exhausted. Sleep well. Shout if you need anything."

"Good night," Veronica said. A peaked terry hood shaded her face. "Now I'm brushing my teeth for two minutes."

"They taught her at school," Greta said. "She's very particular. We have a timer."

"That's great," I told Veronica. "You should always brush your teeth. I mean, not always. Once a day. Or twice." I had no idea how to talk to this child.

I need to know what I want.

SLEEP AT NIGHT

At the turn of the century, passports were optional, especially for those whom any official would know on sight to be respectable—those like Ennis and Florence, white and rich and American;

married women, moreover, never had one, since married women would not think of traveling without a male protector. After World War I, the United States, along with some other countries, began to regularize identification documents, bureaucratizing out of worry over enemies and immigrants and those who could not be identified as acceptable members of the polity through their appearance alone. By then, Florence, widowed, filled out her own application, the one headed "Form for Native Citizen," which asked about travel plans, concluded with an "oath of allegiance" (all enemies, foreign and domestic), and provided blanks on the reverse for a "description of applicant": "forehead," "eyes," "nose," "mouth," "chin," "hair," "complexion," "face." Her chin was "unassuming." Ships' logs are the more complete record of travel, throughout the period, and in 1909, Florence's name appeared in one: "New York to Plymouth; 42, no profession, United States." Ennis had at that point been dead less than a year.

I didn't eat with them the next evening; my napkin went unused in its terra-cotta ring and I came in late, after a convenience store hot dog. Greta sat in the dining room, wearing large headphones in front of her laptop. "Laura." She brightened when she saw me and freed her ears. "Good day? Have a seat."

"You're working."

"Not really."

"You're doing something."

"Hating the sound of my own voice? Among other things." She laughed, unclipped her hair, ran her fingers through, reclipped. "It's my own form of torture. Right? I'm captured, I'm brought in for questioning, I'm all, '*You're getting nothing*'; and then the torturer comes back with '*How about we make you listen to your own voice very slowly over and over for several hours?*' Suddenly, I'm, '*Okay, okay, I'll tell you whatever you want to know.*'"

A normal tone: "I'm sorting through a bunch of interviews I did this past summer."

"Sounds productive." I suspected that Greta in fact enjoyed listening to her own voice. I suspected the complaining was part of her enjoyment.

"I have too much data." She sighed, then spun her laptop around. "What do you think of this?"

In spite of myself, I stepped farther into the room to see. The stacks of papers on the table had grown since last evening. Her computer balanced on one of them. "This" was a pink skateboard, child-size. Twenty-nine dollars, the screen said. "For Ronnie?"

"Yep. I want her to have more confidence! Do you think it would work?"

"Skateboarding."

"Why not!"

"I don't know anything about children."

"Oh, children are just tiny humans."

"I don't know anything about humans, either."

Greta laughed. "Right, right. Well, that settles it." I had no idea what was settled. She pointed to the box of sweets open on a different stack. "These chocolates you brought, by the way, do not mess around. I've had about four."

"Homemade."

"Really."

"There's a little shop near where my mother lives. The woman who runs it stirs a pot of chocolate in the back."

"I thought you were going to say your mother made them. Now I know she's a *cook*." The inflection said that she had tricked this information out of me and was mulling it over in an evolving process of deduction. She peered back at the laptop. "Come in and have one."

"No, I'm fine." She cannot help it, I thought, this eager extension in others' presence.

"I have to leave the computer open, by the way; don't be offended. I'm waiting for an email. Though let's not talk about *that*."

"Okay." She cannot help it and it makes her life better.

"A student of mine who's in a very messed-up situation. An ex? Stalkerish? Male, of course. You know how it goes."

"That sounds serious." And others' lives. It makes other people's lives better, too.

"She left me a message. I'm waiting to make sure she's safe."

"Should you call the police?" She wasn't worried about herself, so she could be helpful to others.

"Maybe. I try not to. I don't know how I get myself in these situations."

"She's lucky to have you." She wasn't worried about whether she was doing the right thing, or enough of it, or too much of it, or in the wrong way, so she could be helpful to others.

"Eh. Yeah, I guess. But you. What about you?"

"Me?" I should be more like that.

"How was your day? You find a lot of stuff?" She stood up and stretched. "You want some coffee, by the way?"

"I'm good."

Greta didn't seem to hear my refusal; she pulled her sleeves down, padded into the kitchen toward a kettle, filled it at the tap. She was wearing a long beaded necklace over her turquoise sweatshirt, and she fingered it as she turned on the stove. A new drawing was up on the fridge.

"My day was fine," I told her.

"Lots about Ennis?"

"Almost nothing about Ennis. Or his wife."

"His *wife?*"

"You seem surprised."

"Did I know about a wife?" Greta was sloppily spooning grounds from a silver canister into the carafe of her coffeemaker. "Did those weird historical fellowship Christmas cards mention a wife?"

"She's the reason for those weird historical fellowship Christmas cards. She started the foundation."

"It was Ennis's name, though." Greta clarified the situation for both of us. "And it was Ennis's money." She closed the canister again with a satisfied tap. "Ennis's sugar money. Ha! He was a sugar daddy."

"She was the older one," I said. "Like six years older."

"Weird."

"I guess." I discovered I wanted to change the subject. "The coffee smells really good."

"It *is* really good." Greta laughed. "Judith told me I spend too much at Starbucks and should make coffee at home. So I thought, If I'm making it at home, I should at least make the good stuff. Now I drink twice as much because I buy Starbucks *and* I make this, and the entire scheme has been a total waste of time and thought and hard-earned cash." Her joy in this outcome was pure. "You take cream? Sugar?"

"Just a little milk, I guess."

"Oh, okay." She rooted around in the fridge. "I take Splenda. Don't tell."

"I won't." I discovered I wanted to change the subject back. "Florence tried to get rid of the money," I said. "After the crash, after Ennis died. She wanted to get rid of all the Weatherfield money. That's why she started the foundation."

"Hmm." Greta was dubious. "She said this?" The water boiled and she snapped off the burner. Steam rose, and a deeper scent of coffee, liberated and rich. "Wrote it, whatever?"

I inhaled. "No, not exactly."

"Yeah." Greta shook her head. "I don't buy it. Giving some-thing away—" She put the kettle back down. "You don't need to be a trained anthropologist to know that gifts are all about power."

The only document I had that Florence herself may have composed was the typed one-paragraph letter directing the establishment of a foundation named after her husband that would have charge of the six million dollars she'd inherited on his death. Its concision seemed to me to skirt the border of legality. It did not include any of the language about ambi-tion and promise and inspiration and enrichment and society at large. All that came later, after World War I, when philanthropy needed a more magnanimous and worldly vision.

"You're probably right," I said. "You're definitely right. And no, I'm not trained."

"*That's* not what I mean." Greta fetched mugs. "It's just—we've got some rich white people putting their names on things? Whatever. It's not complicated!"

"I guess not."

"What *is* your field?" Greta asked. "You teach literature, right? What kind?"

I blew on my coffee. *I wish to have no influence or connection to the legacy beyond my knowledge that it will be doing something not unacceptable to the person whose money it was.* That was the last sentence I had from Florence Weatherfield. The only sen-tence. "Late nineteenth, early twentieth."

"So the Weatherfield dates."

"That's hardly a qualification. But I'm not teaching."

"What?"

"I don't have a job."

Greta stopped, looking at me over her cup of coffee, eyes wide. "I thought you were at Royce!"

"No. I mean, I am, but that's because my mother works there. I'm staying with her."

"Oh, God. *Laura*."

"I was adjuncting. Then I wasn't renewed."

"That sucks."

"I'm okay."

"You'll find something." Greta slurped. "You'll definitely find something. You want me to ask around here?"

"No, no, that's very kind of you, no—you don't even know my work."

"Oh, please. I'm sure you're a great teacher."

I tried to give a little laugh. "I'm less sure."

"See." Greta pointed. "That's what I mean. The teachers who worry they're not good are the best teachers. It's like with parents. The ones who have it all figured out—theirs are the kids who'll be filling the therapy waiting rooms in twenty years. Ten years. Five!" She nodded as if confirming a point I had just established. "Hardest job in the world."

Which one? "Well—"

Greta sat down at her computer. "And different every day," she said happily.

I was still standing in the doorway with my coffee.

"But still—we're the lucky ones, right?" She stretched. "I think about it all the time."

"About luck?"

"Like, I listen to the news, okay this awful thing, that awful thing, this awful person, that awful person, and I'm all, My hair is going prematurely gray and I'm driving a hatchback, but at least I can sleep at night, you know?" She didn't wait for an answer. "You know what I'm saying."

I did sometimes try to articulate, to myself, the value of what I taught, but no one asked me for those justifications, because the classes I led were the ones eighteen-year-olds took for a requirement: They had to pass this course to get a degree, and they had to get a degree to get the sort of job they wanted, and they had to get the sort of job they wanted to have the sort of life they wanted, and they had to have the sort of life they wanted because getting what they wanted, those modest, reasonable, ordinary wants, constituted the plan and practice of their lives. I had no reason or occasion or method to argue them out of this. "I would probably agree if I taught something like anthropology," I said. I looked down at my empty coffee mug. "I've been reading a lot of anthropology, actually."

Greta nodded. "Yeah, I'm lucky in my subject." The voices: "*Are you human? Did you come out of someone's vagina? I must admit I am and I did. Then let me tell you about the study of human cultural practice regarding childbirth!*" She chuckled. "But literature—that's the fun stuff, right? Imagination!"

I left that aside: the fun, the imagination. None of my students found Henry James fun or imaginative. I wasn't sure I did. "I worry—" I began. I tried to put together a sentence that would make sense. "I worry about teaching as—I don't know—a pyramid scheme."

Greta was confused. "A what?"

"I convince myself that what I do is worthwhile, or what I have done is worthwhile, by convincing other people to do it."

"Are you serious?"

"Or maybe that's just life." I stopped myself. Parenthood.

Greta shook her head. "That's the weirdest thing I've ever heard."

"Sorry."

"Hang on." Greta looked at her computer screen, read, and clicked on something. "Oh, good. She's okay."

"The one with the stalker?"

"Yep! I thought it would all work out."

And it did. "I'll let you finish with your data, then," I said. "I'm going to get some sleep."

"You're leaving early tomorrow? It's been great to have you here. I'm sorry I didn't realize earlier about your job situation." Greta grimaced. "I should have. Of course that's why you're doing this shitty gig work for the foundation. Ugh."

I almost began a few sentences.

I need to make things less complicated.

GOOD THOUGHTS

In 1908, when Ennis died, the "certificate and record of death" for New York included "sex" and "color" and age and marital status and occupation and birthplace, as well as the birthplace of father and mother, along with the time of death, the place of death, and the "character of premises." In 1947, when Florence died, the certificate among other alterations changed "cause of death" to "causes," above the line where a medical examiner would type in the respiratory failure due to pneumonia, the ischemic stroke due to atherosclerosis, the hepatic failure due to cancer of the liver—though the goal was a chain of causation with a definitive end, rather than a collection of causes with a doubtful relation. The certificate prevented doubt. Not, necessarily, falsehood or obfuscation: Suicide was commonly termed "accident" ("crushed chest, hemothorax, automobile crash," in Ennis's case), and the precision of standardization might confer, paradoxically, a covering anonymity. Florence and Ennis, together, lived through the age of standardization. By the 1940s, the World Health Organization maintained a supposedly complete list called

the "International Classification of Diseases." The age of records.
Records establish that Florence died of a heart attack.

"Speaking of ugh," Greta went on. "Did you know Heather is now on the Weatherfield *board?*" She raised her voice to reach me at the sink, where I was rinsing my mug. I turned back into the dining room. "She emailed me. One of those personal fund-raising appeals that you can tell are copied and pasted."

I said, "Heather is the one who gave me this job."

"I should have guessed."

"Actually, Heather asked Justin first. Justin couldn't make the deadline."

Greta rolled her eyes. "I should have *guessed.*"

"I thought you were friends with Justin." I didn't say anything about Heather.

"Eh." Greta waved her hand. "We were close enough for me to figure out he wasn't as smart as he thinks he is."

"Oh."

"He resented me, frankly. That's what I would say now." Greta adjusted her hair again. Then her hands lingered over the keyboard. "Plus, he had a *lot* of ideas about what was best for Mark. Who was best for Mark."

"Mark? You mean—"

"Mark and me? Yeah." She smiled. "We slept together that first year. You know, when we were all going a little crazy. Not you, of course. You were always sane."

"No." Somehow I was out of complete sentences in this conversation.

"Onetime thing. Okay, maybe three-time thing. Mark decided pretty quick that I was too much work." She raised one eyebrow, cocked her head in a "What can I say?" gesture. The voices: "*Perhaps she is like this only when she meets someone new?*

No, I believe she is like this all the time. Also"—normal voice again—"he and Justin were weird, frankly. I wonder if they ever slept together."

"I thought Mark was dating Caroline."

"Dating!" Greta waved one hand. "Ha. That's one word for it. Caroline was smarter than I was anyway. Thank God that part of my life is over."

My backpack had slid from my shoulder again. I sat down.

"You really didn't know this?" Greta was delighted at my surprise. "I thought . . ." She paused. "Hang on." She held up a hand.

I waited.

Greta did, too. A noise from upstairs. She narrowed her eyes.

After a moment a small blond three-year-old appeared at the dining room door.

"Veronica." Greta's voice was almost menacing.

"Mommy, I—"

"You're not supposed to be awake."

"I had a bad dream." The child sounded guilty but adamant. She stood with one foot on top of the other.

"Really? You're sure?"

A nod.

"You really had a dream?"

"I promise."

"Okay, come here. Do you want to talk about it?" She shook her head no, trotting over. She was wearing blue pajamas with white trim, a short-sleeved shirt and floppy pants. "You want some water?" Greta held her at arm's length, examining her face. "Here, sit with Laura at the table while I get it for you. Okay?"

"Yes."

"But after you drink it you have to go back to bed. Right?"

"I promise."

"Now try to think good thoughts. The dream isn't real. Remember?"

"I remember," Veronica said.

"You mind, Laura?" Greta asked me. I shook my head no, of course not. Greta picked up her daughter and placed her in my lap.

My mind was still circling around a ten-year-old bit of news, Greta and Mark, Mark and Justin, circling without settling. I moved my frayed nylon backpack nearer to my feet. I felt the hard right-angle thunk of my computer, the shift of my cardboard and paper notebook. Veronica sighed and settled on my lap.

I could smell the sleep-sweat aroma of her scalp and see the back of her tiny ears. I could feel her spine against my stomach. Greta returned with a glass. To me: "Don't let her have candy."

"I won't." I touched my hand briefly to Veronica's hair. Her gullet made small undulations as she sipped. I could hear the ticking of the hallway clock. Greta stood with her arms folded, somewhat apart, as if assessing the two of us together. Veronica drank again.

Judith appeared, wearing a thin printed robe and flip-flops and glasses. "Everything okay?"

"Bad dream," Greta explained. "She's finishing her water. She's just about ready to go back to bed. Right, Ronnie?"

The child nodded in my lap. Judith and Greta exchanged glances. We waited. "And how was your day, Laura?" asked Judith—polite, killing time. Her voice was gentle, like a lullaby.

We were all keeping things gentle, for Veronica. I said, "Not very good" in a low, slow tone. "Not very good at all. I didn't learn anything about Florence. The mentions were just other people saying that she or Ennis was supposed to show up somewhere.

And I had to page through a lot of stuff to see that. So." I realized I was not unhappy about this. It may have been the volume
of my voice that calmed me, the weight of the child on my lap,
drinking her water, or it could have been that I remembered
my fruitless hours in the library, the feeling of them—it was
that same feeling of taking things in, the not-quite research, the
not-really work, the forgetful bliss of turning pages and moving
through facts. For that it didn't matter that I had found nothing. The hours of looking and reading were enough. Though
of course they were not. "It was a waste," I went on. "And I still
don't know a thing about how either of them felt."

Judith said, "And that's what you need? How they felt?"

"Maybe." I remembered something. "My adviser once told
me that it's impossible not to overrate or underrate affect." I
could see Renata's face when she'd made this pronouncement—
not a pronouncement, more of a regret. It came with a sigh. I
added, "Affect being feelings, of course."

Judith took all this in. "And you would agree?" But she didn't
wait for an answer, because Veronica had put down her water
glass, looked up. "Oh, I'll take her to bed now," Judith said.
"Thank you."

"Sure." I realized the full warm heft of her body only when
that weight was lifted from me. Veronica folded her arms
around Judith's neck.

"Here we go," Judith said to her gently. Greta and I watched
them leave.

Silence for a moment. Then: "We've been having trouble
with this," Greta said to me as they reached the top of the stairs.
"She pretends to have bad dreams because she wants to get up
and be with us."

"Ah, I see."

"She'll probably just grow out of it."

"Probably."

"You can grow out of anything!"

"I've heard."

"Now what were we talking about?" Greta frowned lightly.

"Nothing."

"Mark," she said. "No. Your job."

I said, "I think you were about to tell me that I need to stop fucking around and get to work on something that actually does good for people."

"I said that?" She smiled at me. "I really need to stop cursing in front of the kid."

When I woke up in the middle of the night, my mind circling around something about Mark, or something about Florence, and when to stop thinking I hauled myself up from the air mattress to the bathroom to splash water on my cheeks, I paused on my way back at the cracked door of Veronica's room. I looked in. She lay on her back, one elbow up behind her head, so that her forearm framed her face. Her curls made a soft cloud. How does Greta know, I thought, that her child was lying about having bad dreams.

But I need to do something real.

5

MY MOTHER GOT PREGNANT WITH ME to get out of a job she hated.

No, that's not true, she says.

My mother got pregnant with me to quit a good job and take a worse one.

No, that's not—

I always knew I wanted to be a mother. This is what she tells me several times. I didn't get pregnant to change jobs. Sweetheart.

I believe you, Mom, I say. I believe you. So would you say motherhood is your vocation, then?

She says, No. Yes. I don't know. I don't think I have a vocation. I don't really know what that means! She laughs a little. Why are you asking these questions, again?

Are my questions annoying?

No.

I feel like I should already have this information.

(I have information only about my father. I never knew him. My father took the job at Royce College because he had failed to finish his dissertation about twentieth-century political history, year after embarrassing year, and while he tried to finish he earned money supervising residential housing in various dorms at his graduate university. When someone hated their roommate or stole something from the common area or refused to shower for weeks, he got a call and set up a meeting and made arrangements. Then he answered a listing for a full-time post doing the same thing at Royce. The job didn't pay much, but he didn't press for more because it was so short-term. Only till he finished his degree. He was almost done. Then he would apply for faculty positions. Plus, the residential staff post did come with reduced rent on a house the college owned. I was born the third year. My father was killed by a drunk driver in the fourth. Royce College promised me a scholarship, after this tragedy, which is how I went to college without loans. And my mother still rents the house at a reduced rate.)

Not annoying, my mother repeats. My mother is happy to answer my questions; it's just that she doesn't have much to say. She found jobs where my father was. While he was still in graduate school, she cataloged in the Columbia music and arts library, for which she wrote call numbers on rectangles of white paper, then coated one side of the rectangles with a smelly glue, then stuck them on the library-bound spines—deep maroon, deep green, deep blue, pebbly, durable stuff—of musical scores. My mother does not read music. But she liked her library work a lot, except for the number 9, which was hard to get right. She often had to redo labels with a 9. When she came to Royce, she assumed she should look for office jobs, and applied for the first one she saw, which was in the development division. The interview required her to write a timed paragraph explaining why someone might donate money to the school. She wrote such a good paragraph, she was hired on the spot, and then found out the job would consist mostly of writing more such paragraphs, which she hated. You had to talk about money, she tells me, without ever mentioning money. It made me feel terrible. I didn't realize the interview was testing me on the things I would actually have to do. Which was so silly.

I say, I understand that.

But she couldn't quit the development job. Or, she *felt* she couldn't quit because she didn't want to offend anyone. After a maternity leave, though, she could simply ... not go back? And everyone would assume it was because of the baby. She looked for a job that was as different as possible and she settled on Dining Services. She didn't have any experience with kitchens, but she applied repeatedly for three different openings in about nine weeks and the head of Dining Services eventually took pity on her. He was a big man named Frank and he liked to do favors for people, especially women. He assigned her to the bakery. Frank seemed to think the schedule was tough and would scare her away. But to my mother it was the perfect routine. She worked from 4:30 to 9:30 in the morning. She woke at 3:45 and nursed me before she left. A few hours later my father woke and gave me a morning bottle. He took care of me until she returned. When he left for work my mother would feed me again, and then both she and I would go to sleep for a while. Then we would wake and sleep until the evening, when she got dressed for my father and made dinner.

Also the bakery smelled good. And it was so quiet. She really liked the quiet.

After my father was killed her bakery schedule was no longer possible, because my mother couldn't find a babysitter who was available from 4:30 to 9:30 in the morning. She switched to alternating lunch and dinner shifts, which were noisier and full of people. Frank was always around. Frank was incompetent. I gather this from the way my mother speaks about him. She speaks about him with great fondness. I began to help Frank with planning, she says. Things that needed doing. She was still a prep cook, and she was not paid for the planning work, but she enjoyed it. She smiles when she describes it, the kind of private smile marking a pleasure no one else will understand, but that's okay, they don't need to understand. It was like a puzzle, she says, to use the ingredients left over from one meal in another, and make sure of variety, and always a vegetarian option, a vegan option, a kosher option. She invented some dishes. She estimated quantities. She kept track of how much students consumed at various times of the day and various seasons of the year. During that time, I knew a lot about the eating habits of twenty-year-olds, she says matter-of-factly.

Her knowledge went nowhere. Frank told her often that when he retired she would take over, but he apparently did not tell the college vice president the same thing, and when Frank died of lung cancer my mother was not promoted. Instead Royce hired a man with a master's degree in business administration who decided the school's Dining Services should be run by a food-management corporation headquartered in Delaware. Ingredients and plans came from there. All chefs and cooks had to interview again, to convince the new head they deserved to keep their jobs. Some didn't—keep them, I mean. My mother did. I think they let me stay, she says, mostly because I had one of the lowest salaries. It made sense. I ask her how she felt about this. Oh, I never expected to be head of Dining Services, she says. Why didn't you? I ask. I don't know, she says.

My mother apologizes. Maybe you should ask someone else these questions. I don't think I'm the right person.

Then I apologize.

Then she apologizes again.

She tries to help. When I was younger, she says, I was living with my grandparents. You know this part of the story. I had five older siblings, or half siblings, and they were always in trouble. They were doing drugs, or in jail, or losing their jobs, or dropping out of things, and my grandparents, well, my grandparents were good people, but they couldn't cope. I was always alone, growing up, but I wasn't alone, because I was related to people doing bad things far away, and I didn't know these people and I didn't have anything to do with them but I was . . . tied to them. It felt like the worst of both worlds, because I had no one and I had too many people. So when I was young and I thought about the future, I didn't imagine a particular job or success; I just imagined being safe and not worrying. I knew I would work, and I wanted to work; I wanted to save money and pay rent. That's all I really thought. So the way it happened with Dining Services was fine for me.

I understand, I say. I understand.

I wanted just a few people who were close by, she says. Just two people, really. Just you and your dad.

Okay.

I wish I were better at these questions. Or maybe you can tell me what you need, what kind of answers you're looking for.

No, no, I say. Forget it. It's my fault.

I never really thought much about my life, she says.

Yes.

I think that's the way it is for many people. People who aren't as smart as you.

Stop it.

I can see what it's like for you. It's very difficult for you.

No, I'm just—

And you will find a job. I know you will, sweetheart. You will find the right job. You deserve it. Others, though—for others, a job is just a job.

I'm sorry, I say.

She looks confused. Don't apologize, she says.

I'm silent.

You need work you care about, she says. That's a good thing.

I'm silent.

And then I say that in fact, no, I don't think I need work I care about. I always worked, I say, but not because I cared; I mean, I cared about *work*, but not *the* work—if that makes sense—and the work I've been doing doesn't matter, and when I was spending all my time on it, I think I knew it didn't matter; in fact, I think I always knew how much work meant to me; I knew work would save me, and I didn't think hard about what I was doing *because* of that, I was too scared.

Scared? My mother is looking at me. Half of her face is ready to dissolve into open worry. The other half is trying to figure out the way that this will be okay. This is an exaggeration of her most common expression. You've done so well, she says.

I don't bother to deny this. I have more to say. Anything you do is part of something, some institution, system, way of oper-ating, and all of these ways are founded on cruelty or heading for a crash or they have no use for you. Or all three. Have no use for me. I mean *me* when I say *you*. I'm sorry for dragging you into this. I don't know what I was thinking.

Are you going to be okay? my mother asks.

It feels like I'm trapped in something I don't want to be part of, and that something has also rejected me, and also I can't escape it.

Do you mean being a professor?

I'm not a professor.

Oh.

I don't have a career.

It's all right, my mother says. You can stay here at home as long as you need.

I know, I say miserably. I'm very lucky.

Maybe get a little rest, my mother says.

I turned fifteen hundred words in to the Weatherfield Foundation yesterday.

o O o

I do not expect the website for Welcome House to be as complicated as it is. I stare at links for guests and volunteers and donors and press and public. The link for volunteers opens an application. I type into white squares. I feel better, typing into these white squares. Name, phone, email address, postal address. Gender and age. Religious affiliation. "None." Place of employment. "None." "Does your employer have a volunteer matching program?" "N/A." "Can you drive a car?" "Can you lift a weight of forty pounds or less?" "Can you stand for up to an hour?" "Yes," I tick. "Yes." "Yes." I feel better.

I haven't volunteered at anything in a long time. Of course I did in college. Everyone volunteered in college. In college, it was called "service." Service was a section of your résumé. I was suspicious of that section. I didn't trust those who took pleasure in the soul-deepening profundity of their service. Also I didn't trust those who manufactured a pose of generosity from what was really an extension of their own leisure. The Ultimate Frisbee league for troubled youth and the Makeover Night for housebound seniors. Or maybe I was wrong; maybe it was all genuinely caring; maybe troubled youth really got into the spirit of the game; maybe housebound seniors really wanted to learn contouring; what did I know. Back when I did good things I was very cynical. Now that I've stopped doing them I'm not, not so much.

I don't want to be. I want to get as close as possible to the provision of basic needs—food and shelter—in ways that consider my own personality and preferences not at all. I do not want to bring anything of me to the work except for my ability to stand for an hour or more and lift up to forty pounds. I am almost at the end of the questions. "Why do you wish to volunteer at Welcome House?" There is no drop-down. I look for a drop-down. I want an "N/A." I write, "I wish to help the homeless." Is that self-aggrandizing? Self-deceiving? "I wish to feel less useless." That is definitely self-aggrandizing, self-aggrandizement through self-abasement, the worst kind. "I wish to understand what it's like to do something both effective and uncomplicatedly good, so I might know what I am supposed to look for in other areas of my life." I delete that last sentence. Blank, again. "I wish to help the homeless." I click "Submit."

"Next Steps," the web page reads. There are several. I have to complete a Saturday-morning orientation. After that I can sign up for a shift. I will then receive a confirmation of my shift from a volunteer coordinator. And then complete my shift and log my hours. And then sign up for more shifts. Perhaps there is a different shelter with fewer steps. At the same time, the steps are comforting.

I decide on Welcome House because the Royce kitchens donate leftovers there every Tuesday and Friday. You can ride with the driver, my mother says, when he comes to get the food. Though the driver comes very early, she adds. My mother seems more careful than usual these days. Why would I care about early? I ask. I don't know, she says; I thought you might. I take her car to the orientation; I drive clenching the steering wheel with two hands, glancing down at directions. The weather gets colder every day now, temperatures dropping steadily, not even the pretense of subtlety in their decline anymore. No. After daylight saving time ends the whole world gives in.

I enter New Haven on the cracked asphalt of an access road

bordered by chain-link fences and rail tracks, pass a downtown
district of what look like warehouses, a few shops eyelidded
with roll-up metal gates, and keep following my directions into
an area where trash drifts and subsides in the gutters and most
structures seem abandoned. A block from the address, I see a
small crowd of people waiting, some with shopping carts and
some with large bags. I already feel the squeeze of hypocrisy in
my stomach. I am only, technically, nonhomeless because of my
mother. The building is yellow-brown stone and brown aluminum. It looks like a school. A fabric banner, frayed at one corner,
hangs over the door. WELCOME. I park.

The first floor is warm, miasmed with the smell of old soup
and laundry and disinfectant. There are a few chairs in the
entrance hallway—folding chairs, placed there it seems tempo-
rarily, holding people who sleep sitting up. Around them others
move purposefully in several directions, one in a wheelchair,
one crutching along. The space is loud and close. My guilt has
curdled, typically, into nausea. This is an old problem. I like to
think I am tough about things like bad smells and tastes but
I am not. I am squeamish; then—overcompensating—severe.
My mother's house has always been clean and quiet. An atten-
dant at the front desk slumps on a high stool behind a pane of
smeared plastic and eyes me suspiciously. Through a horizon-
tal security slot he passes me a binder to sign in. I follow the
direction of his finger to the right, to the Gathering Space. The
Gathering Space is filled with long benches of wood and turquoise vinyl scuffed and in a few places cracked open, showing
white filling. A dozen people, more or less, are already there. I
sit in the back. A few minutes after I arrive, a group of teenagers
comes in, laughing. They wear matching T-shirts. Older than
teenagers. College students. I can't see what the shirts say.

Two women at the front clear their throats and tap

clipboards, about to talk. People, the older one begins. She is tall, with wavy hair and square blue glasses on a chain. She puts on her glasses and claps her hands. People. The room quiets. She is waiting for us to settle down. PEOPLE.

The first thing you've got to know, she says once it's calm enough to be heard, is Thanksgiving is *done*. She raises one finger in warning. So if you want Thanksgiving, you can leave *now*. A pause and a silence. Her glance is almost threatening. I do not know what she means. It is November 12. No one says anything. The teenagers look around also. I feel implicated in their obvious lack of knowledge, their slapdash approach to this orientation, their disregard for its requirements and commitments. I am not like them. I should have sat farther forward. But if I move now I will seem fastidious. I focus on the front of the room.

Now the older woman smiles. Apparently she is glad no one left at her invitation to leave. I don't know what it is about Thanksgiving! she tells us, almost jovial suddenly. Folks think if you volunteer on Thanksgiving you have a guaranteed ticket to heaven, or something. I mean. She laughs at this idiocy and invites us to share in her laughter. At the dais where she is standing are several banners. The left one reads WELCOME and the right HOUSE. In the middle, COME TO ME, ALL YOU WHO ARE WEARY AND BURDENED, AND I WILL GIVE YOU REST. MATTHEW 11:28. It is constructed from felt cut-out letters, roundish, fluffy, and messily stitched. Beneath the letters are hands in many colors reaching up. Red, yellow, blue, green, orange. The older woman says, Not even Christmas is as bad as Thanksgiving. Thanksgiving is *bad*. Then she pats the younger woman on the arm and turns to go. That was all she needed to say. Now she has more important places to be. That was Anne Stevens, says the younger woman; she's our director of services.

The younger woman, now in charge, is Paige. Paige has fair hair and skin and wears a plain gold cross on a chain. She has a slight southern accent. Or perhaps that is simply training, since something about the way she uses "y'all" and "folks" suggests such language is policy. The way she uses "friends and neighbors" is definitely policy. Right now we're serving breakfast to our friends and neighbors who have stayed the night. Paige is going to run through a few things real quick, she tells us, and then we'll have a tour. She is real grateful to us all for coming out. As Paige talks, I look up on my phone the remainder of the chapter, Matthew 11. The verse that follows "I will give you rest" runs this way: "Take my yoke upon you and learn from me, for I am gentle and humble in heart, and you will find rest for your souls." This does not seem to follow. In my view the whole chapter is hard to follow. Rest or a yoke? "For my yoke is easy and my burden is light." This is the end of the chapter. I have missed some of the brief monologue in which Paige outlined the different volunteer opportunities.

She is explaining different levels of commitment. For example, maybe you want to volunteer from your own home. In that case, you can call and thank donors. This sounds like a useless job. Paige stresses how important this job is. There's also admin work, or work in the kitchen, or work in the day care, or work with the reading group. The important thing is to remember there is something for everyone. Paige has said these things many times before. Now I'm going to run through a few rules real quick. These rules are for your safety and for the safety of our friends and neighbors. Be punctual for your volunteer shift. Always sign in. Always report injuries if injuries occur. And we ask that you dress modestly, so that means no shorts, no tank tops, no sweats, no open-toed shoes, no tight clothing, no saggy clothing, no holes, no skirts above the knee. Paige rattles this off.

I am impressed at her memory. I look down at my jeans, which have a hole and might be too saggy in some parts and too tight in others. It is hard to tell. Paige continues. It's real important that you don't offer any advice or counseling to our friends and neighbors. This can disturb their progress. It is also important to have supportive conversations. So no foul language or negative talk. Above all, don't exchange personal information or socialize off-site. This is a safety precaution.

Paige smiles at us. Paige is much younger than I and she has a good job in which she is helping people.

The tour begins. We lurk together, waiting to be directed. I look at the teenagers' T-shirts. They are a service group from a local community college. None of them is wearing open-toed shoes or baggy or tight clothing or jeans with holes. I see now that they are purposeful and focused. They understand why they are here. I have misread them. I fall back so they can lead the way as the tour begins. Paige takes us upstairs. So here's a dorm, she says. The bunk beds are close enough to one another that sleepers would be barely arm's length apart. Each bed is made up with a gray-green blanket and white sheets. The ceiling is so low, the top sleeper wouldn't be able to sit up. Could you request a bottom bunk, I wonder, so you could read in bed? I would want to read in bed. I catch myself. I am not here to imagine myself in this homeless shelter. Or am I? Is this empathy or paranoia or narcissism? Perhaps empathy is always a kind of narcissism. Paranoia, too. Fourteen days, Paige tells us brightly, is the longest any one person can stay. Fourteen days in, seven days out. We don't want anyone to grow dependent on us.

We move from the dormitory to the admission area. Paige doesn't stop; she walks backward, moving us through. This is where we check for bugs and drugs. And then we provide a clean set of pajamas. The pajamas are stacked on metal shelves.

Paige shakes out a pair for us to see. Pale green, something like hospital scrubs but more faded, less ready for hard use. Paige is moving. Then our friends and neighbors can get a shower, here. Moving again. We see the laundry, the gym, the rec area. We end in the kitchen, all clean steel tables and ranges and refrigerators, with a tiled floor that slopes down to a drain. Paige wraps up the tour, handing around sheets on which we are meant to put our names down for shifts. I sign up for Tuesday and Friday breakfast.

We file back into the Gathering Space to hear from the head of the Board of Directors of Welcome House, a balding man in baggy khakis and a button-down shirt. The head of the Board of Directors tells us how glad he is that we are here, each of us. He wants to tell us what he knows we already know, which is that Welcome House is a very special place. We already know because we have already volunteered. But you won't really know, he says, you won't really know how special, until you let it change you. You should not be afraid of being changed. Then Welcome House can help *us* as we help Welcome House. He wants to tell us a little bit about how Welcome House helped him. He started in the army, he says, and then went to college and business school on the GI Bill, and then worked as a consultant, but after a long career in the financial sector he realized it was time to give back, so he retired and began to think about what mattered. It wasn't just money he wanted to give, he realized; he wanted to give something more meaningful. Time. Himself. And every one of us is also making that gift. We, too, are giving ourselves.

Next we hear from a former friend and neighbor of Welcome House, a skinny, smiling man in dark jeans and a long-sleeved T-shirt. This person also tells us how glad he is that each of us is here. Also how much a place like this can mean to people; he should know, because he was one of them. He did two tours in Iraq, got a metal pin put in his leg (he points to his hip), and when he came back his life fell apart; they took his kids away from him, he got into the booze, into the dope (he uses these words—*booze, dope*—as if he is trapped in a public-safety message from fifty years ago), and he just kept going into that downward spiral, you know, that downward spiral (his hands move in graceful circles from shoulder to waist). And blaming everything, he adds, cussing this, cussing that, cussing the other thing (he uses the word *cussing*)—but not facing it, you know, facing himself. And that's what the program is all about; that's what the program can do for you—he should know; he did it three times (here he laughs, the sound bubbling up, ingenuous)—it gets you to face yourself. So that's what y'all are a part of now; it's saving lives. He should know.

There's one more person to speak. She comes from the audience; she steps forward from the benches where all of us are sitting. She has been leading the group of teenagers I noticed, and she has on a T-shirt like theirs, but she's older, maybe sixty, and gray-haired, wearing on her lower half a long chambray skirt and cowboy boots. Her palms press together in front of her as if she is praying or nervous, and what she says seems smooth enough to be scripted, if it were not so earnest and plain. She's been working for justice a long time. When she was younger, she lived and worked for ten years on a cooperative farm in the South, helping people there learn to grow food to feed themselves, until it was wrecked by an eminent domain claim for a chemical plant, and after that she got a degree in social work, and spent ten years in Washington, D.C., working at a nonprofit that tried to influence national policy on hunger, during which time she lived in a halfway house for women and children, but then her nonprofit folded, so she went abroad for about fifteen years, living in different countries, working with a Christian mission. But now she lives in the city here, because she is married again—her first marriage, she says by way of a calm digression, ended in divorce—and her husband is here, so she is living with him and waiting to see what the Lord has in store for her next. She has been asked to lead us all in an ecumenical prayer, she says, to conclude our orientation, but more important than anything any of us can say is what we all can hear, in our heart of hearts, and what we speak there, what we promise there, so instead of any prayer, she would like to pause for thirty seconds in silence together.

During the silence I look down at my phone, at the website where I looked up the Bible verse, and switch versions in the drop-down menu at the top, selecting the King James Version, which I was accustomed to using in college and grad school for no good reason, really, other than it sounds better. "Come unto me, all ye that labor and are heavy laden, and I will give you rest."

o   O   o

On Tuesday morning, the driver arrives at six, pulling in behind the wide cafeteria door near the Dumpsters. I am ready. I will load, unload, pack, whatever has to happen. But the driver only gets out wordlessly with a lighter and a pack of Camels. So I stand, also wordless, while he pinches a cigarette between his thumb and forefinger, inhaling, exhaling, not speaking, his face down. Our separate clouds of breath are soft white in the darkness. The thermometer by my mother's back door read twenty-eight degrees this morning. The driver digs his other hand into his jacket pocket and jiggles his feet a few times.

I cross my hands into my armpits. No words have been spoken and he does not offer me a cigarette. I watch the etching of frost on the pavement and count the empty cans of cooking oil stacked nearby. When he tosses away his butt he looks at me with aggression, as if I am about to accuse him of violating a rule, as if he is about to defy my accusation. In fact I think smoking is illegal on school grounds. He opens the back door of his van and pulls out five large silver trays and as many large metal spoons, along with a box of gloves. The van is painted on both sides with the name of an electrical business, perhaps his, perhaps his boss's—he has the general demeanor of a man who often thinks he's being cheated, but the thought could be directed against his customers as read-ily as his employers. It could be directed at both. He moves inside. I have not been addressed. I follow. In the kitchens he pulls on a pair of gloves and hands two to me, grunting. Last night's leftovers are waiting for us, a few big cauldrons of baked ziti and a few of vegetarian rice pilaf. We spoon each into the dented trays, which are very clean, then cover them with huge clattering lids. I lift two back to the truck. Food is surprisingly heavy. The driver arranges these metal rectangles on the floor of his van and secures them with bungee cords. The rest of the space remains cluttered with metal tool caddies, spools of cord and wire, white plastic buckets, the contents of which I can't identify, and two folded stepladders. He nods at me. You can sit up in the front, he says. He makes this concession seem magnanimous. Up in the front is the only seat.

My mother comes out in her coverall and hairnet, holding a doughnut wrapped in a paper napkin and coffee in a card-board to-go cup. She stands by the open driver's window with these offerings. I've already had coffee and three of her dough-nuts. Hello, Craig, my mother says. How are you? Would you like some breakfast? The sharp smell of black coffee mixes with the fat, yeasty scent of the doughnut. Craig says, No thanks.

He says that he's got to get going, and with one arm out the window, he bangs the side of his van twice, as if it were the flank of a horse he is spurring to gallop. We pull off. Craig is small and thin with a small, thin beard. He wears a mesh ball cap. He drives with an exaggeratedly confident style, leaning back, one thumb adjusting our direction. We are on the highway; we drive past two quick exits; the van rattles and squeals faintly as its roof racks persist through the wind. The other vehicles around us have the particularly headlong, reckless appearance cars acquire in the dark. Craig changes lanes without signaling or looking much and grunts as another truck speeds past. Bungeed into the back are the pasta and rice my mother made, the tomato sauce she dumped in, the ricotta cheese she stirred, the onions and peas she slit free from their plastic pouch. Morning is seeping into the windshield with its watery green light. Craig drops me off at the WELCOME banner. He says, I'll take the food to the back door. There is something of a rebuke in his expression, as if he knows I am not qualified for this part of the operation.

I am not. I must stand in line again in front of the plastic booth and sign a black binder and get a volunteer badge and make my way down the hall to the cafeteria. The cafeteria is full of activity. About a dozen people are already there. They move boxes, vats, pitchers, chairs, and stacks of trays. One man who seems to be in charge stops me to ask, You here for breakfast? No, I almost say, I'm here to volunteer. Then, aloud: Yes, I am here for breakfast. You're okay on the serving line? He doesn't wait for an answer. He points to a box of blue plastic hairnets, a box of clear plastic gloves. Get those on. Apron? He is friendly and solicitous, but he is mostly efficient, looking me over to make sure my clothing is suitable, to make sure I can manage. I do not know, even, what qualities I should try to project. Apparently, I pass, because the man in charge doesn't say anything more.

I put on my plastic. The serving line has two identical sections for two separate queues of people, skeining in from the sides and converging in the middle, where large square urns of iced water are waiting beside stacks of opaque brown cups. Each line is composed of one high metal shelf, along which a person can move a tray, guarded by a shield, and below that a counter with heated wells for large dishes. Three volunteers are already stationed on the right side when I arrive. They are wearing their mitts and bonnets. They are waiting with spoons. I stand in an open spot. You've got bread, one of them tells me. Watch your back! a voice screams at the same time. Behind us, a large man wields a big tray of fried potatoes. It is the same type of dish into which Craig and I spooned the Royce College leftovers. The man slams it down hard into a well. Then another dish comes, next to it; this one is full of thick whitish gray fluid flecked with bits of brown. I do not know what this is supposed to be. It smells of warmth and fat and not much else. My stomach doesn't seem to require any distinction in a smell to recoil from it. Is that— I start to ask. Gravy, says the worker next to me. He seems unperturbed by its aroma or appearance. He is used to this work. On my other side another volunteer stands ready to hand out slices of cantaloupe. The cantaloupe doesn't look ripe yet—a green sketch along the rind, a green smile along the curve of each piece. Watch your back! comes the voice again. Bread is here. It comes in a garbage pail, slid in front of me, a plastic bin lined with a clear bag and filled with cut-up rounds of a vaguely French or Italian loaf. Next to me also appears a large cardboard carton of wrapped sandwiches. I feel the bread through my plastic gloves. It is mostly hard.

The supervisor moves briskly along the line, checking on

supplies, making sure of our tasks. Five minutes, people, he says. The supervisor takes a quick look at the fruit person, but the fruit person needs nothing more than a nod of confirmation. My position is more problematic. The supervisor looks at the bread bucket. He evaluates. For quantity, I realize. The only question is quantity. He says to me, We have plenty of this. I say, Okay. I sense the experience in that assessment, as well as the stakes; it would not be good to be wrong, but he will not be wrong. You can give everyone two slices of bread. Should I start with one? I ask. Sure, he says. It doesn't matter. Then he looks at the box of sandwiches. This requires a longer reckoning. You're going to have to handle this, too, he says to me. I nod. These are . . . He is not expecting the question. He picks up a wrapper and reads it. It says sausage and egg biscuit, he tells me. The wrappers are printed with the name of a local convenience store. Okay, I say. Sausage and egg biscuit.

Now the supervisor steps back, nodding—food is in place, tables are in place, and we are already a little bit behind, nothing major, but he needs to move things along. *Okay!* he shouts. His voice is thunderous when he wants it to be. *Handicapped trays! Handicapped trays!* Several people in gloves and hairnets scurry over, pulling plastic rectangles off the stack and forming a line. The volunteer next to me explains, briefly, that thirty meals are prepared first and placed at a special table, so people with disabilities do not have to come through the lines themselves. I am grateful for these, a practice run, in which I can determine which square of tray to use for the sausage and egg biscuit and which to use for the pieces of bread so as not to inadvertently slop either into the borders of the white-brown gravy while leaving some clean and dry space for fruit. One or two? I ask, holding up a piece of bread. One or two? The answer has to come quickly. Rummaging, I seek out the best of the bread, the softest pieces. One or two? The trays are complete. Noise has already overtaken the cafeteria, and the doors are open; the line is full. There are dozens of people, already, instantly, waiting behind the counter to get breakfast. Sausage and egg biscuit? I ask. One or two? I ask.

The sausage and egg biscuits, when I pick them up, feel flattened; they give off the too-long-refrigerated scent of stale coolant and old grease. But everyone says yes to the biscuit. Many people say no to the bread. No thanks. No thank you. Others say yes to both. Yes, thank you. Yes, God bless. Many say, Can I have two of *those* instead? indicating the biscuits. Yes, I say. I give out two biscuits. Halfway through the line I realize I will run out of biscuits. I have made a mistake. Someone without a biscuit will notice that others have two. I am glad the supervisor is not seeing this. The supervisor is somewhere else. He is in a lot of different places. He is shouting various rules amiably, because everyone knows these rules, and his job is not to let anyone think he doesn't see them when they break the rules they know. Yo! Wait your turn! Then: You right there! You've got to put your silverware in the bucket! I begin to see faces I have already seen once, now back for a second breakfast. More of the bland gravy. More of this stale bread. More of this unripe fruit. Thank you. Oh, yes. God bless. The level of noise in the room continues to rise. It is hard to make myself heard. One or two? It is hard to find bread that is still a little bit soft. The noise is cheerful, aggressive but satisfied; it is full of the sounds of people eating, the rustle and chew and swish, beneath words and laughter and shouts. Someone has brought a portable radio and it thumps away. No, two people, two different portable radios, competing doggedly. Neither is mad but neither is giving in. Nothing is giving in. Not the noise, not the smells. The smells grow and grow. Urine, sweat, fat, meat, dirt. Food and bodies. I wonder if there is a maximum to this combination of smell, which seems to be increasing gently, and I wonder how long it would take for me not to notice this smell at all, were I to be around it always. Fifteen minutes! comes the shout. People! We've got fifteen minutes!

Fifteen minutes means the meal is almost over and everyone has just a quarter of an hour left to finish and clear out. It seems barely to have begun. But so many have already eaten. The cafeteria tables are brown metal, with benches attached, and a lever allows them to fold in the middle. The wheels on either end catch and then the whole contraption, hunched like a mantis, can be rolled to one side of the room. Several people are jacking up empty tables in this way, one smooth movement each, as they become empty. Underneath are crusts and papers and wrappers and napkins and rinds. Those of us on the serving line are motioned out to help with the cleanup. Someone who knows what he is doing has wheeled out two bright yellow industrial mop buckets, one in each hand, and two brooms, one in each armpit. The shout is now Ten minutes! Ten minutes! Wrap it up, people! The water in the buckets is already gray and flat. I take one of the brooms instead, a long capital T of an industrial broom, and push the trash on the floor into something like a mound. The floor is smeared and stained. Someone else appears with a huge plastic dustpan. Someone behind me is mopping. In a few minutes the floor is clean. No, in a few minutes the floor is free of visible garbage and shining wet with a solution that includes bleach. Five minutes! One worker is squirting something on the tables and wiping them down with a rag. Another is hauling the tub of dirty silverware, sloshing with water, to the back kitchen. Everyone knows what to do. I do not know what to do. All right! That's it! Everyone out! The supervisor is leaning against the counter at the front of the food line. His legs are crossed. His arms are folded. His eyes might be closed. Another meal done.

I throw away my hairnet and gloves and I peel off my volunteer sticker. Our stickers are the last pieces of trash in the large mound the breakfast has produced. For a moment I wonder if there is something mean about the way feeding someone keeps them alive until they need food again. *Mean* in the old sense. In all the senses. Of course I am wrong to feel that. Some of the people who just ate are in the Gathering Space for morning prayer. Some of them sit now on the same bench I sat on for orientation. I am outside. The cold of it shocks. A relief to be smelling and tasting the hard, strong city cold. I stand to one side of the door, loitering.

What are you doing? I imagine someone asking, someone who is suspicious of my loitering. Oh, just waiting for my ride home.

o O o

On the Tuesday before Thanksgiving almost everyone at Royce clears out. The campus empties and I can love it a little, forlorn and purposeless, even if the library is closed. I can love the library, closed; look at this dark building full of *books*. Of all useless things. Yesterday, my mother prepared and served to the Royce students and teachers and staff a holiday dinner of turkey, turkey gravy, vegan nut loaf, vegan gravy, cranberry sauce, sweet potatoes, succotash, mashed potatoes, green salad, dressing, rolls, butter, pumpkin pie, apple pie, and whipped cream. The dinner is the largest of the year and the only one for which the food-management company does not set the menu, because the same menu has been served for fifty years, always in four shifts, always with the hall decorated in gourds and honeycombed banners of brown and orange and red, always with a student string group playing an arrangement of "Over the River and Through the Woods" and an arrangement of *Appalachian Spring*. At the end of the evening, more than four thousand utensils have been washed.

For our Thanksgiving, my mother says to me on Tuesday evening, I have been thinking. I might not cook a completely traditional menu. Would that be all right with you?

Yes, I tell her, that would be very much all right with me.

We are in the grocery store together. This is the first time we have shopped together since I came back to Royce. I push the cart. My mother has a list, each item of which she regards and revises as she goes. Perhaps a chicken, she says.

A whole different bird, I respond. I shake my head.

You think that's bad?

I'm joking.

Oh, she says, good. Hand me that little carton of cream. No, we better have two cartons. For dessert I will try something without so much pumpkin.

I hate pumpkin, I say.

Really? My mother looks alarmed.

No, not really, I say, and my mother says, Oh! and then asks me if we need potatoes; she's going to make wild rice, but should we *also*— No one needs potatoes, I say. Can you imagine needing potatoes? True necessity, about potatoes?

You're in quite a mood, she says.

Am I? Would you say it's a good mood? By the way I'm buying.

You've already bought a lot, she says. Can you afford to?

That's very rude, I tell her.

She smiles. She reminds me we're cooking for five. I invited a few people over, she says.

Ah. What people are those?

She says, I invited those who don't have a family to go to.

But we don't have a family to go to.

What do you mean? She looks up from her list. Of course we do.

I let that go. I say again, What people?

College people. Professors, like you, she says. I let this go, too. She continues: Turn left here; we need to pick out some nuts. . . . A physics professor. He's from Ghana. And a Japanese woman. And oh, someone else who's a visiting scholar in Russian history, I think. Or international affairs. I don't know all the different departments.

I push the cart past the nuts and wait and ask her if they want to come, these people, and she asks what I mean, and I say it seems very pitiful—a dinner for those who don't have anything else; I say that *I* wouldn't want to go to such a dinner.

But you are going, she says.

That stops me, but I mutter that she knows what I mean. Then I nod at her choice of cashews. Cashews are an underrated nut, we can both agree. They are unexpected. They have more flavor than you think they will have.

It's not a dinner for those who don't have anything else, my mother adds.

I thought you just said it was, I reply. I thought those were your words, a few moments ago.

My mother is very concerned, suddenly, in front of some brussels sprouts.

I honestly never thought of it that way, she says. Do you think the people I invited will take it that way?

I am even more ashamed of myself. I say, No, probably not.

Maybe they will. Maybe they will take offense.

No, they won't, I say. No, stop it. I was wrong. Forget what I said.

I can't uninvite them now, she says. I thought asking would be better than not asking, all in all.

I tell her of course that's correct. Forgive me, I say. Ignore me. I arrange the two bags of brussels sprouts in the cart. My mother cannot serve sprouts at the college—students don't like them, on the whole—so she will cook them at home. I tell her, It's like you said, a moment ago. I'm just in a weird mood.

Are you okay? she asks.

The Friday after I sent in my historical essay, someone from the foundation wrote and explained that everyone appreciated my work but that the program would be going in a different direction. After reading Justin's essay, the people at the foundation solicited more first-person accounts from former fellows, and the gala program would showcase these instead of anything about the Weatherfields; authors of these personal accounts would also read from them at the gala dinner. The foundation is, again, thankful for my help, but they won't be using my contribution. Is this a relief? Is this a defeat? I don't know. I decide not to make that ruling in the middle of a grocery store. I'm fine, I say to my mother.

Heather wrote to me separately. I'm sorry this didn't work out, she said. She wanted to assure me that I would be paid, as agreed.

Are you going to Welcome House on Friday? my mother asks me.

Also, Heather sent me a ticket to the gala. I don't think so, I say to my mother.

It's not open?

It's open, I say. I'm just not sure I'll keep going.

She says, I thought you enjoyed it. She backtracks. I know *enjoy* is not the right word. I thought you found it valuable.

No, I say. But that's not the point. Valuable.

When I say this I can't believe how awful I sound. I stop the cart. Sorry, I tell her.

My mother hasn't noticed. She's checking her list one last time. Can you think of anything else we need?

We steer to the checkout.

My mother is unloading food. Here, she says, here, here. We're pulling out the reusable canvas bags my mother has stashed on the lower level of the cart, and the checker is ready to make small talk with us, how are you, all ready for Thanksgiving, and I smile and take the bags and pack up the items as she scans them, so as not to respond; doing well, my mother tells her, and just about. It's dark by the time we emerge from the store, burdened by all the things to eat that I have purchased with money I don't have, and cold, so cold that we don't talk anymore, just look forward to the small, fleeting pleasure of going back to a lit-up house and pushing into a warm kitchen, even this worn, stained, and cracked kitchen, and thumping down bags and opening cupboards and putting away boxes and stashing vegetables. It's a small, fleeting pleasure to wash the pears my mother has chosen and put them in a bowl. It's a small, fleeting pleasure, thirty-six hours later, to clean the wrinkly pink bodies of two slender chickens, pat them dry with a clean towel, smear them with bright white-gold butter and chopped herbs, and then watch them turn brown in the oven. It's a small, fleeting pleasure to stand next to my mother as she pours hot water into the bain-marie pan around the waiting pallor of a custard. And to shuck a few tough outer leaves off each sprout, as if feeling them for weakness, and then chop each of their green-layered worlds cleanly in two. It's a small, fleeting pleasure to wait among the slowly toasting scent of cooking rice.

You like cooking, I say to my mother, finally, on Thursday, after the meal is done. It's a question and not. And then: Isn't it funny I didn't ask you that before?

When we were talking about my life? she asks.

When we were talking about your work, I reply. It seems like the main question and I didn't ask it. You like cooking?

Not very much, my mother says.

You're kidding me, I say.

She doesn't respond.

I wait. Really?

I'm sorry, she says. You look disappointed. She frowns.

I confirm, You don't like cooking?

She says, I think it's as good as anything else. I've shocked you?

A little.

I'm sorry, she says again.

No, no ... She's already moving away. We have food to spoon into storage dishes, plates to lift from sudsy sink water and scrub and rinse, glasses to dry, a table and counters to wipe, floors to sweep; we have to clean everything up. And by the time we are sitting in darkness it no longer seems important what anyone likes to do, or doesn't, or will, or won't.

I ask instead about Craig. Who is he, Craig? I say. I wonder about him.

My mother shakes her head. He's been picking up food for years, she says. Five years. He's very reliable. That's all I know.

And he doesn't eat doughnuts.

Oh, sometimes he takes the doughnut, my mother assures me. So I always offer. The doughnuts used to be better. We get them from a supplier now, frozen. They haven't been the same. I have the feeling Craig disapproves.

No, Craig likes you a lot.

Really? She is pleased at this news. How do you know?

We were driving home the other day, and he said out of the blue that I was lucky to have you for family, because you were a good woman.

He said that? she asks. I can't imagine.

I know. It was quite a speech for him.

That's sweet. How funny.

Tell me what you're going to do with the rest of the weekend, I say.

Well, I thought I would go with you to the shelter tomorrow, she says. If you're still going.

I'm still going.

Don't let me change your mind, she says quickly. You should do what you like.

Of course I should let you change my mind, I say.

My mother looks confused.

But I don't think we should go tomorrow, I say. They have plenty of volunteers this weekend. Everyone volunteers on Thanksgiving. This weekend, I think you should rest and enjoy yourself.

What does that mean?

Whatever you want. You deserve it.

I don't know about that, she says.

I do, I say.

Well, I just don't like thinking about it that way, she explains. Deserving. Then she adds, How about you? What will you do?

I say, I don't know.

I thought you would want to work.

I shake my head. No, I say.

She looks at me.

I don't have any work, I say. I explain about the Weatherfield Foundation. They rejected the essay. Or not rejected. It just . . . wasn't useful anymore.

I'm so sorry, she says. I'm sure it was good. I'm sure you did a good job.

That's not—

I put my head down. I can't manage the rest of the sentence.

Oh, my mother says. Oh. Sweetheart. Don't cry. It will be okay.

I'm not crying about that, I say. I'm not crying about the essay.

My mother waits. She hands me a box of Kleenex.

I don't know, I say. Maybe I am crying about that. I try to wipe my eyes. But not in the way you think, I say.

My mother makes a low *sssh*. Just let yourself cry, she says. Don't try to talk.

I shouldn't take their money, I say. But I have to leave. I'm not supposed to be here. This was temporary. I have to start— I wipe my eyes more. I blow my nose. My tears have not stopped.

You mean here at home?

Yes.

But I thought you liked being here, my mother says. I thought Thanksgiving was nice.

It was nice, I manage to say. It was actually very nice, having strangers over for a meal.

My mother nods. When I said you would want to work, she says. I meant your real work. Before the foundation, she adds, clarifying.

Oh, I can't go back to that, I say. That's what I mean. I can't— I stop talking again. The tears have returned.

You don't need to say anything now, my mother tells me.

6

I. *I can imagine it, maybe, as conversion*—a development both logical and disproportionate. Though she had always been religious—an Episcopalian—her practice as a child had been distant and obligatory: She went each Sunday to Grace Church, watching dust motes in the soft jewels of stained-glass sunshine and noting enough of what was uttered from the pulpit to report her thoughts on the sermon at luncheon, following her grandmother's questions—her grandmother believed women should think for themselves. Her grandmother herself barely needed the pretense of a reply to share her own thinking on the minister's performance—the "new minister," she called him for the twenty years of his tenure through which she lived; he was learned, she conceded, but he did not have the proper stature; she liked a voice with a bit of timbre to it; and when Florence's father, whose infirmity kept him from church, or rather, provided enough of an excuse for him to indulge his aversion to it, replied from across the table that he agreed, certainly, in a tone full of conviction and absent of interest, religious observance concluded for another week. Her grandmother died the summer Florence matriculated at the new college called Bryn Mawr. This left her father alone in the Irving Place house but for the cook, the furnace man, the maid, and his valet, and settled the question of anyone from that address pretending to care about weekly sermons ever again. While in college, Florence certainly attended services with the other girls; she even wrote an essay in her theology course about the order of books in the Old Testament, which earned a good mark from the peevish instructor, a woman who walked five miles to and from the campus in a tweed skirt and jacket to teach one subject. "The Hebrew language is the most vital the world has ever known," she insisted without emotion to her mostly uncomprehending pupils. But when Florence, after she graduated, after she returned to her father's household, learned that the round of a spinster in New York brought her into various positions presuming her Christian faith, she did not feel especially keen about the presumption, if she never felt especially compromised about it, either. She considered, say, the Christian mission of the Guild (for which she collected donations and subscriptions) in the light of her observations at its drafty building, where she surreptitiously admired the practical speed of dark-skinned immigrant women sorting bins of used clothing, tossing away flimsy organdy overskirts and lacy shirtwaists to finger triple-layered overcoats and wide-hemmed wool trousers, or the shy determination of children arriving for an English lesson with half a cold potato in their pockets. When she thought about these people and their lives, she felt the particular denomination of any religion to be decidedly beside the point. She felt even a basic religiosity beside the point. What was the point? Goodness? Truth? Goodness was too variable, Florence felt, and truth too abstract for either to seem apposite; both were also too large for her life, her small life. Perhaps it was ritual? *That* she should be able to grasp; her life included plenty of diminutively sized rites; indeed, when, every evening, she appeared in the doorway of her father's library with a small tumbler of whiskey and water and a small pill, when, every evening, he said, "Why, thank you, my dear, how kind," and then sipped and swallowed the drink and medicine, which he could easily have rung for, or procured himself, her gesture could stand for many that made up her days—too slight to be called an act of charity, too gratuitous to be called an act of necessity, and yet just substantial enough to be missed.

Then after her marriage. Mr. Weatherfield, Ennis—"You must call me Ennis," she remembered him saying solemnly—was nominally Catholic. This was one of the objections Florence could see playing through her father's kind, clouded eyes when he was apprised of the young man's intentions, one of the considerations against which, she knew, he weighed the fact that she was nearly thirty-five and, before now, had not presented any serious prospects of marriage at all. "Yes, Catholic, but—" Religious belief was not important to Ennis, she told her father honestly; he did not believe in God. He did believe in matrimony, as Ennis took care to explain when he proposed, anticipating a question, as if this were something she would need to ascertain before she said yes. He thought it was one of the few institutions designed, overall, perhaps surprisingly, for improving human pleasure. She did not remember how she responded to this. For weeks she had listened to his musings on pleasure; it was his aim in life to understand it, to promote its appreciation—since, as he explained over tea, American culture distrusted pleasure, in general, which prevented American philosophy from ever reckoning with pleasure as an ideal, even though such was the principal reckoning needful right now. The nineteenth century had conquered the basic material conditions of life, he told her, and in so doing put the spiritual, the philosophical conditions on entirely new ground; humanity needed to undertake a rigorous investigation of its hedonic impulses. Ennis paused after this formulation. He licked his lips and on Schopenhauer—the stranger near Florence in the lobby scowled so much, she risked the impoliteness of inquiring if he were ill; he was not, and fortunately a distaste for Schopenhauer, or at least a distaste for the followers of Schopenhauer, passed quickly—but he had only recently returned to the country from Oxford and Paris, and he wished to settle again in Europe as soon as he could. A culture of aristocracy, he told her, was more conducive to a life of sensibility or intellect; a culture of democracy favored only a career in politics or, worse, commerce. She nodded at this. It made sense. Later, when he repeated this conviction, she wanted to ask him about how a culture of aristocracy related to a dilation of pleasure, but she did not. Ennis added that the dreadful religiosity of the United States was an attempt to address the lack of an aristocracy that only made things worse; this was clear when one spent time in Europe and this was part of what made life there, for an American, so essential. For now, he was confined, alas, to the United States; after his father's passing, his mother would not allow him to leave, too distraught at the prospect of an ocean between her and her favorite son, especially since Hugh, Ennis's older brother, busy with his banking position, five club memberships, two houses, several children, and one wife, seemed not inclined to be dutiful. Ennis was dutiful. Hearing all this, Florence felt pride in fulfilling *her* duty to this strange young man who seemed to have become part of her life for a strange, brief time. She was prosecuting a responsibility. She was ushering him through a world she knew well, the world after a parent's death, the world she had been consigned to for a long time and one he was just entering in groping ignorance; he needed her comfort, her questions and silences and dim back parlor and plates of varied, deliberated, unenticing cakes before he would emerge into the sunshine again, before he would leave her behind in the place she had always been. Before he left for Europe, or was married, or both. Both, certainly. She steeled herself. And then he asked her, one day, gravely, if he might speak to her father.

After the wedding, she could not say, exactly, what her churchgoing habits were—no, she could; they were not habits at all, for she had no habits anymore. Married life made her realize, by its contrast—by its repeated, unexpected bursts of confusion—precisely how habitual her life before had been. The investigation of pleasure, she learned, was effortful and restless. Ennis contemplated and scrutinized and rejected many things—mostly places and houses, also vases and cushions and rugs they did not need, books he did not read; he engaged in long correspondences with estate agents about property, with tailors and art dealers about the specifications of a new suit or the colors of a new plate, the results of which were always unsuitable or proved, when they arrived, so dissatisfying that he must begin again, with a new merchant, on new grounds. Florence, while sometimes murmuring commiseration at the mismatch of his own meticulous expenditures of taste and the disappointingly slipshod returns they elicited, tried mostly not to impede, not to interfere. She learned not to quickly. Their household, managed as it was by the inconsistencies of her husband's firm resolutions—for or against breakfast, or noise, or light, or open windows, or closed windows, all explained in the most reasonable of tones, all changing often, without acknowledgment of the change—ran more smoothly, if it ever ran anything like smoothly, without her intervention. And Ennis wanted only to think. He repeated this often. He felt he could not think, and if only he could, he said—well, he seemed perpetually to be on the verge of settling or deciding something; Florence could not even quite say what it might be, but resolution was imminent.

Which made it difficult for her to know or settle anything of her own; certainly she could not engage in anything like the staid, settled duties she had undertaken when she lived with her father. Her alliance with Ennis was *meant* to signal a departure from those, anyway, and a link to something less readily comprehensible but more ultimately meaningful, something that wrapped her and her husband into one unified, if to outsiders unconventional, truth; this had been her assumption before she was married. But though she had taken her assumption to be a careful humility, she soon realized it had been a dangerous presumption; worse, she could not explain or admit the error to Ennis; she could not liberate him from what seemed, clearly, to be the mistake of his attachment to her.

It was soon after she formulated this tragedy to herself that she wandered, one summer during their stay at a seaside house Ennis had chosen for its seclusion and then castigated for its rusticity, into a small and seemingly forgotten chapel nestled among the dunes of eastern Long Island. Weathered, uninsistent, the building from the outside seemed deserted—but in its cool interior, after she entered at what she thought was a safe hour of the afternoon, she found a service being held, with two dozen mostly lone but not at all impecunious (in appearance) parishioners, scattered among the pews, murmuring their responses to the robed man who stood with his back to them at the altar. She sat in the last row, kept her head bowed, and barely listened to, let alone tried to decode, what was being said; still, she waited until the concluding rite to slip away. Later, she looked back at that day of calm despair as something embryonic. And after Ennis died, when she traveled to France and then to England for the first time, to visit the two places on Earth in which she knew her husband had been happy, or in which she knew he had reported himself to have been happy—when she found herself, one sleepy Oxford morning, with a free few hours, she made her way to a Catholic church near St. Giles on the Woodstock Road. She proceeded as if she were simply taking a walk, and had not spotted her destination beforehand; arriving, she told herself that if her efforts in this trip were to discover the places her husband had known, then this address might well be a logical part of her itinerary; perhaps it was here he departed for good from the religion of his forefathers? Speaking to a frocked minister inside (a priest? a monk? she wasn't sure of the names), she even asked conscientiously if he remembered a parishioner by the name of Ennis Weatherfield, some years before, coming to services, a young man, pale . . . He did not. Of course he did not. She murmured her thanks and a good-bye, then moved off, as if examining more closely a row of candles in front of a statue, and dropped too many coins in the box, with gratitude that she had found no evidence of her husband in this space, that he had never been part of this cold, dark, ancient cavern of stone. Her relief worried her. She had traveled to Europe, with her own money, as some kind of final memorial—final expiation? she couldn't be certain—before she returned to New York to live alone on the small income she had been left in her grandmother's will. As if to test her motives, her desires, on the last day of her visit to Oxford—by which point she had returned to the Oratory three times, and attended two Masses—she mustered her courage enough to request an appointment with a chaplain and ask him about the possibility of services for one deceased; several months later, in New York, when she received a letter from one of the fathers thanking her for her donation and assuring her of prayers offered for the repose of Ennis's soul, she felt less uneasy. Her motives had been made clear. When she composed her grateful reply, she could ask without much fuss, in a final

savored them, but she did not bother much about comprehension. She underlined: "And yet it was in my power to withdraw
from Thee, O my Lord, that I might serve Thee better!" The
way of contemplation, she learned, lived by the conviction that
seclusion from the world enacted a more worthy, a more effica-
cious connection to it. She wrote again—this was several years
on, now—to the priest from Oxford who had sent her a message
about Masses for Ennis's soul. She wrote a long letter.

She did not undertake the next step until after her father
died. She did not intend to lie to anyone about her motives or
meanings. And in the end, once again, nothing of the sort was
required. "I do not want," she said in answer to the Mother
Superior's question when she presented herself as a postulant
for the New York Carmelite Sisters, "to live in the world others live in," and

*On the first of the month, with the Weatherfield money in
my account, I move a few blocks farther out in Royce into what is
advertised on Craigslist as an in-law apartment. I don't know what
in-law apartment means, but this one is a spare room in the half
basement of a man called Len Holland, with a microwave and sink
and mini fridge in one corner. The bathroom is down a hall. Month
to month, only $350 per. He doesn't even want a credit check. Len
used to coach track—or "cross-country," as he says; I don't know
the differences between different types of running. As far as I can
tell Len just runs. He runs every morning, early. At 6:30, I can see
through the narrow window at the top of my low-ceilinged bedroom
the end of his run. He turns into the frozen dirt ruts of the driveway,
going hard, then drops to a swift walk, then shakes out his arms and
looks at his watch. It's under twenty degrees at that hour. Len is tall
and about as thin as a person could look and still look strong, tan
even into winter, with a crew cut, deep furrows, sunken hazel eyes.
He wears two pairs of shorts on top of each other, one tight and one*

loose, and a long-sleeved solid T-shirt under a down vest. On his feet he wears beige trail-running shoes and low, functional socks. Running as Len does seems to me like a possible solution, expenditure going nowhere, without expectation of

the faces across from her, in their habits, smiled and bowed slightly in understanding.

II. *Or I can imagine it, sometimes, as exploration;* she traced its beginning to a dinner at Oxford. "I'll expect you for some exploring tomorrow, then," said the elderly figure on her right; this was long after the port had wandered down the table, stoppered in thick glass, accompanied by carved silver boxes of snuff. "No?" said the figure to her left, a much younger man with a careful part and slender build, who seemed to have determined she was not, after all, worthy of much notice, this middle-aged American woman, despite any suspicion of the middle-aged American's millions. Florence spent most of the dinner confined to nodding at the man on her right, at his monologue on the deficiencies of the soup course, the fish course, the roast—interspersed with the sounds of his satisfaction at consuming the soup course, the fish course, the roast. Encouraged by her murmurs of approbation, he could move seamlessly from opinions about the decline of high-table menus to other diminishments only too evident to anyone who could notice—for example, how several new buildings ruined parts of a skyline that was one of the chief beauties of European architecture. None of his points about the university's recent failings, as far as Florence could tell, registered intellectual objections, and when she asked him with almost embarrassment, near the end of the meal—the first time she had a chance to do so—about his area of scholarship, he reared slightly at the indecorous turn their conversation had taken: Yes, she had been told the English did not like to talk about work, even the most nominal of work; they left that to uncouth Americans. She flushed. He, collecting himself and making allowances for her gender, nationality, and appearance, told her briefly that he was assistant curator at the Pitt Rivers Museum. "Ah," she said. "The Pitt Rivers; it's a museum for . . ." For *anthropology*, he told her. But, he added, she should come round and see it. "You might find something to your liking. We have some wonderful costumes, as well as plenty of pretty things." He smiled pityingly. She answered that yes, she would like to see. Tomorrow? He blanched again, recovered again. "Of course, of course," he said, and she apologized; he had not meant her to say yes. But he waved aside her apology; caught in what might be seen as even a momentary loss of gentlemanly self-possession, he protested, in reaction, overmuch, *insisting* she come, absolutely, and he would take her around personally.

Miserably, she agreed; miserably, they made plans neither now wanted for the following day. She returned to her rooms, weary, dyspeptic (the dinner had been, in fact, rather bad, the fish particularly so), and tried to write Susan Dawes a letter she never mailed, one that would make her visit so far seem amusing. Had Ennis really found this city congenial? Was this actually the place of which he had dreamed? At the museum the following day, with Mr. Smithson—that was his name, she remembered in a lucky rush when he came to greet her—she looked mostly at the shadowy reflection of her own face in glass cases. Smithson led her past what seemed like endless dim exhibits; he had also arranged for some items in particular to be set out for examination in a sort of storeroom: Ah, here were four rows of knives, each with an identificatory card. "There is so little *left* of primitive culture from this part of the world," Mr. Smithson exulted. He was enjoying himself. She wanted only to leave, to sip a cup of tea in the sitting room of her lodgings and spend a few hours in perfect silence. But on turning to find an excuse to go, she found her glance caught by a round of scuffed brass near the edge of one of the displays and, in spite of herself, inquired about it. "Oh, that," Mr. Smithson said, "that's not properly part of the collection. Paraphernalia, but we keep it labeled. One must be thorough." He was proud of his thoroughness, though he frowned at its object in this instance. "Used in an expedition. It came engraved with initials, though they weren't the admiral's. Matched his wife's, actually, though they may just as well be those of another relative, father, grandfather, handed down to him. Or someone else's entirely, of course." She gestured; might she—then blushed at her temerity, but he was unruffled. "Why not; this isn't very valuable." He placed it in her palm. It was heavier than she expected, the metal cool to the touch, cloudy, but the arrows inside moved as she passed her hand gently from side to side. "A sundial," he explained to her, "as well as the standard compass. If we were out and about, I could tell you exactly where we were." "Yes, of course you could," she agreed soothingly, handing the artifact back to him, thanking him for the honor of touching it.

And from there the plan, enacted after her return to New York, formed without effort; it seemed to float up to the surface of her life like some placid sea creature. She would go east first, the Long Island Rail route that she and Ennis had taken so often, but farther than they had taken it before—and then she would go farther still, out toward the lighthouse, to what she knew (from her novel collection of travel brochures) was a single, mostly forgotten tourist establishment aimed, it seemed, at businessmen of middling income who still wanted to hook or spear animals for diversion rather than livelihood, as well as scientists of even more modest means who needed the least fussy way to collect . . . specimens, samples? She booked a room. She did not need to explain her trip. It seemed to be the main boon of widowhood, the privilege of removing her choices from the opportunity for questioning—she could mention, merely, that some travel might "do her good," a useful phrase; she needed good done to her all the time now. Her carriage, shuddering along the dirt road, passed a steep-roofed wooden structure labeled LIFE-SAVING STATION. A few sheep and cattle grazed nearby. On the front porch of the inn, at the top of three bowed steps worn down from white paint to a soft fingerprint of weather, a row of boots stood complacently amid various tin pails, traps, white-painted buoys, nets, and walking sticks; she had time to observe as she stood there, holding her bag, waiting (she rang a bell she later learned did not work) for the sunburned girl—maid? daughter? she could not tell—to appear and take her upstairs, to set her bag down in a chilly room furnished with an iron bed, an oval rug that was too small, a washstand that was too big, a rocker cradling a lumpen crocheted cushion. Looking through the uncurtained windows, Florence could watch the light from the point come around like a cautious pulse, sweeping its cone of bright across the profile of the coast. It was October. "You'll want something to eat," said the girl, not ungenerously, and led the way down the back stairs—distinctions of front and back stairs, Florence learned quickly, were not observed here—to a kitchen, where she fixed a plate of thick buttered bread dabbed with thick strawberry jam, set down next to a thick gray mug of warm rum and water. Florence felt more genuine hunger than she had in quite some time. Her compass was in her pocket. She touched its weight. These new gyroscope compasses, the salesman at the emporium had told her, were quite advanced, marvels really, and while he didn't quite understand them himself, he was certain this was the best on the market; he knew that much. "That's what I need," she said.

She learned to use it in the days that followed—days of

nothing more than walking out into a late-summer waste of air and sun and grass, through the scrabbly beach-plum bushes, their branches splitting like an old woman's veins, or along the deserted beach, listening to the resigned crash of breakers, the complaints of the gulls. She paused to eat a paper packet of hard-boiled eggs, which the same taciturn kitchen girl had prepared for her, watching the tilt of sun for inclinations of when to return and following the dial of her instrument for instructions how. After dinner, at which she quietly consumed the substantial plate of fish stew and corn bread that appeared in front of her, then an equally substantial plate of blueberry grunt and cream that appeared after, with more rum, then tea, then even more rum, warm again, she sat and rocked in the drafty parlor, a shawl pulled across her shoulders, the compass hidden in her fist; she had brought a novel and needlework but took out neither. She avoided a group talking over the blue-fish catch of the previous spring and waited, calculating, though unsure in her own mind of what she was calculating about, until on the fifth night of her stay she dared say hello to a man who sat nearby with a thick brown volume and seemed oblivious of the aroma of diffident fishiness clouding his wool jacket and vest even in the after-dinner hour. She knew he set out terrifically early each morning, and returned always with a faintly sloshing row of metal boxes. He researched the habitats of crustacea, he said with some hesitation when she asked, then explained with greater and greater relish, to her encouraging and barely comprehending nods, his minor but essential additions to the scientific understanding of these creatures' various parts. Her questions gently guided him away from details of cephalo-thoraxes to the places he had been in order to look at them: Newfoundland, the Carolinas, the Gulf of Mexico, Monterey Bay. . . . The next morning, after rising to a knock at half-past what she tested of survival in her hands and chapped cheeks and aching feet. What interest in, what connection to the sea had she any right to claim? She thought about this, chewing dried beef in an Arizona camp, and decided that the closest she might come was Tommy, an occasional hand at a sailing club on Long Island—whom she pictured, when she pictured him, standing in the solarium of their summer house, holding a shell. She had seen him just so, for a moment, on one of the many afternoons Ennis had persuaded him back for gin and conversation after one of their long sails together; Tommy—what was his last name? Something Polish she could never say or write properly. He was freckled but dark haired, with a rough forehead, big jaw, thick hands; indoors, he always seemed on the verge of knocking something over, bearing down too heavily on something inanimate, misperceiving distance and force, though when he was on or in or even near salt water—jamming a rudder, undoing a rope from a cleat, squinting at a triangle of canvas, or propelling himself through waves, his stroke a modest, muscled rhythm—he seemed not to waste an ounce of wind or breath, not to move any object except deliberately, swiftly, and just as it wished to be moved. Twenty-five the summer their paths crossed, and as tall since he was thirteen, he told them, he'd never had a job that wasn't boats and ships, though he didn't say much about this past; he combined a lifetime's discretion with what seemed an eternal youthfulness, a perpetual cheer. Ennis, despite protestations from Tommy that he was no good with learning—his brain couldn't do it, he said; he had tried—misinterpreted his geniality as eagerness, and took him home often to press on him books, more books. "When I look at that boy," he told Florence, "I understand the importance of a liberal education." Florence pointed out that if Tommy was a boy, Ennis himself was hardly older, and her husband frowned, as if their similarities were something not to be noticed or at least not to be remarked on in polite company. Florence demurred; she made sure Tommy always got dinner, too, when he came for what Ennis wanted to believe was intellectual talk.

These visits made her wonder again what sort of father Ennis might have been. She had stopped thinking about this, she realized, sometime after their marriage, though she'd thought about it—worried about it—intensely before; when they were engaged, she tried obliquely to remind Ennis that she might be too old to bear a child, and he waved these attempted warnings away: "I don't think of your age, my dear." Between the two of them, during the heady affianced time, there seemed to exist a kind of confidence in reverse, a faith that certain things would never be confided; she felt it to be a species of integrity, though later she realized it was cowardice—cowardice, and hope. Perhaps she was not too old. Perhaps. By the time they met Tommy, by the time he was coming in for a glass of gin several nights a week and laughing too hard—mockingly?—at Ennis's questions and answers in the delicate solarium where Ennis liked to drink, it had been five years since Florence's wedding night, at an uncomfortable hotel, where Ennis remarked on the heat and went to bed early, a cool cloth on his forehead. Florence thought nothing of this turn of events, assuming that the duties of marriage would unfold in time. Not, she conceded as days passed, not perhaps during their honeymoon, since everything was in disarray during their honeymoon, with its unfamiliar hotels, its calls and visitings, its excursions to notable sights, all of which left them worn, confused, with so much and yet so little to say to each other; rather, when they were settled, when they had a home of their own, or perhaps when they returned to Europe, to Oxford, to Paris—of course they would—perhaps then Ennis would feel . . . But Ennis seemed no longer to think about Oxford or Paris much, and no longer to count on the enrichment of expatriation—in consideration of his mother's feelings, he said. And after his mother died, suddenly—she had seemed till the very day of her death to be in excellent health, so different from his father, who had spent years grumbling about the chalky concoctions he took to soothe his stomach, Ennis reported—after the normal round of mourning and the tedious sorting of effects, well, Ennis seemed withdrawn from every-thing, even his normal complaints about the horrors of Amer-ican civilization. That is, he seemed that way until he took up sailing, an enthusiasm about which Florence almost held her breath, she was so anxious not to disturb it, not to say anything that would draw Ennis's consciousness and then his dissatis-faction and then his disgust (she knew the inevitable sequence now). In short, it was not ever quite the time, was it, to expect whatever it was she was *supposed* to expect of marital intimacy? And if she were to answer to the contrary, what would that matter? Her duty clearly lay in patience, no more or less; it was always better to hold one's tongue.

Not to mention that Tommy—she conjured again the pic-ture of him, alone with the shell, the creamy china-smooth mineral swirl in his big hands like an unexpectedly inherited heirloom he planned to sell at the first chance—brought peace to their household, even if she hadn't been prepared to admit before he came that peace was needful; it seemed she and Ennis required a third person not, as the conventional argu-ments for progeny would have it, to repeat and even emphasize the determined meaning of their union, but, rather, to forget about whatever it was the two of them were supposed to have meant. Tommy told them details of whales, crabs, giant squid, and poisonous jellyfish; also legends of brave smugglers, lying fishermen, wrecks, and duplicitous mermaids—and they encouraged him, half-knowingly, with their effete incredulity and fragile urban ignorance. His smile cracked quick as the splash of glass on a hard floor. He moved to the Cape, the following winter, to join his brother-in-law in a business venture—he seemed to have married very quickly; Florence assumed this was to make the business venture easier—and they never saw him again. The following autumn Ennis was dead. She imagined Tomasz Wisniewski now, lithe on his bad leg as he moved across the deck of his own ship. Alone, finally, in the middle of the country, on what might once have been seabed, under a bright embroidery of stars with a tin cup of bad coffee in her hand, Florence thought about what she would say, what she had said, if anyone asked her about her interest in the effects and remains of the ocean: She had no interest, really. She simply wanted

Len knocks on my door the second night to offer me a heater. "Are you cold?" He looks down at my slippers. The room is carpeted in a thin gray layer, industrial, but the furnishings manage to be homey, mismatched, and solid. Len says, "We had some problems with damp down here." I wonder about the we. "But this thing is noisy," he adds; "I'm warning you." He turns it on and the hum is barely audible. "I can't stand noise," Len explains. "It gets worse the older I get. Just can't stand it." I ask if he runs with music, then, and he looks at me. "No!" Scorn. I tell him I'm not a runner, as if not running at all is better than running with the accompaniment of pleasant sounds. "It's the best exercise there is," he says. "What I tell the kids is you get out what you put in. That's it." This seems like a lot for Len to offer all at once, and to do it, he looks away from me. I ask him how long he has been running. Forty-one years. He has this number ready. "Started when I was twelve. My parents split and I figured I had two choices. I could go to hell or I could pull myself together. That's it." I want to ask who used to

live in the in-law apartment, but he is already leaving. Len works
at the medical-supply warehouse and drives there in an old Ford
truck—which he repaints himself, I think, because I saw the paint
in the garage, labeled with a strip of silver duct tape and black block
capitals: FORD. *The truck is dark blue. He leaves at 7:30 A.M. with*
a Nalgene bottle in one hand and returns around 6:00 P.M. I don't
know what he does in the evenings; he could

to get away as far as possible, in time and space, as far as
possible from everything.

III. *Or I can imagine it, sometimes, as illness;* in widowhood,
the decline happened so gradually, so naturally, that in a year she
could not remember the last time she'd ordered a carriage, been
to the theater, kept an appointment with her dressmaker; more,
she could not remember how these and dozens of other exter-
nal responsibilities had taken so much of her time, how they
had seemed so much of a life, and could not quite fathom why
it had ever been necessary to call on a relative or stop in at the
butcher or take a turn around the park. The delicate corsetry
that excursions had once provided to her days, she was grateful
to discover, was hardly necessary; she did not feel that her time,
stripped by illness of what might have been its battens, notably
sagged or crumpled or leaked; on the contrary, she felt her days
finally had integrity, a posture of their own. "You are bearing up
splendidly," her doctor told her, patting her arm. She thanked
him. "Your heart is strong," he added. He listened to its thumping with his stethoscope, gravely, during every visit, before rec-
ommending again that she be patient; she would be well soon,
very soon. "Don't worry yourself. That will make everything
worse. You mustn't become nervous. Or hysterical." No, she
agreed, it wouldn't do to become hysterical, but she had never
been less in danger of hysteria in her life. Her doctor was glad

to hear it. He cleared his throat before the next question, as if it were delicate, or required his careful approach, though the tone he ended up choosing was gruff enough: "Are there any changes in the symptoms?" She smiled, hoping to soothe him. No, there were no changes in the symptoms, she told him, and when he began to mutter about iron, tonics, massage, electric stimulus, she reminded him of his own prescription; they were waiting to see, and they were sure she was improving. She felt very solicitous of the doctor; she wanted him to remain cheerful, because he meant well and took such good care of her, because it was not his fault that her condition lay beyond the boundaries of his, of anyone's, professional medical knowledge.

And of course they were practicing a time-honored version of the sexes' mutual dissembling, each protecting the other from their own awareness, since she thought she knew, and would not tell him, of what *he* thought he knew: Her condition was only an overwrought woman's somaticized grief—understandable, wasn't it, with her husband's death so sudden, and no children to comfort her? It would never do to discuss this with her, though; it was better to let her rest. And he could well be right, Florence conceded happily to herself. Very likely he was right. She had first fallen ill three months after Ennis, drunk, left their summerhouse one light evening in his new car, a Pierce-Arrow that reminded Florence of a spaniel with its tongue hanging out, and crashed into an oak tree, dying instantly; it was at Oxford, to which she had traveled for the first time only when the man who'd told her he loved Oxford would never travel again, that she felt compelled also for the first time to spend a full day in bed. It was, in fact, the day after she had determined to sign away Ennis's fortune that she spoke to her Oxford housekeeper—a small, round woman who entered the room every morning of Florence's stay at seven precisely, bringing a cup of tea but mostly, Florence thought, expressing through the force of the energy with which she drew back the curtains her suspicion of anyone who was not already up at this hour—it was at Oxford she spoke to her housekeeper a sentence of unadorned truth: "I am in no condition to rise today, I'm afraid." To the immediate shift of Mrs. Lewis's demeanor, from censorious to concerned—Was she feverish? Had she caught cold? Did she need a hot-water bottle? A compress?—Florence replied that she was not contagious and there was no need to worry, but she *did* need to be as still as possible and to rest. These words were more effective than even her hazy intentions could have hoped for. Indeed, the remainder of her visit was spent mostly in a more or less reclining position as she usefully established how much could be eradicated from an itinerary, any itinerary—at least in the case of a life like hers. Which was the life she must live, after all. At home, once two different New York doctors had made concerned, noncommittal noises at her bedside, she repeated the demonstration; acquaintances and associates were remarkably understanding: so much grief to bear, you know, to lose a husband so young. That is, Ennis was so young. Yes.

There were moments, however, in which Florence actively hoped the doctor was wrong—that is, she hoped that the physical afflictions keeping her to the divan and four-poster were not at all a consequence, however attenuated, of Ennis's death. Because it was too infelicitous an irony: A wife discovers what would have allowed her marriage to continue only as a condition of its definitive end. It could have been key to her union with Ennis, some sickness, some *state*. It was her last small pride, she allowed—to hypothesize on what would have been possible had she fallen ill with Ennis as her husband. Or if perhaps, what was even better to imagine, if *he* had fallen ill with her as his wife. He would not have had to drink so much; she would not have had to look helplessly across the breakfast table, quelling again the useless suggestions she had made and he had mocked so many times by now—Perhaps to Europe? To South America? Was he really so very trapped? But of course, yes, you know best; I don't mean to question ... —as she noted a deeper restlessness and shame in his vague eyes, edged below, those last few months, with purplish half circles, and only brightened into something like life when they darted through the brief peak of an alcoholic daze she was rarely near enough to see. The year after Tommy married, the increase in his drinking was matched by the increase in his absence. But absence, physical absence, was not the point. The need of getting away from everything was not the need of keeping everything else away.

And she was not solitary, in her current condition. Nor did she even wish to be solitary, but when visitors came, with their news already edited into conversational, piquant snatches, with the complaints they could confide only to someone who was no longer actively engaged with those to be complained about, with wishes and might-haves that the suppositional air of a sickroom kept from the need for any pragmatic steps, they brought these into *her* world. She was not entering anyone else's. It was a small realm, the back room on the second floor that had once been her mother's library—before Florence's time—but it contained what she needed; she sometimes took to calling it, in private, her office. Women didn't have offices, of course, not women without a position. Ennis's mother had had one, but then, Ennis's mother had been unusual—a small, fierce Englishwoman, born the fifth of seven daughters of a dishonorable minor peer, a girl who had married an even less respectable but much more determined Irishman and followed him through a course of emigration, industry, banking, and fortune building that did absolutely nothing to regain her former status as a European aristocrat and everything to make it, in her new country, irrelevant. Ennis had put it this way to Florence, after Florence had one day during their engagement been asked to tea with her future mother-in-law. While Ennis's comments about Hugh Weatherfield, Sr., and about all his unimaginative American success, seemed to vary only between the indulgent and the openly scornful—to make money was all he was good for, and he wasn't even, in that pursuit, one of the true visionaries, the Havemeyers and Morgans and Carnegies who transform their worlds—Ennis's comments about his mother seemed uncertain of the tack they wished to take, darting between cowed and vicious, flip and serious: "I have never known anything to defeat her," but also, "She will smoke herself away, one of these days; we will enter that infernal room to see a puff of gray leaving the window, talking as it does."

The image did not seem likely to Florence, given her own observations, though Esmerelda Weatherfield was one of those women who wizened rather than softened with age, and though she did pull on a cigarette, via a long mother-of-pearl holder with a gold tip, throughout the entirety of that first conversation. Mrs. Weatherfield was too intent, too full of intention, to evanesce. She would always be here, clutching one arm of her leather chair—"Do you like my little office? Good. Ennis has not told me very much about you"—exhaling. "Though I am certain marriage will be good for him, very good for him. I don't much care what Ennis puts his mind to as long as he puts it to something. What matters is the commitment." Florence was not sure how she should respond to this, so she maintained the mild smile she had been practicing, which seemed to have no effect on her interlocutor. "Pour the tea, girl. Don't wait. Pour the tea. Take one of those biscuits. You'll like those. Ennis has all the flaws of his intelligence.

He takes after me, I'm afraid. You know this? Thank you—"
taking the cup and saucer extended to her, putting it aside and
instead inhaling again—"and you'll forgive the smoke. It's my
vice. It concentrates the mind. At my age, everyone is allowed
one vice. Every woman especially." When Florence asked
Ennis if his mother had wanted more children, girls, Ennis
told her that two girls before him had died very young, which
was, in his opinion, for the best: "I can't imagine ours was a
household for girls." He didn't explain further, but Florence
thought she might have something of an idea why when Mrs.
Weatherfield laid down her cigarette and began to recount an
assessment of Ennis's character—his waywardness, his bril-
liance, his caprice, his taste—in a tone of such careful disapproval that Florence only then understood the depth and
comprehensiveness of her adoration: "Now's the time, now's
the time; he should strike. He should make his move"—Mrs.
Weatherfield plunged one small fist into the opposite palm.
"Marriage is a good sign. I'm sure you'll agree." For a moment,
Florence was invited to regard this disinterestedly, as if Ennis's
marriage had nothing to do with her, and moved to answer
before she was stopped by the older woman's left hand, clot-
ted with four large rings, clutching at her lower wrist. "Now,
don't misunderstand me; I am not saying *business*, in particular, if that's not to his liking; it might not be, and Ennis has
quite enough to live on, as you must know by now. We don't
need to tiptoe around that. I don't believe for a moment you
are marrying him for his money; that would be conventional,
and I can't imagine you have waited this long for a husband
only to be conventional; the money is beside the point." She
raised a finger. "Action. To *commit*. You see." Florence was not
sure she did; she nodded. "His father, bless him, thought it
would be fitting to have a lawyer in the family. I'm not sure.

Certainly Ennis might enjoy the intellectual aspects of the law. But is it active enough? *Active.* I discovered early in my life, thank heavens, that we are made to contribute to the goings-on of the world. It doesn't do to resist. Leads to perversion. The nerves. The nerves go." Florence nodded. "It was the boon of my marriage to Mr. Weatherfield, the chance to take action, and I don't mind showing my pride in it, I can tell you." She waved her hand. "All this . . ." Florence looked around at the room's handsome furnishings—the large vase in one corner, the standing lamps and cushions and wicker basket, the dark rugs overlapping on the floor, the stools brought closer, as if perpetually seeking an audience, with a settee in one corner looking on disapprovingly, even the gilt-framed chain of landscapes marching down the wall opposite the window. Florence wasn't sure how to respond. "Action," said her future mother-in-law again, nodding. Florence did not speak to her much in private after her marriage to Ennis, though Ennis visited his mother once a week, coming back each time always grimmer than he had left; he refused Florence's offers of accompaniment.

And then she died. *Action* was an odd word. Nine years after Florence was widowed, when she began her letter writing to young men during the war, some of the names in the list she received bore the denotation after them "wounded in action," and she reflected again on the oddities. She would emphasize, in these messages, her wishes for a speedy recovery and hopes of comfort and rest, though otherwise they did not differ much from the letters she sent to privates still on the battle-field—that is, in action—where, she learned from the replies she sometimes received, they acted little, and often spent their time waiting, amid the rats and mud of the French trenches, or amid the butterflies and wildflowers of the French fields.

"We spent the evening popping lice in the fire and trying to forget another cold, wet night to come," one wrote; "We spent the morning tramping through the most beautiful country I have ever seen," another told her. "We are grateful," she ended all her notes, regardless, "for your patriotic service and hope for your victorious return very soon." Soon she requested to correspond only with the wounded, those to whom it seemed less incongruous to send—along with the string of meaningless daily details about her inconsistent furnace, a proposed new streetcar line, the rumors of fresh adulterations in flour and milk—the record of her pain, an enumeration of its shifts and gradations. In return, among details equally banal to the writers—iodine smells, wet wool, a new nurse, old magazines, the lights in the ward that made sleep impossible—came all of the soldiers' pain, as well. Some lines had been struck out in black by censors, which jarred her not with anger about what she therefore missed, but with a startle that others read the notes; this gentle record of suffering, she felt, was so private, a matter only for her and those strangers far away who through their writing entered her tiny room, her office, for a brief span. "There will be a limp, but he got most of the shrapnel out, so I guess I got off easy, and gosh, some of the fellows here have lost an arm or something worse." The goal was to keep up their spirits, Josephine explained—Josephine was involved in so many good causes; Florence knew her from their time together working for the women's vote—and to take their minds away from immediate circumstances, and to remind them that people cared for them back home; they would be grateful. Florence did not think about soldiers' gratitude. And only when the armistice was declared, as she listened through her window that early morning to the whistles and church bells and cheers, then settled back against her cushions, did she allow herself to feel her own thanks, detailed precisely by the absence now settling inexorably around her.

About action, she realized too late, she should have spoken with her father, he who had lived every moment of his life after the age of twenty with a wound from Chancellorsville gnawing into his leg, who could walk down stairs only with the aid of his cane and a valet, and who did so—though he never needed to, strictly speaking—daily. Tell me, she should have said—but what? And she had not. She still remembered the feeling of his hand on hers, the morning of her mother's funeral, perhaps the last time he had touched her for that long—the dry palm resting there throughout the carriage ride and into the church, whereupon they were separated, or surrounded, by a sea of others. She remembered how, at the moment of their parting, she thrust that same hand into the pocket of her coat and felt two wintergreen drops, already rather sticky, from a package her father had given her several days before, when the house was in confusion and he would enter the nursery at odd hours to pat her and offer small things she did not quite know what to do with—a doll, a picture book, a bag of sweets—and at once, almost instinctively, there in the vestibule, she put the candy under her tongue. She realized on doing so that if it was improper to *possess* such a substance in church, and at a funeral, it was even more improper to *consume* such a substance in so sacred a space. But there was nothing to be done about her impropriety, once committed, but to keep her lips pressed tight, her mouth carefully, warmly, softly concealing its contents, and to enjoy a slow, warm loosening of flavor, spreading out and down the back of her mouth, throughout the service, before she swallowed the last and was ready to be kissed on a now innocent cheek by a seeming parade of women who looked at her and said, "Poor dear." With her father gone, with Ennis gone, she was not sure what she had to conceal. What was melting now, within her, and keeping her, even in the midst of life, far away. Her heart,

    Len is one of those unscholarly people whose respect for scholarship runs deep. As deep as his scorn. He thinks everyone should get a real job, pay the bills; look at his son, twenty five: "He has a degree in art history, wants a position in a museum. He can't find one. What about a position on a construction site?" That is Len's question, because every contractor Len knows needs help. But then he asks me about the Ph.D., shyly: "How long did that take?" He tells me he never finished college. I tell him he could go back. He ignores that. This is Sunday, in the garage, with the door open, where we're trying to fix a bike I purchased for sixty dollars. Len is trying. He fetches a tool. "What do you teach?" he asks. I say I don't anymore. "What is it then"—he gropes for the word— "research?" I say not that, either. He doesn't respond. "I think you may have been ripped off with this bike," he says finally. "It is art that makes life," Henry James once wrote. I should tell Len that all I have done for the past week is reread novels and imagine. I should tell him that imagining is not what I want. I know that failed academics are supposed to find refuge in imagination; they are supposed to realize that books are more important than scholarship about books. But they're also supposed to find refuge, the failed academics, in life; they are supposed to realize that the world is better than any words. I don't want either part of this contradiction. I don't say any of this to Len. I tell him that I have applied to be a part-time shelver in the Royce library, which is true. He nods. I tell him that should buy me enough time, maybe, to do

the doctor told her on his now infrequent visits, was still strong, and tomorrow, perhaps, she would go out.

7

character

The applicant's mother didn't want to leave her children, but the recruiters who showed up told women like her that in just a few months they could earn as much as they made in a year here at home, since Dubai was full of millionaires who needed haircuts and manicures, and salaries were high and tips plentiful. They just had to pay a small fee. Well, it wasn't small. But the applicant's mother was one of the several dozen women from her neighborhood in Manila who paid and signed paperwork and gave up their passports and boarded a plane. The planes went from Dubai to Baghdad and the passports were not returned. The women became third-country nationals, neither Iraqi nor American; contract labor, neither citizens nor soldiers. They worked technically not for a government, but for one of the vast corporations that had been hired to do the work of a government, keeping the pseudostate of a military operation fed and housed and tended. They were to sleep on thin, dirty mattresses in trailer barracks on the far edge of the base, at which they were to work long shifts, caring for soldiers in a salon designed to offer military personnel some comforts of home. Smile more, they were told. Also how to put on body armor quickly in the event of mortar fire. After one of the women was raped twice by her shift manager, after he threatened to return and do it again, after the applicant's mother and two others refused to work so they could stay behind as guards, supervisors sent in security personnel, who pushed the applicant's mother against a wall and choked her. "Security personnel" is how they were referred to in the report. The corporation seemed to agree that this incident was unfortunate, because the applicant's mother was allowed to leave, travel fares taken from her wages, which were less than she had been promised, which left her, on her return home, with nothing. The applicant's mother began to write letters. She wrote to the U.S. State Department and Defense Department, explaining what was happening—they must not know was happening. But U.S. officials could do nothing but contact the corporation, and the corporation could do nothing but reiterate its policies forbidding sexual harassment and its commitment to honoring the terms of each contract. No, the applicant's mother did not have a copy of the contract. She remembered a fuzzy photocopy the recruiter had held out on a clipboard. The corporation could not be responsible for recruitment tactics that occurred before someone was formally employed. After a time, the applicant's mother mostly abandoned justice; also, most of the other women were reluctant to join her, ashamed as they were of being duped. She told herself that at least she was safe now. At least she was with her children. I wanted to know if it could be part of my job, after December, to figure out how to help one of those children earn a scholarship to a U.S. institution of higher education.

incident

I went to New York the second weekend in December to attend a training in scholarship and fellowship advising.

What happened was that the librarian at Royce forwarded my application to the fellowships office because she thought I would be perfect for an opening she knew they had. I met the coordinator in the same building where my father once worked. "A homecoming!" said the coordinator when he heard. I was not the one who told him. The building was one of those turn-of-the-century houses along Elm Street that the college had converted into administrative space, parlors and bedrooms divided by soft gray partitions, the steep third-floor stairs covered in industrial carpet, cords and cables snaking along the molding to overloaded outlets. The coordinator was careful to tell me the post was part-time. Everyone at Royce assumed I had other more important things to do. Part-time and temporary, because it was paid for by a temporary grant, earmarked for programs to help students of limited opportunity. "But it might lead to something larger, so it's very important we meet our deliverables." I hadn't applied for this job, I reminded him politely, and didn't have any experience. "But you have your own experience!" He was already adding my class year and Weatherfield year to the end of my name on emails and memos. I removed the numbers when I replied. The coordinator sent me information about the training but told me that unfortunately the grant could not pay overtime for a weekend event. I didn't mind, I said; I had to be in New York anyway.

character

I went to New York the second weekend in December to see Heather. "I really need your advice on a number of things," she said. "Personal and professional!" Great, I told her; that worked out because I had to be in New York anyway.

incident

I went to New York the second weekend in December to listen
to a talk by Justin. "Remember I said I was doing this?" he wrote
above a forwarded message. "Look who followed through on
something." I didn't respond. But I would go; why not; I had to
be in New York anyway.

character

When I went to New York, I also had an appointment to see the
great-niece of Florence and Ennis Weatherfield.

I'd contacted her weeks earlier, of course, before the
Weatherfield gala program went in a different direction. Hugh
Weatherfield, Jr., had made up for Ennis's lack of offspring with
three children and then four grandchildren, two dead by now of
cancer and what seemed to have been an overdose; but I found
a number for a Hugh Weatherfield III, a confused eighty-three-
year old in California who couldn't remember anything about
his great-aunt before confirming—barely—that his cousin
might. "Lois?" he said to me through the phone. "Oh yes, *Lois*.
You could talk to her, I suppose." When I called Lois the voice
mail answered in that automated voice that suggested no one
checked. The suspicion seemed accurate, for a time.

But then: "You called me?" I was at a temporary cubicle at
Royce. I picked up because I thought a New York number on
my cell might be something to do with the fellowship training
I'd just registered for. "Laura Graham?" The voice was clear,
high, petulant. "You left me a message?"

"Oh! Yes. Thank you for returning—I'm sorry to bother—"
A little gurgle of awkwardness that I tried to mop up quickly.
"Are you Lois Richards?"

"*Ricard*."

"Oh, right." I had made it worse.

"What are you looking for, exactly?"

I explained, as quickly as I could, what I had been doing when I left her a message. "But it's fine, really, if you don't have time, because I no longer—"

"Yes yes." She cut me off again. "I have time. I just don't like the telephone. I'm old, you see."

"Of course," I said, before realizing I should not agree to that. "I don't like the telephone, either."

"If you wanted to meet, perhaps. I find meeting in person to be less draining, on the whole."

"You're in New York?"

"Yes yes." She added in my pause, "It's up to you really."

I mentioned December 10. Saturday afternoon, when I had to be there anyway.

incident

The training began at eight that morning at a community college in Queens, a corner room with linoleum flooring and blinds hanging crookedly from the windows next to their tangled strings. Two dozen-odd orange chair and desk combinations stood in several desultory groupings. Up front was a trim man in a checked shirt and thin woven tie. He was already dragging furniture around. "Welcome, welcome; just setting up." I moved to help, which seemed visibly to agitate him, though his smile grew only more insistent. "Thanks. I've got this. Make yourself comfortable! Almost ready." He clicked at a laptop and tried various cords to connect to a black rectangular console in the corner, amid bouts of hauling a few more chairs into position. The chairs screeched. He fixed his tie, which had turned over in his exertions. "We may have to do this the old-fashioned way. Technology, right?" No response from his audience— me, a stout bald man in jeans looking at his phone, a young woman with wet hair sipping from a gargantuan Styrofoam coffee cup. Our leader fixed his tie again. I sat down. Others trickled in. The feeling was groggy compulsion, students who didn't care enough to protest their Saturday-morning detention. Dan—"I'm Dan, by the way, Dan Finch, facilitator of this workshop"—had finished or abandoned his setup; he urged us into the seating now laid out up front: "Don't be shy, folks. Room for everyone up here."

We moved up. Dan passed out an agenda as he asked us to introduce ourselves and say something about our backgrounds. No one did, exactly. We stated instead our names and the name of a college or high school for which we worked. A round of personal and institutional names. I told those in the room I was part-time at Royce, working on a short-term grant. When I said this aloud, the words *part-time* and *short-term* sounded defensive. "Excellent," Dan said under his breath, as if these responses were better than he could have hoped for. "So glad you all—" And then a whir and a beep; a machine came on and colors appeared on a white patch over the blackboard. "What do you know!" Dan sprang up. Relieved, he could now press the button that presented the first of his uniformly bordered slides, the one with his name, followed by commas, M.A., Ph.D., the credentials one couldn't exactly announce. "There we are." A click. I opened my notebook. Dan: "And you probably want to know why you should listen to anything this stranger says—" He looked around for laughing confirmation, nodding at the few smiles. I wrote down his name. "Let me first say I've been in higher education for over twenty years." I wrote down "higher ed." "Passionate about the science of student success." In my notebook: "science of success." "So eventually, my personal investments pulled me from research to teaching to people." I drew little arrows between the words *research* and *teaching* and *people.* "And then—" He clicked through to a culminating slide, a list of acronyms, ending with the NACFO, National Center for Fellowship Opportunity, which happened to be one of the fastest-growing educational nonprofits in the country, press in the *Times*, the *Chronicle*; Dan was pretty pleased to be part of the team. I wrote down "growth, press, team" as he clicked to the next slide—which said "Questions?"—and he spread his hands: "Questions?"

I stayed quiet. Already an unspoken pact had formed among those of us in the cramped orange chairs—to say or do nothing that would extend the session a minute, a second longer than it needed to be. "So let's start with why we're all here today," Dan said.

character

Lois's address was an Upper West Side building of about a dozen floors, another turn-of-the-century structure, this one fading into distinguished shabbiness around the preservation, at least, of its most valuable materials: gilt-rimmed mirrors in the lobby, marble floors. The doorman nodded and showed me to a small, lurching elevator. I emerged after seven flights into a foyer with more mirrors and three doors.

One of them opened. "You found me," said Lois.

She was thin and small, with white hair floating mildly around her head; she wore a pair of gray canvas overalls spattered with paint, a turtleneck sweater beneath that, and grayish woven wool shoes that might have been slippers. Her glasses were round and gold. I followed her though the door and a narrow hallway, at the back of which was the suggestion of a bedroom, with a big living room to the left and a small kitchen beyond. Towering into the light from two large windows was a gawky plant; nearby, an easel stood on the puddled rumple of a drop cloth, also a tall metal stool daubed in paint drips and a steel industrial cart filled with jars, brushes in jars, cloths, spray bottles, trowels, crumpled and folded tubes of paint. There was nothing on the easel, but stacks of canvases leaned against a baseboard near the kitchen, the naked pine and staples of their back sides facing out, and on the large wall opposite a love seat hung a dozen paintings in a grid of small framed squares. They were so similar that the accumulation only accentuated the garish qualities of each individually— the bright synthetic colors globbed and daubed into abstract but vaguely corporeal shapes.

"You're an artist," I said at the same time she asked, "What was your name again?"

"I'm a painter," she said to my comment. I was already familiar with this firm tone of correction from Lois. "Also drawing, I suppose. Yes yes. Sketches." She looked at me. "In fact." She shook her head slightly, but not as if to deny something, more as if to shake something loose.

"I'm Laura Graham," I told her.

"And where are you from? Did you tell me? The foundation. You can sit down. I got something recently from the foundation. I don't pay much attention." She was hanging up my coat. "It's all very good work, I'm sure."

I sat on the edge of the green velvet love seat. "I worked for the foundation, yes. Briefly. Not anymore. This is now—this is a personal interest."

Her glance was doubtful. "Florence is a personal interest?"

incident

"We're all here today," Dan went on, "because we care about the same thing. And that thing is"—he clicked his slide—"helping students *tell their stories.*" In light, above us, the machine breathing hard, came the words *Telling Your Story.*

character

"Kind of," I told Lois.

Lois gave a small shrug, provisional, as if we could come back to this later, but in the meantime we had more important things to settle: "Here's my proposal," she said to me.

incident

"I didn't think you'd be here," Justin said to me after his talk finished. "Walk with me? You have time? I have like half an hour. I'm supposed to meet someone at seven. I need a drink. Why are you here again?"

character

"Laura!!" Greta's email was effusive. "That's GREAT. I should have thought of something like this! Yes, I bet Haverford is interested. Or should be. I'll put you in touch with the person. Watch for a cc. Sounds awesome."

I sent her an email of thanks and she responded with capital letters and exclamation points: "It was SO great seeing you! Judith loves you and she doesn't love ANYONE. Also, Ronnie is mildly obsessed, I think?" I had seen no evidence of either reaction. "We'll have to do it again soon. Tell me what you're up to!!" I archived that email without responding, but two weeks later, in my cubicle at Royce, I unarchived it. This was the day Lois called. One of the deliverables in our grant asked us to involve other schools; this would help students, in the end, and it was my job to help them. I wrote back to Greta.

incident

I waited for the proposal. Lois stood with hands folded, her small feet turned out to a woolly first position in those wide gray shoes. "I'll answer your questions. You said you had questions. If I can answer them." She tilted her head again, looking at me. "And I sketch as we talk."

"Sketch?"

"Yes yes."

"Sketch me."

"You object?"

"I, uh—"

"You're not a model." She waved her hand. "Good. I don't like hiring models. A waste of time and money. I prefer to take advantage of a situation when it comes. Real people. Serendipity."

"But—"

"Don't worry; no one will recognize you." She pointed to the wall of paintings. "In my work, a human figure is just the beginning."

"I see that."

"So. Would you like some water? I should have asked. Seltzer? Tea?" She was already assembling a pad and pencil, moving around her easel, clipping something up. "Something to eat?"

"No, I'm fine."

She glanced up for a moment. "Of course you're allowed to refuse. Not everyone can stand to be looked at."

character

I had a picture of the applicant—dark eyes looking out from a fringe of dark bangs—clipped to a printed-out pdf of his application essay, what the form called a "personal statement." I had those documents in a shiny folder in my backpack. The folder also contained a copy of Florence's engagement photo, the only photo of her I had, a list of the boxes I had searched in the Dawes collection, the torn-off sheet of notes from the workshop that morning, and an article I'd haphazardly noticed about sugar in the European Union. The problem with never admitting what you are doing, I thought, the problem with never identifying what you are doing, is that you can never get better at it. The folder was the one I'd been given by the publicist at the Weatherfield factory. I think her business card was still tucked into the slit in the pocket. It was a sturdy folder, and I don't like to waste things.

incident

Greta's email: "And if that person doesn't respond, just pester me and I will pester them!! I am good at email pestering. But forgetful. I think my New Year's resolution will be to answer emails on time. Honest. 2012 is the year for a better me."

character

The seats were mostly full when I arrived for the talk, mostly rustling with easy time-killing chatter. I could see Justin at the front of the room, in jeans and a blazer, listening to a woman in a neat black dress. The talk was held in a private library near midtown that I hadn't known existed before now, lined on four sides with bookshelves running to the ceilings, two rolling ladders promising ascent to the upper reaches, rimmed wooden trays around waist height proffering magazines and journals. In one corner were the long mahogany rods on which newspapers could rest like dignified indoor versions of drying bedsheets. Chairs had been positioned in a series of shallow arcs, as if up-and-down rows were too severe; the program hosting Justin was called "Contemporary Conversations." Soon the

of his success, proving that guidance counselor wrong, proving wrong everyone who thought the path to success was doing what one was told to do. Justin was good at this. Anyway, he continued easily, "See, that's sort of what I want to talk to you about—finding yourself." He fingered the paper. This was the real talk. No, it was all the real talk. "This may be the next book," Justin confided to us. He wasn't sure. The not being sure was also the real talk. He leaned forward over the podium, arms at the lower left and upper right corners and elbows almost extended, a position of relaxed command. "It's a weird phrase, isn't it, 'finding yourself.'" The audience nodded again, agreeing, as if they could assume as their own Justin's obvious intelligence and grace, the modesty and seriousness of his position. "And identity, a weird concept." Justin's voice kept moving forward— he barely looked down at his paper—through a summary of different philosophical projects related to that weird concept, through a revelatory contrast of Rousseau and Fanon, through a discussion of slave narratives and a skeptical but respectful analysis of the rise of the scientific process, through mentions of Charles Taylor and Kwame Anthony Appiah, through an opposition of Obama's autobiography and Augustine's *Confessions* that was also unexpected and, as far as I could take it all in among his quickly passing phrases, also revelatory. "We often assume," he began after a pause to sip water, but then smiled and stopped himself and talked about how sloppy it was to use the word *we*. He would take that segue, he said. Why not. He talked about the problems of politics as such. The audience nodded. They seemed to appreciate the way Justin included them all in both the accusers and the accused. Included us all. I was part of the audience. Justin was circling back now through thinkers and writers he had mentioned, pointing out the problem of collectivity and individuality, the problem and the necessities—he wasn't going to pretend this was something that could be solved. But he wasn't going to pretend that we shouldn't go on trying to solve it. He looked down, then up. "That's all I've got, folks." The applause was long and appreciative. Justin smiled and stepped back from the podium and made a little "Okay, stop, you're embarrassing me now" wave to the clapping so that the moderator could begin the question and answer period. I think I read, once, about a psychology study that found how hard it is not to return a smile. The response is innate. Could that be right? The questions were starting. "What do you say," asked someone in the first row, "about the charge that identity politics means more and more division? Do we need to exaggerate our differences? Do we need to split ourselves into smaller and smaller groups?" "What do you say," asked someone near the back, "about the fact that self-discovery is a privilege some people can't afford?" "What do you say," asked a hesitant elderly woman near the front, "about people who don't want to be labeled at all? Isn't that the case? Some people don't want to be labeled?" The questions didn't seem to be responding to what Justin had just explained. Perhaps they weren't supposed to. Justin didn't seem to expect anything different. He started with how good the questions were. He thought more differences meant more points of contact, too, and he didn't think it was a zero-sum game. He thought solidarity wasn't about reducing our complexity, but extending our empathy. He absolutely acknowledged the importance of material circumstances but didn't want to reduce identity to a privilege, something you get to do after you take care of the real stuff, because, he said, identity was the real stuff. "You know, I just want people to be able to be themselves," Justin said. The moderator stepped in. "I think that's a good place to end," she said. The audience agreed. Most were ready to go. They had what they'd come for. Applause once more, briefly this time, as people began to collect coats, gloves, the ends of scarves, already confirming to those sitting next to them and with whom they'd come that this had been a really good talk, hadn't it? Yes. A few people approached Justin at the front of the room: They had another thought to offer, a reference to confirm; they had the name of a friend of a friend they needed to drop. I waited at the back. I didn't know if Justin had seen me, and I didn't think I would try to see him. I thought about the last moments of his talk. Do I just want people to be themselves? Well, I thought to myself. Why would I *not* want that?

incident

I said to Lois, "Okay, I'll do it."

"Yes yes," she said. She never doubted my agreement. She clapped her hands together with a brisk "Let's get started" demeanor.

"Where should I stand? Sit?"

character

"The biggest mistake I see, over and over again," Dan told us, shaking his head a little in regret, "is that students think success is about numbers. Quantity. Well, it's quality, folks. It's all about quality. It's all about *narrative*."

incident

"That went okay?" Justin said. We were in a dull, dark bar near Times Square. The first one Justin saw. He ordered Manhattans and a cheese plate while muttering anger at someone in his texts; he wanted to know how many minutes of human existence people wasted in little half hours after 5:00 P.M. waiting for others to show up, in this fucking city at least. "You think that went okay?" His question the first words for a while directed surely at me. I forgot how Justin could make rudeness seem like intimacy. "My talk, I mean."

"It went more than okay," I said. "It went well."

"You can be honest."

"They loved you."

"All right, let's not get carried away."

"Don't worry."

"Who said I was worried?"

"No one."

He relaxed a little and unwrapped his scarf. "Yeah, it was fine. I was surprised you came. How did you know about this?"

"You told me."

"Oh." He looked up. "Right."

"I was in the city anyway."

"More research?"

"No, that's over."

He raised an eyebrow, momentarily interested. "You quit?"

character

Lois told me to stand near the window. To relax. "Yes yes, look out, that gaze, that's good, try to keep that. But don't think too much about me drawing. Let the moment achieve itself. It's best if you just ignore the process altogether."

"I see."

"Yes yes. Don't worry. I do this all the time. Now we can talk. Florence. I only knew her for a very few years, of course, at the end of her life. What year did she die?"

"Um—1947." She was behind me, to one side; I couldn't see her. Would I feel more or less awkward, speaking to someone I couldn't see? My view was the small courtyard of Lois's building, a window opposite, a hint of dingy wintry sky through the gap in the buildings. "August."

"I was six."

"Right. Your brother was ten." Less awkward. I didn't have to react. I was being sketched. This must be what psychoanalysis is like, I thought.

Lois said, "You have all the facts, don't you."

"All I could find. Very few. That's why I'm here."

"Yes yes." Lois sounded pleased at that. "Well, she was quite old when I knew her." I tried to do the math in my head; she wasn't that much older than Lois now—I didn't say this. Lois continued: "And I was very young. So I don't remember much. Children are not very observant, you know. People who know nothing about observation are always saying children are wonderfully observant, that artists should train their minds to be young again. That's nonsense. Children are mostly absorbed in themselves. Hmm." She paused briefly; some complication had emerged in the sketch. "In general my memory is very good."

I said, "I'm not surprised."

"It's true I don't see much point in dwelling on the past. I have always been a rather future-oriented person."

"Well, you can't—"

"Yes yes." She wasn't finished. "Added to which my parents and I were estranged for much of my life."

"I'm sorry."

"Don't be. It doesn't have to mean anything tragic. Some people don't like each other. And sometimes those people are related. That's how I look at this question."

"Uh—right." I shifted my weight just a little. I tried not to move.

"My mother hated her parents, too. Alas, she couldn't admit it." Lois made a small sigh. "They treated her awfully, yes yes, but still." A pause. I wasn't sure of the implication. But still, despite awful treatment, she should admit her hatred? "My father didn't help. He just wanted the money."

"Right."

"My mother never thought we had enough. Anxious. Grasping. Such a horrible quality. And so silly. There was plenty."

Her tone implied there is always plenty. I wondered if Lois's estrangement included an estrangement from the family money. "Right," I said. Who was I to talk.

"When you called I remembered that box from the basement and I did go and fetch it up. Clippings, I think. Someone sent it to me after she died. My mother, I mean. I suppose there is no one else."

"Clippings?" I did turn my head at that, a little, before remembering. "Sorry." I looked back again at empty courtyard and blank sky. To that view I said, "These are family papers?"

"Something like that. I've only just glanced. It seems quite random. Don't expect much."

"Is there anything in there from Florence?"

"Oh yes, Florence," Lois said, as if I were slightly rude or tiresome for bringing the conversation back to its ostensible subject. "Perhaps. I doubt it. It's all right over there," she added, oblivious to the fact that her gestures indicating direction meant nothing to me when I could not, posing, turn my head.

"Could I—could I look at the papers? Would you mind?"

incident

I did not quit, I told Justin. I explained about the project. His essay, I told him.

"Really? Shit. Sorry, I guess. Wait, should I be sorry?"

"It's better this way."

"Yeah. Good." Justin was done with that topic. "You think

it was too long, the talk? Too short? Come on. You're holding something back."

character

Lois said she would not mind. "You can tell me what's there. If there's anything of value. I suppose some old papers are valuable, right?"

"Um—maybe. Some."

"Ah, that gesture you just made. Wonderful. Yes yes."

I wasn't aware of having made a gesture. I scrambled for something to say. I was supposed to be asking her questions about Florence.

"Now," Lois said. "Tell me the rest of what you know about my great-aunt."

incident

I told Justin no, I was not holding anything back. "I was going to say—I was surprised by all the philosophy."

"You were surprised I quoted so many white people."

"Ah—maybe." And to his look: "All the ideas? No, that's not right—"

"Yeah, you're just digging the hole deeper." Justin smiled. He enjoyed my discomfort. "It's fine, don't worry."

"You know what I mean."

"Not really, but it doesn't matter." He pointed at the last piece of cheese on the plate in front of us. "Try that one. It's good."

I ignored him. "I just didn't think you were interested in ideas."

"Put the honey stuff on top."

"I thought it was people," I continued. "No, you take it. I don't like sweet things."

"Everyone likes sweet things." He shook his head. "It's biological. All these women telling me they don't like sweet things. It doesn't make you a worse person or something."

"Wow." I smeared a brown pearl of honey on the slice of cheese I was holding.

"Plus it's honey; it's natural and shit."

"You're kind of a bully."

"Where did you get that I wasn't interested in ideas?"

"I don't know," I said. "I was dumb. Tell me something."

He didn't respond. He was looking at his phone.

"Have you ever taken a writing class?"

character

Specifically, according to Dan and the slides that followed, *narrative* meant an essay in which the young person happens to want to do what they happen to be uniquely good at and what their experiences so far have uniquely prepared them for. It was also very important, according to Dan at the workshop, if at all possible, for an applicant to show how they had overcome adversity. The overcoming of adversity was something of a formula, true. But it was still vital. More and more schools and fellowship programs were interested in character, he said. "Character over credentials!" Overcoming adversity was a measure of character.

incident

Justin looked up and narrowed his eyes. "Are you saying my writing sucks?"

"No, no, not at all—"

"I'm kidding. Ease up. In college I did. Writing class, yeah, easy A."

"I didn't," I went on. "I read a textbook, though. This

textbook says a character needs to do something because a story is a character actively wanting things and making decisions."

"Sure." He ranged over the remains of the plate.

"My question is, does that happen? In life. In real experience. How often do you actively want something and make decisions to get it?"

"Um." Justin gave me a puzzled look. "A lot, I think? Like all the time?"

I was still holding the slice of cheese he had made me take. "Oh," I said. "Right. Of course."

I took a bite. He was staring at me.

I said, "Forget it. Dumb question. This honey is good, by the way."

"I told you."

"I'm working now on advising for scholarships and fellowships," I said. The words were meant to cover my embarrassment. They didn't. "It's all about story. Apparently. Anyway. I'm trying to learn. To, you know, help students—kids—those who—"

Justin supplied the words: "The disadvantaged." His voice was dry.

"Right, but—"

"Underrepresented."

"Well—"

"Minorities."

"Please stop."

"It all sounds very valuable."

He smiled to underline his scorn. After his talk, for a moment, I thought about asking if he had ever considered that these assumptions about being someone, someone with a story, a story of choices and decisions, choices and decisions only *this* person could or would make, seemed to emerge with the capacity to originate systems and structures that, once created, could not be controlled, could not be prevented from erasing and undoing and obviating in unforeseen ways the very chance for choices and decisions, the very legibility of any story, so that the proof of being ourselves was our recognition we could not be, had prevented ourselves from being, ever again—and I was glad that I had not said anything about this. It was so obviously dumb. Sometimes I couldn't believe how little I knew.

I said to Justin, "It's just something I can do."

character

"But how does this work?" Greta's note. "Are you in charge? Can I send you some names, basically. My friends in Philly. Will they qualify?? We need to get them SOMETHING. Right? These kids, what they've been through, you will not BELIEVE."

I wanted to write that I would, I would believe, but of course my belief was not the point.

incident

"I know almost nothing," I said to Lois. "I tried first to learn something about sugar, because sugar is where the money came from."

"Well, the sugar *business* is where the money came from."

"But my assignment was Ennis, because he was the source of the money."

"His death," Lois said.

"And Florence was the one who gave it away, the Weatherfield money, your family's money. So I wanted to know more about her. I could find almost nothing." I stopped. "I'm going to scratch my forehead for a second, if that's okay."

"Yes yes, do whatever you'd like."

"All I had was the fact of her giving it all away. I mean she wasn't involved. That part was interesting to me. I wanted to understand it." I put my hand down and resumed my motionless stance. I was talking to the view. "I saw in it something definitive, I guess, something strong."

Lois said, "Oh, well, *that's* completely erroneous."

I heard a whisper of paper. She was turning a page. "It is?" I said.

"Yes yes." She was calm, preoccupied, her tone that of someone engaged in a task and giving only half a mind to her words. "My great-aunt was a very weak person."

"She was?"

"She was."

"Do you know that?" I sounded feeble. "You were only five. Six."

"Oh, I was old enough." Lois was unoffended. "We visited her every few weeks, out at her place on Long Island. Out near Glen Cove? You probably have those facts, too. It seemed like a long drive to me then, so strange, perhaps because no one wanted to go. I don't think even Florence enjoyed those afternoons. Mostly she spent the time complaining. Though perhaps she enjoyed the complaining." She paused. "Do you need to scratch anymore?"

"No."

"This is going quite well, I have to say."

"That's good," I said. "I'm glad." I added, "And what did Florence complain about?"

"Oh, everything, nothing. She had no one to talk to. She had Emilia, but that was different."

"Emilia?"

"So when we were there, she went on and on. It was frightening, to a little child like me, but in a pathetic sort of way. Sometimes my brother and I were herded into her bedroom, which was always dark. She would put in her teeth while we watched. Then she would go downstairs and feed us these cheap candies from a glass jar that we were meant to be grateful for."

"That sounds—yes."

"My parents, I think, tried to get her to do things. She was in fairly good shape for her age, you know. She wasn't weak physically. She talked endlessly about things she hated without trying to change them. I'm sure you know those kinds of people. Endlessly dissatisfied and incapable of doing anything. There comes a point."

I made a sound that I hoped was the right response to this point.

"She hated the damp out there by the ocean but she wouldn't move; she had some old friends, I think, or would have, but she couldn't make a phone call, write a letter; she listened to silly radio programs about angels, I remember, which left her even more bigoted than she was anyway. In all, I suppose she seemed to me deeply silly." She paused. "Silly or fearful. If there's a difference."

"I see. Do you think," I tried, "that she was shaken by Ennis's death?"

"I wouldn't know," said Lois firmly. "Before my time. From my parents' opinions I would say, not much. I think he was a weak sort, too."

"Well, there was also the war."

"The war?"

"It must have been hard."

"Which war? I don't think Florence could blame her personality on the war."

I persisted. "But do you think she was different when she was younger?"

"Not really," said Lois mildly. "At least I doubt it. Anything is possible, of course. But in my experience people don't change much."

"No?"

"No no. How you start is how you go on. Circumstances change. But I've never thought that circumstances mattered that much." She paused. "Is any of this useful to you?"

"Of course," I said. "Very useful. Thank you."

character

I wrote back to Greta that I thought her friends would qualify. They would help our deliverables, for the grant. The deliverables, in fact, specified domestic students, within the United States; the questions surrounding visas and foreign schools and different records were just too complicated and heterogeneous. The advising coordinator had explained this to me when I asked her about the possibility of an applicant from, for example, a former U.S. colony with an economy still tied to the sugar trade where women could be forced through general conditions of the international economy and specific practices of international corporations to expose themselves to the danger of yet another war by working for the men of an occupying American army in Iraq. I didn't ask in precisely those terms. I found the file first in a database, where it seemed to be languishing. It was probably languishing because we needed to focus on domestic students, the advising coordinator said. I agreed that this made sense. Nor would such a focus be difficult. There were plenty of files, plenty of obstacles overcome, plenty of stories.

incident

"Good," Lois said. "We're almost finished here," she added. She meant her drawing. "I want to try one more page."

"That's fine," I said. There was something else I wanted to

mention, but I had forgotten what it was. Being a subject had turned my mind vacuous. I wanted a pen, desperately, a piece of paper, though nothing she had said was worth writing down— was it? "How long have you been an artist?" I asked, to cover the silence. It would come to me.

A decade, Lois said. She dated her beginnings as an artist from the moment she decided to draw every day. She had drawn every day for a decade.

"Ten years."

Yes, ten years. Consistency is paramount, she reminded me. Inspiration is a myth. I had heard this before, and so firm a consensus about the worthlessness of inspiration made me fairly certain that random, uncontrollable inspiration must be overwhelmingly important, but as Lois talked I considered the more humdrum problem of drawing every day for a decade and achieving only the ability to make what I saw on the walls. Ten years. Lois continued to talk. Yes, it took her a long time to come to her vocation. She was an actress first; she left home to act. "I met a director."

"You were how old?"

"Eighteen. I matured early. Yes yes. I knew what I wanted." She married the director right away. They had a studio in the Village and a lovely life together; they did a terrific *Antigone* at a festival, some other projects. But neither of them was very domestic, it turned out, and both were sleeping around, which wouldn't have been a problem, except Gerald was still stifled by notions of propriety. Lois came home one night and told him she thought they should be honest with each other, "to be adult about the arrangement." She was twenty-two. Gerald couldn't agree, about honesty or adulthood, and that was that, though they didn't get divorced officially until much later, and she kept his name because she liked the rhythm and she had done work she was rather proud of under that name. After, she said, she was sure she needed the challenge of a new environment, so she talked herself into a job in a theater in San Francisco, where she answered the phones and regrouped. The pay wasn't much, but when you're young, you don't need much; she slept on the couch in the living room of the woman who ran the place, another director. A generous soul, Lois explained, but unfortunately Lois fell in love with the woman's brother, who was already married to someone else, children too, and so Lois had to leave.

"You didn't want to break up the marriage," I summarized.

"No no, that marriage was doomed." The brother left with her; they went to Seattle. Sam worked on a fishing boat. Which was not ideal, because he was away so often and Lois was lonely; Seattle can be a lonely city. Lois took belly-dancing lessons from a woman whose cousin ran a farm, and eventually Lois went to work there, at the farm. They were doing what might now be called "organic," though they didn't use that term; Lois thought it wasn't in fashion yet. Lois did not know anything about farming but felt very in touch with the energy of the place and was allowed to take home all the fresh vegetables she could carry. She was a vegetarian then. Vegetarianism can be useful to determine what's best for one's body, she explained, but everything is so individual; it's all trial and error, "yes yes, until you get very in tune with your own biofeedback." She herself had been a vegetarian and a vegan and then she did macrobiotic. Now she ate mainly broth and rice and fish. At the time on the farm, she was coming into her thirties, when a woman's energy changes so much. "You must know how that goes," she told me. "You must be exploring that now."

"Ah—yes," I said. "Right." I scratched my face again. Lois didn't seem to notice.

"And then we were in California for a while," she continued. One of the men who worked on the farm left to start a different operation in Humboldt County, and Lois persuaded Sam, when he was back from a fishing job, to come along; there were eight of them, experimenting with intentional living on about three acres. It worked very well, Lois said, mostly because they sold a lot of marijuana. That was when she learned about herbs. Oh, and her son was born there. Jeremy. But it all fell apart in a few years. Lois left for Japan. Sam's sister took care of Jeremy for a month. Lois wasn't ready to be a mother and needed some time to herself. "And would you mind one last change? A few moments, if you could *lean*—yes yes yes. There."

While she was in Japan Lois went to a lot of temples, she said, and realized she needed to go back to school; she returned to California and began to read mystic texts and decided to get a master's degree in religious studies. But she had never gone to college, so she needed a bachelor's first, and decided to move to Austin because the state university there was good, or it used to be very good, and not too expensive. "Did Sam come along?" I asked.

"Sam." The name was far off now. No, Sam was no longer in the picture. She and Jeremy went to Austin. Austin in those days was growing so quickly, so much *sprawl*; it wasn't at all like what Lois thought it would be, but they rented a tiny bungalow in the back of an enormous property owned by a reclusive millionaire, Tim, who raised horses. His heart had been broken, Lois explained matter-of-factly, so he and Lois were kindred spirits. Tim asked Lois to do his chart, and when she did she was flabbergasted, astonished by how well they fit together, and soon enough they fell in love. "What is your sign, by the way?" she asked. "Aries?" I told her it was Scorpio. She said she should have known I wasn't an Aries. I wasn't stubborn.

"I'm not?"

"No no." Lois was certain. She was a Cancer; I had probably guessed. Tim was thirty years older and had promised himself he would die on his ranch, but he agreed to move with Lois and Jeremy to Chicago once Lois had been accepted at a theological program there. That's where she converted, Lois explained. She thought Judaism would help resolve questions she had about her womanhood, and it did, for a time, but then it didn't, and so she left school. She paused to ask me to move a bit to the right. "There," she said. Actually, she was still a credit short of her B.A. degree when she moved from Austin, and it was just luck the seminary never asked her for an official diploma, but they probably would have before she finished the graduate program, so it was a good thing she quit.

"And that's how I got back to New York." Lois spoke as if that had been her clear, pursued goal during the whole of the previous story. Lois had been lucky enough to find a very strong group of theater activists, and began to work with them—they staged interventions, mostly about the environmental movement; they sewed tin cans onto jumpsuits, she said, and did interpretive dances, interactive performances, demonstrations. It was a truly amazing bunch of people. The leader was a beautiful man named Jorge, who had served time for dealing heroin, or maybe LSD, no, heroin—anyway, a beautiful man. She and Tim were not getting along then, she added, but by the time they realized they should split up Tim was quite sick and moved to a convalescent home in Rhode Island. And after Tim passed on, Lois added, she decided she wasn't going to commit to a monogamous relationship again.

"So Tim didn't die on his ranch," I said.

"No!" Lois said. She seemed surprised at my remembering this, but after a brief pause she continued: It was through her theater activism that she came to painting. First she discovered art therapy, when someone in the group set up a nonprofit to teach social justice and conflict resolution with movement and role-playing and acrylic on canvas, and she worked at that organization for a time, before she realized she had already spent too much of her life giving energy away. But during one of the classes Lois also realized how much she loved painting and how good at it she was. It was what she had always been meant to do. She spent six months taking classes from a genius in Tribeca—a true genius, she assured me, and she learned all she could from him—and she had been painting ever since. She paused.

"Wow," I said.

"Done," she said. She meant the sketch. "Done done done. You can move."

character

And Justin was finished embarrassing me; he had to go. He had that other, important person to meet. He stood up. "The book is in, by the way."

"Book?"

"Um, mine? My book?"

"Oh, right! Your book! Great. Congratulations, I mean. What are you writing now?"

"Listen to you. Always the next thing."

"Sorry. You're taking a break. That's good."

"Actually, I'm writing a novel."

"A novel?"

He laughed at my expression. "Is that so weird?"

incident

I turned around. I could look wherever I wanted now. Lois was peering at the page she had just drawn. "Yes. This went well."

I had the urge to tell her a story of my own, or not my own, Joshua's story—that was his name, the applicant I couldn't help. I didn't say anything, though. The desire came from the wrong place: spite, maybe, revenge, defense. Also it wasn't mine to tell.

character

I told Justin it wasn't weird at all.

"Glad to hear it." He was winding his scarf again. "In the meantime more talks. Let me know about that, okay? I mean Royce or wherever you're teaching."

I skipped over that. "You really should get in touch with Greta."

"Oh, yeah. Greta."

"She has a real academic job. She would be able to make some connections, I'm sure."

Justin stood up and swallowed the last of his drink. "Actually I was just thinking about Greta," he said. "Because of that email from Mark."

"An email from Mark?"

"Right, Mark's people." Justin rolled his eyes. "The package that is Mark, now."

I said, "What?"

"I mean I'm glad he finally decided to run. Get on with it. It was clear from the beginning."

"Mark is running for office," I said, clarifying. At his look I added, "I didn't get the email."

"Oh, I thought you were on there. I guess I assumed we all were."

"No."

"Greta wrote me, anyway, like, get a load of this." He smiled. "I think we had a bet or something."

I wasn't thinking about the fact that I hadn't gotten the email. I was thinking about "clear from the beginning" and "finally decided." I was thinking these seemed like contradictions.

incident

But I didn't know if I could promise anything, I wrote to Greta, because my role was quite small; I was just part-time, a cog. She responded with "We're all just doing our best!!"

character

In fact Joshua did not write, in his personal statement, about his mother's experience in Iraq, or her exploitation, or her efforts at justice. Such details came in a separate memo, from an international organization trying to help refugees from the Iraq War, and while his mother didn't qualify, something might be done, the writer of this memo thought, for him. Joshua's personal statement was about photography, because he wanted to document the world and he wanted to turn it into art.

incident

Lois asked if I wanted to see.

"Not particularly."

She held up a page anyway.

It was divided into six patches, rough unmarked squares, holding six penciled figures without distinguishing features or marking—barely, awkwardly identifiable as human, like the shapes framed in color on the wall opposite. I could tell that three of them corresponded to the first pose I'd made, and three to the second; otherwise, nothing about the work seemed to index anything of me in particular. The whole page was slightly blurred, as if showing several small variations on the pose at once, or illustrating the principle of animation, badly.

"What do you think?" Lois asked.

"I, uh—they seem to be in motion."

"Yes yes."

"But I didn't move."

She nodded in satisfaction. "I've been working a lot on motion lately." She folded the paper. "I will paint this tomorrow. But you need to leave." I had looked at my phone. "I've kept you." She smiled—condescending, almost. "You're meeting someone."

"Not really. I'm—oh." I remembered then what it was I wanted to ask. "You mentioned someone called Emilia?"

character

"There is an old-fashioned distinction between the novel of character and the novel of incident," wrote Henry James, in an essay called "The Art of Fiction." I read this quotation in the textbook about stories. James did not think much of this distinction between character and incident. He wrote that "the terms may be transposed at will. What is character but the determination of incident? What is incident but the illustration of character?" The quotation in the book about stories ends there. James went on, though: "What is either a picture or a novel that is *not* of character? What else do we seek in it and find in it?" At the end of the paragraph, he concluded that "the only classification of the novel that I can understand is into that which has life and that which has it not."

incident

"Emilia," Lois said. "Oh. Florence's—what would you call her—" She shrugged. "Her manager. Her companion. Emilia was the majordomo of that little household."

"She worked for Florence."

"Well, yes. I don't know the exact arrangement. But she wasn't some sort of domestic servant." Lois wrinkled her nose at the prejudice she already detected in me. "She had been employed at the company first. I think she did accounts."

"The company."

"The American. My impression was that she was terrifically smart. You see." Lois wanted to make sure I understood.

"The American. The American Sugar Refining Company?"

"Yes yes."

"I didn't know your family had anything to do with it. I mean, after—"

Lois was puzzled. "My father worked for the company all his life."

"Your father—oh. I wasn't aware."

Lois shook her head briefly at my ignorance, then continued. "As I said, I wasn't clear on the exact arrangement. But my understanding was that Emilia needed a place to go. Very suddenly. A marriage gone bad or some other little catastrophe."

"Right."

"And Florence needed—somebody. So the two pieces came together."

"She and Florence."

"Yes yes."

"Did they like each other?"

Lois considered. "It was convenient. My parents knew if Emilia were there, Florence wouldn't fall downstairs or forget to eat for several days in a row." Lois shook her head. "*I* liked her, though."

She offered this pointedly, as if I should have asked about her feelings. I said, "Emilia."

"She smoked lovely cigarettes. I remember the box. Also I

remember her high heels, buckled." Lois made a small gesture with both hands of buckling something. "You see, I was very attuned to beauty, even as a child. But no, I didn't see her much. She withdrew whenever we visited, very proper. Still, I remember her high heels. She was a socialist," Lois added.

"A socialist?"

"So my parents said. I overheard them talking—you know what it's like when you're a child. That one was a *socialist*, they said. I didn't know what the word meant, of course. For a while, I had the idea that a socialist was someone glamorous."

"Right. Yes." I was trying to organize my questions. I had too many questions.

"And Florence must have liked her well enough," Lois added. "Depended on her anyway. She couldn't bear to be apart. That's how she came to die down there"—Lois gestured—"in San Juan."

"What?"

"She was there with Emilia."

"Florence died in San Juan."

Lois nodded again. "Emilia had to travel back to see about some family matter, and Florence went with her and died suddenly. A heart attack, I think. I'm sure you already have these facts."

"No." More and more questions. "I mean yes. The death certificate says heart attack."

"There you are."

"But it has New York. It's from New York."

Lois gave one of her small shrugs. She wasn't interested in the death certificate.

"That could be wrong, of course," I added quickly. My next question also came out as a statement: "Emilia was from Puerto Rico."

"Yes yes." Lois said this as if she had already explained. "I do remember her dying quite clearly because much later when my parents talked about it we thought that it vindicated all of Florence's fears, all of her silly prejudices. About travel, pain, Catholicism. Dying like that—it was ironic. Or pathetic, really."

"Pathetic." I was repeating, rote. "Yes."

Lois nodded.

"But what happened to Emilia after Florence died?"

"What happened to Emilia ..." Lois had to be recalled to the name. "I have no idea." She sighed. "These things are never easy. Family. At a certain point, my parents or my uncle should have taken her in. Taken in Florence, I mean. But they didn't want to, and came up with this arrangement instead. I can't say I fault them for that. No no. I think doing things out of obligation is always a mistake, frankly. Charity, duty—these are not healthy emotions between relations." She considered. "Or anybody."

"Right," I said. I didn't care about Lois's ideas regarding emotions between people. I needed other information. "Do you know her last name?"

"Emilia's?"

"Yes, do you—"

"Oh, I never knew anything about her, really," Lois said. She was ready to be done. "But you should go. Do you still want the box? Florence?"

character

The box, Florence.

I couldn't take it with me to Justin's talk. Could I take it with me back to Heather's apartment? I said, "I can't carry it now; I have—" Too much explanation. "But I could come back tomorrow?"

She explained that she would be working. "Painting." She did not like to be interrupted when painting. She would leave the box with the doorman.

"Good," I said. "Thank you. I don't want to disturb."

"I will be painting *you!*" Lois smiled.

I couldn't think of a response. "I don't want to disturb," I said again.

8

I HAD AGREED ONLY TO SHOPPING WITH HEATHER; I would watch her choose something and buy it, which would not require much from me and not involve any new people, certainly. But here we were at the foundation offices in midtown, talking to Lexie. "Lexie's the one who's dragging us into the twenty-first century," Heather said.

Lexie smiled. She looked impossibly young, her very short hair dyed a reddish black that gave her scalp the impression of velvet. "I'm just sprucing things up a little is all." She was tanned and muscular and wore a stud in her nose and a tight black sweater and tight black ripped jeans. "Did you want to see where we're at?" Her voice had the hint of a southern accent.

"Yes?" Heather said to me, and then to Lexie: "Lexie is fantastic."

Lexie didn't protest. Heather found a chair for herself. The office was four workstations against two walls, a smaller tiny room with a door on the far side, and a printer or supply closet—I could see a refrigerator, metal files, high shelves—opposite. Surprisingly cramped, but this was New York, I reflected; other multimillion-dollar charitable outfits were probably being dragged into the twenty-first century in spaces as shabby as this. Shabbier. Heather hadn't told me we were stopping here until we left her apartment. "It's on our way, really. And you'll meet our Web designer." Lexie was freelance, Heather explained in the subway, and worked mostly on weekends, when she had time. She was from Little Rock, now a public policy major at NYU—did I know about this wonderful program where undergraduates took classes at Wagner? "Such a good opportunity."

Heather's tone, without ever mentioning a disadvantage, seemed somehow to convey that the foundation had been beneficent in giving Lexie work. Her praise of Lexie's expertise only reinforced this impression. I wasn't sure why Heather needed me to affirm it. But I was just there to agree with Heather. "Moral support," we had decided when Heather laid out her Sunday agenda: She needed to buy a dress for the Weatherfield benefit. I reminded her that I was terrible at picking clothing—"you know that"—and Heather said she did not know that, not at all.

"I just need another pair of eyes—unless you have something else to do," she said. "I don't want to keep you."

No, I had nothing to do.

"Moral support is plenty!" Heather told me.

Now I stood near the door as she nodded approvingly at something Lexie pointed out. To cover my awkwardness, I asked if I could use the computer to my left; I clicked open a browser to check my bank balance and clicked yes to the message telling me I was on a new machine and answered some security questions and looked at the row of numbers—what was left, after not just rent and the bike and some food but also the train ticket, a coffee, lunch, a subway card, drinks last night. I had $1,012.21. "Laura," Heather said to me. I clicked the bank window away. "Come take a look. This is where you come in."

"Me."

She smiled encouragingly, as if we had discussed this. "There's a chair, over near—"

I had no choice. The three of us crowded around one screen. "I think half the board didn't even know what a CMS was," Heather said, lightly imitating: "'We have to spend money on *what?*'"

Lexie didn't respond to that, either. She seemed genuinely not to care about the board, in comparison to Heather's more explicit bemusement. Next to Lexie, Heather's good humor seemed strenuous. Lexie sat with both legs planted, knees wide; she smelled faintly of sandalwood and I could see the tight black edge of her underwear at the back of her jeans, also a strip of skin as she leaned forward. "This is just what we've got so far," she said.

I recognized the foundation website. It didn't look much changed. Heather was eager: "Don't forget to show the comparables." Lexie clicked through the other tabs. A trust in England, "dedicated to innovation," and a charity from a health-care fortune in the United States, "devoted to a culture of human flourishing," and another foundation with a surname I didn't recognize, "promoting international understanding." The sites certainly looked of a piece, a banner at the top with a quotation above a picture of, presumably, the good work achieved—the pictures were often of happy young people, smiling, glad to help or be helped. Lexie began, "So, what I pointed out—"

"Here," Heather said, breaking in. "You see. 'History.'"

"History"—sometimes the category appeared under "About" and sometimes under "Who We Are." A paragraph, a black-and-white photo, a time line with more black-and-white photos. "We don't need that much, maybe," Heather said quickly. Lexie was obligingly silent, clicking between pages. "You see,

Laura," Heather added. She and Lexie turned to me. "The work you've done. I felt so bad that nothing came of that."

"Well, in fact—" I stopped. In a little spurt of panic I remembered that I was supposed to pick up the box from Lois's doorman. This morning.

"When Lexie mentioned a 'History' link," Heather went on to say, "I thought, this is perfect. A win-win." She smiled again. Lexie waited.

Could I go later, to pick up the box? I had to. I looked back at Heather and Lexie. I said, "Definitely."

This was enough. We all turned back to the screen. Lexie explained to me that we could pop something in afterward, too. "That part is easy." We could "go live" without the complete text. Heather beamed. Later, on the way to the subway, Heather told me that when she talked with Lexie she felt good about the future.

"Millennials," she added, nodding. "They really are going to save the world"—and when I said, mildly, that Lexie couldn't be much younger than we were: "Oh, it's a whole different generation!"

She seemed happy about this. She had been in a good mood all day. "You're awake!" she'd called to me that morning when I emerged from her office. "Do you want some coffee?" I shook my head no. I pulled my hair back with one hand and rooted in the pocket of my jeans for an elastic. Heather had the sort of clean glow about her that meant just enough makeup—concealer, a little blush, something on the eyes. None of it detectable and all of it operative. "Are you ready? Can we get started?" Getting started meant in the bedroom, the drapes wide; sunlight was just coming through; spread out on the bed were several luxurious outfits. "I so appreciate your help," Heather said. "So I already have *these*. I think we should take a hard look. It may be that one of them is really the best option. Though of course I'd like something new."

I should say something. "Of course."

"To mark the occasion," Heather agreed.

Heather had taken the CFO job. I'd gotten the group email the previous week, a bcc note beginning "Dear friends" before a colon. She was excited and honored to grow the philanthropic work of an institution that had given her and others so much. The transitive *grow*, applied to something other than an agricultural product—this usage was sprouting everywhere, suddenly.

"Any initial thoughts?" Heather asked. She was lifting and lowering fabric. I hesitated.

"I think I do want some coffee after all," I said. "Would that be okay?" Over my shoulder on my way to the kitchen I said, "Gorgeous." I didn't know what I was describing. It could have been Heather.

With a mug I had an excuse to stay safely back, standing in one corner, away from the material on the bed. "Okay, so three real contenders," Heather went on. "You tell me which is best." She held up one after another: the first strapless, a soft textile I couldn't name modifying the severity of the shape; the second black pocked with what looked like tiny white seeds; the third longer and fuller, silvery, with a deep V neck. Heather looked at me. It didn't matter what I said. I was just there to agree. And she would look amazing in any of them. I asked how they felt— that might be important—and Heather nodded generously, as if this were an unusual and useful piece of advice. "I'll try them on then," she said. "Do we have time?" I had all day. My train was later. "And you should of course switch your ticket," Heather said from the bathroom. "You should stay over another night." I didn't answer. She stepped back into the bedroom in the first dress. The fabric lay taut across the bodice and fell in sleek lines around her hips. Her collarbones stretched like wings. She pulled on some heels, one foot at a time cocked behind her, and then picked up her hair to look at the effect.

"Amazing," I said.

Heather regarded herself in the full-length mirror: "Eh." She scrutinized her own reflection with the unbiased appraisal that must come from a lifetime of never needing to deceive yourself about how you look. None of the looped second-guessing that compensates for the proclivity to see things as better than they are as a correction for the proclivity to see things as worse. Heather said, "It's not bad." I began to agree before she added, "I think I can do better." She picked up the second dress to try on. *Would* I stay over? I told her I had to work the next day; I was still looking at her in the dress. Why did I say that? I didn't have to work the next day. "Oh, right," Heather said. And then: "I think it's *great* news, by the way. The job." She was moving toward the bathroom now and called back over her shoulder, "I heard about it from Greta!"

I said, "You talked to Greta?"

But I wasn't sure she registered my question from the bathroom, where she had raised her voice a bit, undressing, continuing: "It's perfect for you and such a good opportunity."

"Well," I said, "I'm supposed to be creating opportunities, not taking them."

"But this is both!" Heather stepped out in the black dress. "Okay, how about this?"

I must have done something with my face.

Heather laughed. "Is it that good?"

Yes, I told her. Definitely that good. She perched on the edge of the bed. She had never worn this one, she said. Not once. She pulled a tag from her armpit. "I always had the feeling it made me seem *harsh*." I asked if that was a bad thing, and she laughed. "Maybe not! Oh, Laura. I knew I could count on you for an honest opinion." She unzipped a seam along one side and moved back into the bathroom. "You and your *harsh* . . . What are *you* wearing? I mean to the benefit."

"Nothing."

"What?"

"I'm not going."

Heather put just her head outside the bathroom door. I could see a bare shoulder: "What?" Hadn't I gotten the ticket? "I sent—"

"I got the ticket. I appreciate the ticket."

Heather waited for me to explain the problem.

I said, "Oh, you don't want me at the benefit." I meant it to be light. But it wasn't, and I moved on quickly, before she could say something reassuring: "Also, I don't have anything to wear."

This was true. And Heather thrilled to hear it, because we would find something for me, together, something great; it would be fun. "No, don't say anything. I'm already excited about this. No, don't protest. I mean it! This is perfect." Heather stepped out again. "Just tell me your criteria. What you look for in a dress. What do you *like*?" I stopped trying to interrupt and pointed to the dress she was wearing and said I liked this one.

"This one?" Heather stopped to look in the mirror. "Really?" She scowled.

I explained: "It makes you look old-fashioned. No. It makes you look mysterious."

"Ugh." Heather frowned at these adjectives and kicked off both heels. She reached a hand to the back of her neck; half-unfastened, fabric flapped behind her. She tossed the previous two dresses on the bed. The tag for the black one swung into my view. Heather had purchased it on sale for $589. "Let's see what *else* is out there," she called from the bathroom, and when she emerged in her jeans and sweater again: "Are you ready to go?"

Not at all. I hadn't even showered. "Sure," I said. "I'll just get dressed."

I did not have a bag other than my knapsack so I pushed my phone and my debit card and my MetroCard into various parts of my down coat. Outside my eyes watered in the cold sun. Heather walked quickly in high-heeled boots, hands in the pockets of her jacket, elbows alert. She kept her head up in the subway. "It's been so long since I had a day off!" she said when we were finally on our way to the department store.

"But we just left your office. One of your offices."

Heather laughed. "I suppose you're right."

The admission only increased her happiness. At the top of the fifth floor escalator in Bergdorf Goodman she began at once to flip through racks, her bag on one arm, narrowing her eyes at some things and raising her eyebrows, nodding slightly, at others. I unzipped my coat and stuffed my hat into a pocket opposite my phone. "All right," Heather said, "let's get serious; divide and conquer." She would take this side, I the other. "If you see something that inspires. Anything. We can use it as a point of departure."

Departure, conquer—I remembered the anxiety that clothing stores produced in me, the sense of waste and wonder at seeing volumes of clean, new stuff. I bought sweaters and shirts for myself at thrift stores, sometimes jeans and dresses, even; when I acquired something firsthand, I did so online, where I could filter by style, size, color, fabric before choosing quickly among what was left. Here instead was a whole floor of various, useless sensuality, all at once, presenting itself for apprehension. But I was just there to agree with Heather. The store smelled good; it smelled like those women who do not use perfume but who always have a faint good scent in their hair, their skin, their things. I touched a few articles of clothing gently. Some of the dresses were too precariously hung to be disturbed. I pulled one out. A sales associate in gray, glasses on a chain around her neck, approached instantly to ask if I needed help, and as I was beginning to back away, Heather approached, dangling from a hand held high a clutch of hangers; yes, the associate could start a dressing room for us, that would be lovely, and of course we would be sure to tell her if she could get us another size. "I only found this," I said to Heather, offering her the green column I had plucked more or less at random for the simplicity and saturation it presented, and Heather told me that was okay, she had plenty for a first round, and oh, also something she wanted me to try.

"Bergdorf's might be too traditional for you," she said. "We should look around Barney's. We'll go there next. Let's share a dressing room, right? We need to zip each other up."

"Whatever is easiest," I said. Moral support.

I tried to crush myself into one corner. I could feel the start of the sweat in various pits and crevices of my body. But removing my puffy jacket would create more volume than I was entitled to. Heather flipped through the different articles of clothing now hanging above us, and I had the thought that materialism is not, first, a drive to accumulate and possess but rather a basic comfort with material, with *things*, a capacity to comport with and sort through the substance of the world, choose what suited you, discard what didn't—this required such confidence. Heather was already unzipping her boots and pulling off her clothes. She folded them quickly. She wore a smooth black bra and a matching pair of underwear. "I thought this one was sort of fun," she said, stepping into the first dress; it was a slim sheath of silk with a high collar, champagne-colored, a vine of reddish embroidery reaching up from the hem: "It's *different*, anyway. Can you zip?" When I moved in to do so I could feel the softness of her skin against the fabric and even more against my clumsy hands. She was looking in the mirror; I was hidden behind her, bent over a delicate zipper I couldn't pluck from its bed of silk, and I told her to hold still; my fingers were too big. Heather wasn't listening. "Okay. Laura. I want to tell you something. Something you can't share."

I made a sound, the aural version of a raised eyebrow, a *hmm?* sound, and she turned around, almost inadvertently, to whisper, "I'm serious—" and I told her not to do that, turn around; it made the thing harder to zip, and she apologized, straightened up again, looking into the mirror: There. She kept her gaze forward. My face was now just behind hers, visible in the mirror over her shoulder. I looked so much larger. She said, "You remember Mark?"

I did, I told her. I did remember Mark. In fact I had seen Mark recently, or in August anyway. "Really!" Yes, it was random, a symposium, up in Cambridge, just before I left. "Oh, that makes sense, actually," Heather said, as if she couldn't credit my news until she had some corroboration; "Mark mentioned your name for the job. The historical work, that job. Of course I had already thought of you," she added quickly when she saw my expression, "but when Mark said . . ." She paused, wriggling the fabric of the dress over her hips, smoothing her hands on her flat belly, her slim thighs, then turning slightly this way and that to see the left and right sides of the impression she made. "What do you think of this one?"

I said, "So you're in touch with Mark."

Heather turned all the way around, craning her head over one shoulder: "Too tight?" I told her no, not too tight; she was gorgeous, of course, if that was the effect she was going for, and she laughed and replied, "I'm definitely going for gorgeous, but you're no help at all, Laura; you have to be critical." I told her I was being critical, and she protested I was not, and so I said I wasn't sure of the impression it made—not of gorgeous, of Orientalist. She cocked her head to one side. "The style, you mean. Chinoiserie." I agreed, sure, but I thought chinoiserie was just for art. Heather said, "I think clothes count." I agreed again, fine, but while we were wondering about whether to extend a legacy of appropriation and exploitation with a purchase at Bergdorf's—we laughed together at my obviously hyperbolic language—she was going to tell me something about Mark? Somehow my voice was wrong. Could Heather hear that, too? She only nodded. "Well, I'm almost afraid to say it. Not that I'm ashamed. But almost as if when I say it, it won't be true." Also it was a secret. She trusted me, though. She knew I didn't repeat secrets. No, I didn't. "Mark and I are—well, we're seeing each other again."

Oh.

I didn't move; we were still together in front of the mirror, but for a moment I couldn't look. I said, "Again?"

"Yes, we were seeing each other the whole first year at Oxford," Heather said. "Before you and I were friends, really. Off and on." She pulled some fabric from a hanger. "Try this, now, while I get out of mine."

My cheeks were hot. The dressing room was stifling. All this clothing, suffocating. "This is the one I picked out for you," Heather continued. "I think it would look great. I'm serious. Just try it. . . ." She pulled the coat from my hands and wiggled the dress in front of me, up and down, as if a shimmying garment would be a more enticing proposition. The dress was black. I couldn't tell much more. I had no powers of will or thought to resist her instructions or make her stop her little dance of entreaty; all of my brain was busy trying to catch and hold and assemble a few jagged little pieces of information: Heather, Mark, off and on, first year. I took off my clogs and socks and unbuttoned my jeans. Heather beamed in front of me. I was wearing white underwear and an old bra of the pink-beige that is marketed as "flesh-colored." I didn't dare glance down at my stomach. Heather was mentioning the designer, a name that sounded to me Japanese, a single word with four or five syllables. "Such an interesting line. I think the shapes would really complement your aesthetic," Heather said. "I could never wear them. I'm jealous of those who can, frankly." I told her that I didn't believe *that*, but my voice was still wrong—flimsy? Heather moved in with cool hands, gathering the fabric above my head and gesturing until I bowed to her, hair flopping, and let her pull the dress down over my shoulders, my waist, my thighs and bottom, as if I were inanimate, or a child: "There's no zipper," she said. "Isn't that genius? It's all one stretchy piece." I was dressed now. I tried to forget the touch of Heather's fingers. "Just look at yourself for a second," Heather told me, "before you say anything else. See how good you look!"

"I don't—"

"Look!"

And she was right; I did look much better than usual. The dress had a wide neckline that set off my abnormally large head to advantage and its sleeves hovered in length on the edge of what might be short and what might be sleeveless, so my thick upper arms looked close to normal, and it stopped about an inch below my knee, before the worst mass of my calves, and cohered around my flesh not in the clinging that reveals bulges and rounds and bumps, but in the embrace that smooths all those into a more or less graceful surface. Its thick fabric was patterned with almost sculptural triangles of black foamlike material, standing gently up from the surface, offering distraction and movement while also eliding the various inadequacies of my body below—as if this dress were a protective covering, or a filter. "I knew it," said Heather; "I knew it would look fabulous." She clasped her hands together triumphantly. She was still standing in bare feet, still wearing her chinoiserie dress; we looked at each other, not eye-to-eye, but mirrored gaze next to mirrored gaze, and through that weird relay of a reflection, a reflection I didn't recognize, I tried to smile back. Then she reminded me that the real question was how it *felt*. "As you told me," she said. "Consider how it feels." I didn't answer; instead I said something about "the whole first year," her words, and Heather said yes, "off and on." I asked when they'd stopped seeing each other, and Heather shook her head—a bad memory, but she had processed it: "That weekend," she explained. "At the hotel. Actually I convinced Mark to go to that weekend." Putnam Marsh. Yes, Heather confirmed: "The last night. That's when he broke up with me. Not broke up, of course; we weren't *together*. But he said we needed to stop doing whatever we were doing. He had a whole speech about it, I remember. Something about honesty. Very philosophical." Heather laughed at this. "And I was devastated. We were so young!" I agreed. "But he was right," Heather continued. "And it was for the best. I don't know if I would have accepted the Putnam Marsh job if Mark hadn't broken my heart like that. I probably have him to thank for my whole career."

I remembered Heather's explanation when she did accept: *You only ever take care of yourself.* I stood in the middle of the fitting room in the garment Heather had found for me. I should have said something more, perhaps, but I still didn't trust the sound of whatever might come out of my mouth.

"Anyway," Heather went on, "we each had our path, Mark

and I, and then we could find each other again." She nodded. "And you, are you going to buy this amazing dress?"

The day continued, somehow. At lunch, Heather resumed her persuasion; $319, an investment; it would honestly be irresponsible not to buy it, given the number of places I could wear it, the number of occasions, weddings, galas, anything black-tie, or even funerals, she reminded me, since it was dark and not disrespectful. I told Heather I had not attended any occasions in the last five years and did not foresee many in my near future, either, and Heather responded that the dress would last forever and would never be out of style. I told her that fat people were not allowed to buy clothes meant to last forever, and Heather said she didn't see what size had to do with anything, the dress was super flattering, and my shape wouldn't change—I wasn't growing. I told her maybe I was. She sighed with exaggeration and smiled at me, a "What am I going to do with you?" smile, and then the server was there to take our order and the conversation was allowed to come naturally to a halt.

I looked down. I would pay for my own lunch this time, I found I had decided, decided at some point between the department store and restaurant, and I could therefore order exactly what I wanted, in exactly the amounts I wanted. We sat in a small Italian place, empty still, the first restaurant we saw when Heather realized on leaving Bergdorf's that her blood sugar was dangerously low—when did healthy nondiabetic people start talking about low blood sugar rather than hunger? I was hungry. That was the feeling I knew, and I let myself feel it with the almost pleasure one can take in wanting when fulfillment is imminent. The menu listed pastas and sauces to mix and match in a straightforward formation of columns. I asked for ravioli, meat sauce, a glass of red wine. Heather *hmmed* over salads and antipasti before settling on angel-hair pasta. She didn't think she should have wine. She ordered sparkling water. "Of course," she began when the server left, "if you hate that dress we can find something else. Do you hate it? I can never tell what you're really thinking about things, I mean when it comes to your own—"

I cut her off. "Weren't you with Wesley?" I asked.

"Oh. Right. Well, you know Wesley." Heather sighed indulgently, as if Wesley were an obstreperous ward she had been managing for years. "Wesley and I are destined to be good friends, I think. We're very supportive of each other."

I said, "So you broke up with Wesley."

Heather shook her head, no, not yet. She added that Wesley had a very good job at the moment. "He's working for a really promising new hedge fund."

I couldn't tell how this was relevant. "So no one knows about you and Mark."

Heather sipped some water. "Well, it's a delicate situation." Mark was thinking about running for office. I told her I had heard. Heather nodded, as if she were aware of my exact level of knowledge, which had been calibrated, somewhere, precisely. "It's important to take into account schedules and plans. Of course I want to do what's best for any possible campaign. Actually"—Heather leaned in closer—"that's how this all started."

I said, "Started again."

"Zac and I were talking about doing a fund-raiser. We both wanted to help with the campaign in its early stages. Mark came to New York for a session of strategy. And then ..." Her voice trailed off in delight. "We just connected." Her tone had moved from serene professionalism to girlish intimacy. She'd always had the ability to combine the two. Mark, that weekend a decade ago, Mark in my room: I would not think of that now. The waiter brought our plates. Heather murmured automatically about how beautiful hers looked, though it did not look especially beautiful—well, hers looked better than mine, since mine looked like a pool of stewed mottled tomatoes, bumpy with drowned pasta and browned meat and pocked with small glints of oil. I accepted cheese and pepper from both sides. I like ravioli particularly for their shape, their repeated small gifts, the iterated relinquishments of steam and aroma. Heather was telling me something about a journey, her journey. I tasted the textured warmth of the sauce against the opaque slicks of cheese and sharp wash of the wine. It was so odd, this practice, eating. Heather explained more of why it was best she and Mark had not stayed together when they first met. "We would have missed each other entirely." He wasn't ready. *She* wasn't ready. She had been underconfident, she said. "I recognize that now." At present, given all she had experienced, she had a clearer picture of her own strengths. "I know what I have to offer." She sighed. "Laura. It's so good to tell someone." She picked up her fork again and looked at me. "Thank you."

"For what?"

"Oh, you know, for—being you."

I swallowed. I tried to smile. We ate in silence for a moment, and then Heather asked if I wanted to know the most amazing thing, the aspect of all this she hadn't expected, that really blew her away. Her tone was conspiratorial again. I said that I did want to know what blew her away, and Heather took another sip of water: "The most amazing thing," she said, "is that it's so physical." She nodded. "I forgot what that's like." I nodded back; I think I made some sort of agreeable noise, some *ah*. I had finished everything on my plate.

And I drank the last of my wine. For a moment I existed in a kind of delirious clarity about my feelings. I was full, slightly tipsy; I was therefore thoroughly comfortable. I was also devastatingly, achingly, terrifyingly unhappy. How could that be, some part of me thought. The combination. How can this be. Some part was left to wonder. Our server approached and asked about dessert; Heather looked at me. "Do you? Well—I think we'd better not." The server went to fetch our check. "So," Heather said, "I don't mean to press, but you *will* write just a little something, for the website?" She waited a second. "It would be useful. And I thought it might be nice for you. I thought it would offer a more satisfying conclusion." The white creased ticket was on our table now, and I reached out to put my hand over it, to claim it, then waited for a moment as the waiter withdrew.

"No," I said.

Heather began to reply that she understood if I was too busy, "but really, it could be—"

"No." I cut her off. "No, it would not be satisfying. It would not be nice. The opposite." I didn't want any part of this, I said. "I want nothing to do with any of it. I want nothing to do with the foundation or the benefit."

Heather looked around almost involuntarily at the others in the restaurant, which was fuller now, to check if they had heard. My voice was too loud, as well as wrong in every other way, but I still didn't seem to be able to control it. "Well," Heather said gently, her volume pitched low as if in compensation, "I was trying—"

"You're trying to salvage something." What did I mean by this? I had no idea. What was I accusing her of trying to salvage? The foundation? The Weatherfields? Me? Somewhere I recognized how incoherent this was. I said, "It's unsalvageable."

"Are you saying . . ." She paused.

"I'm saying that you can stop trying in any way to involve me in any of this."

Heather flushed. "Did I do something?" she asked. "Are you upset with me?"

"Not everything is about you."

"Laura," Heather said. I could hear in the sound of my name her pain, beneath the confusion, also the warning, the pain sharpening into a warning. "I don't think you're being fair."

And as if it pricked me, this edge in her voice, or as if it turned me over into the sun, exposed, I saw for a moment what I was. How I was. Exactly how wrong, how petty, driven by illusions I didn't even admit, cowering under the generosity of others, my own indecision, my own ineffectual inconsequence, counting on that. And as I said "I'll pay," in a kind of desperate assertion of my rectitude and guilt, both, as I realized that I would be paying with the money that Heather made sure I received for work I should never have done, I also found that I did not have my debit card, that I must have left it in the foundation office earlier when I looked at the balance on my account, and I said, my shame rising like bile, "Sorry, I have to—"

I picked up my coat. I left Heather there over our empty plates. I held on to the check.

For several blocks I did not put it on, the coat, as if the cold would be some sort of expiation. I clutched the crumpled white paper. My heartbeat felt insistent, embarrassing. My throat felt tight.

I kept walking. Probably no one would be at the office to let me in, even.

But Lexie's voice was on the other end of the intercom.

She didn't ask for an explanation. I climbed the three flights of stairs. "Did you find some dresses?" she asked when I arrived at the third floor. "Ms. A. said you were looking for something. Any luck?"

No, I managed to say, or rather, yes, Heather might have

found something. I put a hand to my hair, my face, my chest. Here was the grubby room of workstations, again, and Lexie, exactly as she'd been when we left a couple of hours ago.

"All right," Lexie said, a soft little cheer about Heather's success. "Sounds like fun."

And I could see my debit card on the table, just where I had left it.

Lexie noticed my expression then. "Something wrong?"

"Not really."

Lexie said, "You're sure?" She didn't seem concerned at my condition, but kindness was a general condition for her, an off-hand default. "You want some water? There's a fridge back there with some bottled water." She fetched one. "Take a minute, if you like." Her accent was so comforting. I told her about leaving my card. She nodded. This hardly justified my agitation, in her view, but she wasn't going to think much about it. "Canceling accounts is a pain," she said.

I nodded and drank some water. "I'm sorry to disturb you."

"That's okay. You're lucky I was here. I would have been gone before now but I'm trying to find a driver for this printer which I think is like prehistoric?" She was moving between her computer, where she bent over the keyboard, standing, and the small room, where I could hear a machine whining in semioperation. I drank more water and let my mind rest for a moment while watching her fix the problem. She would fix any problem. I could imagine her with pins in her mouth, briskly setting the sleeve of a garment; I could see her driving a backhoe, swiveling the wheels and maneuvering stabilizers to prepare for the next load; I could see her pressing a sheaf of greens under one palm as she cut the leaves to ribbons with the cleaver she held in her opposite hand. Meanwhile I felt incapable of doing the simplest thing I needed to do. I did not know the simplest part of what

I needed to do. Lexie said, "To be honest I'll be glad when this job is done."

I said, "Is that soon?"

"Who knows," she said cheerfully.

I knew I should respond with something; I finally asked how she ended up working here and Lexie explained that a friend of hers had referred her; he had too many clients and he gave her the extra. "He knows I'll take whatever. I mean, if I need it. I'm *lazy*, that's the thing. I do whatever until I have enough to pay the bills." I said something about how she couldn't be lazy, all the work for her classes, her degree—I would go, I promised myself, as soon as I finished the water, but for now I just wanted to watch her sort out the various machines, absorbed—and Lexie said over her shoulder, from the copier room, "Oh I'm not in school—I mean, I was in school, yeah, but I dropped out?" I couldn't quell a noise of surprise at this, but she wasn't bothered. "You know how it is. There didn't seem to be much point. I mean, no offense; I know you're a professor. It's all good," she said as I began to object. "College makes a whole lot of sense for some people. For me it's just a big waste right now. Also, I honestly didn't have the time? I mean not this fall."

I said vaguely, "And what about this fall?"

"You heard of Occupy?"

"Occupy?"

"At the park?"

"Oh, of course, right, I read about—or I know—"

"It's over for now, of course." She was sanguine about that. It had already changed her life. This fall, she and her boyfriend had moved into a room in an apartment in the Financial District owned by a friend of a friend's dad—everyone living there was part of Occupy, too—and they spent all day at the park. "We were there from, like, the beginning. It was great." Lexie stood over the printer. "*Now* we're getting somewhere. Come on—" And I could hear the whir of a sheet of paper, a new sound.

"I should have offered to help," I said. "I'm sorry."

Lexie said, "Nah."

I added, "I probably can't help." I wanted to ask Lexie many questions. I wanted to sit there for a long while and learn from her. "Were you upset at the end of the—the end of the movement?" I asked.

"Yeah. Maybe. I guess it did kind of bum me out a little." She seemed reluctant to admit disappointment of any kind. "We did what we needed to do and all. It's beyond the park now. I mean, it's global; it's historic. All that. But I miss the experience. The experience was really important? I mean it wasn't like *sacrifice*. That wasn't the sort of thing it was. We were all just—creating right there the kind of life we wanted." She summed up: "Now we've just got to make sure everyone can do that all the time." She was back at the computer, sitting sideways so she could prop her feet in their thick-soled boots on a neighboring chair. "All right, let's get this *printed*."

I had protested and rallied before, of course; I remembered gatherings against deforestation and hunger and memorial vigils for various tragedies, and while I could justify vaguely the importance of showing up for such things I had never come close to enjoying any of them. "What about the—" I began, trying to phrase the question.

It was not the right question. Would I ever be able to talk to people in the future? It seemed perhaps not. Had I ever been able to in the past?

"Do you think—"

"Are you *kidding* me." Lexie stood up. She wasn't listening.

Something had stopped working. "Hey, do me a favor and check if that printer crapped out again?"

I did. "It's out of paper," I told her. "Can I fetch more?"

"I've got it." Lexie pulled a folding chair into the little closet next to me. "Of course it's on the highest shelf."

I could smell faintly the warm bite of printer toner. I'd always liked that smell. I opened the bottom drawer. My question was still no more than a little tangle of curiosity about experience, about the kind of life she wanted, the kind of life she created, about where they went to the bathroom and what they ate for lunch, and wasn't it noisy and cold and also wasn't there that one person who seemed to be shouting not at the evil institutions all had gathered to protest, but at some person in particular, some person in his life who had wronged him in an absolutely non-political way, but all this was irrelevant, of course, irrelevant to me, irrelevant to Lexie, who was so certain of—I heard a crash and when I turned around I saw Lexie on the floor.

My mind did not remember that I probably should not move her until I was kneeling with one arm around her shoulders. Had I moved her? Was that wrong? Was touching wrong?

"Are you okay?" I asked. Idiot. The one question to which I had an answer.

A pulse. I should check for a pulse. I felt her neck. Her head had hit a file cabinet. But not hard. Not hard? I felt the back of her head with one hand. I couldn't tell anything. She was still breathing, though her eyes were closed.

Then open. "Oh shit," Lexie said.

I said, "I think you fainted." I let go awkwardly.

Lexie was not awkward. She gave a little laugh. "I'd say so, yeah." She wasn't moving except for her mouth and her eyes.

"Is anything broken?" I asked. "Is anything hurt?"

She took a moment. "Nah," she said finally. "Don't worry. This has happened before."

"It has?"

A nod. "It's a thing. I'll get up in a second."

I said I would call an ambulance, but Lexie protested; she didn't need an ambulance. Please, she said, no ambulances; just let her rest for a second, there, use the chair. "Elevate my legs. Helps the blood or something. I'll be fine." I said we should call someone. "Nah." I said I would feel better if someone else knew. Lexie said she would text her boyfriend in a little bit. She was sitting up now, feet down, her back against the metal of the cabinet. She didn't look hurt. I asked about her head. "I think I'll have a bump. Not too bad."

I googled fainting on my phone; I googled concussion. I tried to read warnings and recommendations. I gave Lexie one of the same bottles of water she had fetched for me earlier. I asked her about dizziness and vision. "You should probably eat something," I said, holding open the fridge door. "Are these things claimed?" Lexie didn't know what was there. I looked. "Uh, some little packets of jam? Not helpful." Lexie agreed. "Also," I added, "a diet bar?" Lexie had moved now to a chair in the main room. "It says ZonePerfect," I clarified. "Oh, well," Lexie agreed, "perfect." I brought it to her. "You can say I took it. I mean, I did."

Lexie peeled back the bar's wrapping and took a slow bite.

We got a cab to her apartment after a few minutes, when Lexie was sure she could make her way downstairs. "You know you don't need to come with," Lexie said to me, but she didn't seem agitated that I did. She texted during the ride—unhurt, apparently, unembarrassed. I was the one flustered, especially when we stopped at her building and I got out of the cab as well, to no apparent purpose.

"Should I, um—" What. "Help you upstairs?"

Lexie looked at me kindly. "I'll be fine," she said. "You've taken enough time."

"Someone's home? Your boyfriend?"

"He's around the corner."

"Okay, then," I said. "I'll pay for the cab"—when she was already moving away toward her door, so my comment was too loud as well as awkward. Of course I would pay for the cab; she hadn't even thought about the cab.

"Thanks!" she called back. "It was real nice meeting you!" Her door shut.

The driver was waiting. "I'll get out here, too," I said, simply because I didn't have an address to give him of where I might possibly go next. I handed over the last of my cash and told him to keep the change.

He drove off. The street was empty.

Wind was picking up. The afternoon had settled into a clouded-over cold, gray and blue-gray and white fuzzing into one another.

I stood in the doorway of a bar that was not yet open. I took out my phone and called Heather.

I didn't let myself think about hitting the icon by her name before I did so. "It's Laura, yeah, and I'm standing outside Lexie's apartment," I told her before she could say more than hello. I explained what had happened. "She says she's fine and she seems fine, but I wanted to know if you think I should make her go to the hospital? I mean, did I do the right thing?" A pause, and in the silence I considered my own voice again, still not right, too loud or— And I had no way of making Lexie go to the hospital if Heather said yes, I should. I didn't even know Lexie's phone number. Her apartment number. I was asking too late. I was asking too late and for the wrong reasons. I didn't even know my reasons: I wanted to hear Heather's words, her complete sentences, her questions, calm and reasonable, from the other end of the line, so I could give calm and reasonable answers, or try, so I could match her tone. "I took her home in a cab.... Yeah. She lives with her boyfriend. Some others, too, I think.... Right. No, she's not injured, not that I could tell, not that she felt; I just don't know. There could be something—internal, I guess. Probably not. I tried to look it up on my phone. *Syncope.* That's the word she used. But the websites all seem kind of vague and bullshit. Sorry. Kind of vague.... Yeah, they would probably say. Okay."

Heather said, "I think we can trust Lexie herself in this situation."

I said again, "Okay."

The Zone bar was most likely Heather's.

Silence. I shifted my phone to the other hand so I could put the one I'd been using in my pocket. My fingers were numb.

"Also don't tell her I told you," I said. "She made a point of saying I shouldn't tell anyone."

Heather said she wouldn't. "You never talked to me," she agreed.

"Thanks," I said. Both hands were numb now. I swallowed. "Heather—"

"You've done as much as you should for Lexie," she said with finality.

"No, not that; I—I'm sorry about lunch. I don't—" Heather broke in. I shouldn't be sorry. She understood. "No," I said, "I really—" Heather continued, talking over me: She hadn't realized my position. She had been insensitive. I had been through a lot. "No, that's not—" Heather continued: I was probably very tired. I gave up explaining. "Ha," I said lightly. Yes, I was tired. "I've been out of work for months. Naturally I'm exhausted."

Heather laughed—thin, brief, but I exhaled. I said, "Thanks for recognizing my busy and demanding schedule."

"Demands come in all different forms," Heather told me.

And I remembered her explaining to me the research about mental stress and physical stress, and I remembered her advising me about love and fear, and I thought about adding a few more options in that calculus: freedom, anger. Freedom probably meant love, though. Anger probably meant fear. Heather said, "Are you coming back uptown?"

"Probably. To get my things. Is that okay or are you—" It was suddenly awkward, that I was staying with Heather; it was suddenly awkward that I had stayed with her so many times before. But Heather was smooth; she had already thought this through. She had a coffee date and then dinner, so she probably wouldn't see me again before I caught my train. She was lying about those appointments, or she had made them in the last half hour, and I expressed my careful sorrow at their necessity, and my thanks for her hospitality, and I hung up.

I walked because I didn't know what else to do. I walked west until I found Broadway, then north. I passed the graveyard for Trinity Church, where I could see through iron bars the side of a building labeled AMERICAN STOCK EXCHANGE, and then I passed Zuccotti Park, a privately owned public space of sunken gray stone and spindly trees and stone benches divided by bars, and then I glimpsed to my left the 9/11 Memorial, a few blocks off, with its solemn pools, but I wasn't thinking about any of this. I kept walking. It was so cold; I hunched against the cold and only felt colder. The streets got busier as I walked north but I didn't notice the people around me. The afternoon dusk grew darker but I didn't notice the light. I walked through Union Square; I veered from Broadway to Fifth Avenue and kept walking; I passed the office building where Heather worked for

Putnam Marsh, the library where Justin had given a talk, probably the doctor's office where Greta had consulted with a pediatric cardiologist, but I wasn't thinking about any of this. I was so cold. I kept walking. Even after I stopped at the department store, I kept walking. North, along the park, past the museums, the museum that now owned most of Henry Havemeyer's art collection, also the place where Florence Weatherfield went to school, the place where Ennis Weatherfield grew up, so that when I remembered about Lois's box again, the box I had forgotten, and when I turned west, and crossed near the reservoir, and found Broadway once more, and walked north and west, from there, to Riverside Drive, and finally to Lois's building, where the doorman looked at me dubiously, at my red face and frizzing hair and my jeans and clogs, I had the dress, covered in plastic, hung over my arm. It was dark by then. I had been walking almost three hours.

Here is what Lois wrote to me in the letter that was in the single brown manila envelope the doorman handed over: "Dear Ms. Graham, I've been thinking about our conversation, which I found very interesting, and I've decided that I do not want to relinquish these papers after all. It seems wrong to let family materials go to someone not related or connected. I don't imagine I'm depriving you of anything valuable in any case, and I appreciate your understanding. Regards, Lois Ricard." Her cursive was clear, traditional, a bit prim—the handwriting of a debutante rather than an artist. "P.S. I include a token of our afternoon together."

Here is what I wrote for the Weatherfield Foundation in a statement I sent to Lexie with a cc to Heather, to be included if acceptable on the website: "The Weatherfield Foundation was established in 1911 with money from Florence Weatherfield in honor of her husband, Ennis Weatherfield, after his accidental death in 1908. The money was Ennis's bequest from profits of Weatherfield Sugar, sold in 1887 to a larger competitor. Throughout its history, up to the present day, the sugar industry has benefited from slavery and indentured servitude and economic exploitation as well as colonization by the United States and other countries; it has also relied on various benefits of wars, tariff regimes, labor laws, and immigration policies in the United States. Florence's stipulation for her founding gift mentions only that it be used for study at the University of Oxford or the Sorbonne, two places at which Ennis had pursued his interest in philosophy. In 1919, after the conclusion of the First World War, the foundation's first board established the current criteria for fellowship support."

"Great," Lexie wrote to me. "You really got it all in."

Yes. That was all I had. The benefit was five days away.

I didn't remember to call the restaurant until almost ten, back in my cold room, where a Post-it on the door in Len's capital letters said the bike wasn't ready: "NEEDS NEW CHAIN. DON'T RIDE." A harried voice at the other end of the phone didn't know what I was talking about, a lunch check; someone else had probably paid. I hung up. I had in my bank account $679.54. *Related or connected.* Lois's words. I looked around at the in-law apartment where I now lived. Above me, dangling in its plastic from the top of my door, hung the dress I now owned.

The token in Lois's envelope was the sheet of sketches: the repeated anonymized figure that could be anyone but was in fact me, taken from a moment at which I was perfectly still yet drawn to imply an infinite range of past and future activity.

9

I SHOULD LEAVE, I THOUGHT WHEN I ARRIVED.

I didn't. I watched the ballroom as it filled. People entered, couples, groups. They recognized and hailed one another. White-clothed tables were arranged in a wide ring, gilt chairs set around them and glassware, flowers clustered on top; above were a line of chandeliers and a layer of gold-rimmed mirrors marking each arch. A quartet of musicians at the front bent over music I couldn't make out. The conversations were numerous enough now to flatten into a general low roar. I could hear someone nearby exclaiming that he had just been talking about some other person, and I could hear both laughing at the odds of this. A voice next to me got louder to affirm the importance of choosing trust over experience. If there's a choice, this voice insisted. When it comes to hiring. I couldn't hear anyone raising an objection. I held a glass of water I had barely drunk. I looked down. The carpet was plain hotel carpet, nylon in shades of brown, designed to conceal things. I should leave, I thought.

I didn't. When an electronic gong sounded, calling everyone to the tables, I found the number 11 in one corner. Already around number 11 were a lawyer who worked "in tech" and his wife, a speech pathologist, and a taciturn professor of finance and his bored, stylish boyfriend. The lawyer had been a fellow, also the finance professor. When we exchanged the years and subjects of our degrees, the speech pathologist said "Literature" with an approving nod and told me eagerly how much her husband read, an hour a day—he even put it on his schedule; his assistant knew not to make an appointment during that time—and her husband told me that reading was the best career development there was, most people didn't realize, and free. I missed my chance to agree vociferously enough. I missed my chance, when they explained that their son was in college and perhaps going to major in English, to ask what college, so they could tell me, modestly, a name of which they were no doubt very proud. I recognized too late that they wanted this. I answered their questions about schools I had attended. I missed my chance to agree that an English degree was particularly wonderful because you could do so much with it—and the tech lawyer should know; he hired people all the time. The Weatherfield was like that, too, prepared you for anything. I failed to offer an anecdote in response. "And so you teach now?" the speech pathologist asked. I should have left already.

I hadn't. But I was saved from the question about teaching by another gong, which began the evening's program, and I watched Heather, in her green dress, go to a small podium near the musicians, and wait for the room to settle into quiet, and tell everyone to please start eating, not to wait, because no one should have to listen on an empty stomach. The first course was in front of us, a composed salad, dark leaves and shaved pale cheese and roasted red peppers on a white plate. Around me people obediently took up their forks. In the fitting room of Bergdorf's Heather had been worried about the green dress; it *was* translucent—though she liked that effect, I pointed out. I reminded her that beneath the filmy surface layers was an opaque nylon column, so that anyone who thought they were looking through to some hidden and forbidden

nakedness would not actually see anything but more material. "I do think I *feel* better in this one," Heather had said.
She looked beautiful, of course, at the podium. I could see the
glint of her bracelet as she welcomed everyone and reflected
with awe and gratitude on the fact of a hundred years. She had
so many people to thank, she said, so many people who had
given generously of their time and talents to make this evening
possible. She listed names. She started a round of applause
that caught on only clumsily as people put down their utensils
to join in. Heather kept going; she introduced without further ado the chairman of the board, who wanted to say a few
things to mark the occasion. Then the chairman was the only
one standing apart from those black-clad servers at the room's
edges who were waiting with water pitchers or bottles of wine.
I didn't think I could leave.

I couldn't. I said no, no wine to a boy who looked barely old
enough to drink. I could see the place at a prominent table that
the chairman had just left, and near his empty chair I could see
Greta, tall even when sitting, with her golden hair piled up on
her head; she was wearing something in dark red with a wide
neck. The chairman had settled in at the podium. He was a
man used to speaking to large crowds, with the easy habit of
scanning for eye contact and finding confirmation wherever his
glance happened to land. He explained that he had been doing
nonprofit work for many years now, letting his audience read
through this offhand summation the substance and length of
his philanthropic power, and in that time he had learned one
important thing, above all, which was this: A successful organization must always change while never changing. It was about
enduring principles, he said, but adapted to new and evolving
times. In the coming months, we would hear a lot more about
how the foundation would accomplish just this endurance and

adaptation. I didn't see Judith at the table. Greta had written me an email the week before saying she probably would go to the gala after all; she hated those things, but she had a MISSION now—she thought the foundation should start an initiative regarding fellowships for low-income students—"I mean, I've been gathering information for your program, and I'm just more and more convinced that we could be doing so much MORE," she wrote. "Don't you think so? I told Heather to put me at a table with someone who could make a difference. Then I can charm them. I want to use my powers for good!!" She added a semicolon winking face and a colon smiling face between these sentences. I wrote back that I thought her plan made sense. "YOU must do the same," Greta responded. I didn't write back to that. The chairman of the board was wrapping up. The servers moved in again, silently. I couldn't leave now.

I didn't. I nodded at the server's quizzical expression over my untouched salad plate, and he took it away. Heather introduced the reading of excerpts from those with essays in the commemorative booklet. The room settled into a different listening expectancy over main courses of steak or salmon or pasta. The teenaged waiter came around with a fistful of jagged knives. A slump-shouldered man shuffled to the podium and unfolded a page and spoke hoarsely about studying chemistry in Oxford just after the war; then another stepped in to detail with platitudinous satisfaction his odyssey from small-town farm boy to Parisian intellectual; then a squat woman who had been a fellow in the eighties read through a few easygoing anecdotes about sexism—a tutor who asked if her husband would allow her to travel—that everyone could scorn with gentle laughter and shaking of heads. Justin was last. He had texted me two days earlier to ask which part of the essay he should read, or mostly to argue with my suggestions, to have the satisfaction of scorning them: "No, too boring"; "No, wouldn't work"; then "None of it really works." I said the essay was very good, and Justin wrote back, "Sure, but will they hate it at the benefit?" I wrote back that he shouldn't worry, he just had to read. "Yeah, that makes no sense," Justin wrote. Listening now, I could tell that the essay was not suited for public performance but that the result was the same as if it had been. He was there to close out the program on a note of artistry and, vaguely, what people might take as progress. His selection was better than the others, anyway, if that was progress. Waiters moved in to remove disheveled plates and smeared silverware. It was that time in a long meal when everyone sighs with satisfaction or disgust at being confronted with the aftereffects of their own consumption. I could leave soon, maybe.

I didn't. To my left was a white-haired woman wearing a brooch of bubbly jewels. "Such a nice evening," she said to me. She took a long and appreciative sip of her wine. Her husband had been a fellow. He passed away last year. But he had loved his experience, talked about it often, always contributed as much as he could, and she tried to keep up with the foundation, in his honor. He studied history, at least that was the subject on the degree, but honestly—she laughed—it seemed in those days the fellowship was mostly about having a good time. "Meeting people," she added, as if that was the same thing. I nodded. He was like that, she said, he had a gift for friendship; and the friends he met at Oxford he kept in touch with his whole life. Friends from around the world. "It was such a good chance, he always said, to broaden one's horizons. To leave America, of course, and also to leave the American worldview. This was the real value, to him." Someone came to collect our butter dish, with its smashed rose of fat. Someone came to collect the salt and pepper. "I imagine you feel the same," the brooched woman continued. "Tell me your name again?" I gave it. She nodded. "Oh! You were thanked, earlier. You were part of the benefit." I said no, not really. Then I said yes, kind of. I leaned back so that a server could remove my plate. The servers did not care to pause anymore to ask if a guest at a table in the back corner was finished with an uneaten main course. They wanted to hurry things along. We should all leave.

We didn't. The brooched woman had more to ask. "And were you a fellow?" What year? she wanted to know. I tried to remember escaping the American worldview. I drank sometimes with a Brazilian student in my master's course who spoke four languages and had spent most of his adulthood in Europe but liked to make sweeping statements about U.S. citizens. The difference between American and European culture, he explained in one tutorial after we read a Hemingway story about the First World War, was that Americans are still Puritans who believe they can live in the world without being of it and Europeans know this is a silly fiction, "perhaps also a dangerous fiction." No one said anything to this; it felt like the kind of thing that couldn't be defended or refuted in a scholarly setting. The widow next to me continued: Did I know Mark Harriman? She thought he was my year. I looked surprised. Mark was thinking of running for Congress, the woman explained, "in our district." She still said *our*. Her husband had been part of the local Democratic committee. He had met Mark once, her husband had, before his death. "He was quite impressed with the young man," she said. "He loved young people, you know. My husband. Is he here?" "Mark?" I asked. She nodded. I scanned the room. I found Mark standing near Heather's table, talking with the chairman of the board. That man I recognized now. He was the one Mark and I had had dinner with back at Oxford. That was how long ago? I pointed Mark out to the brooched woman.

She nodded appreciatively. I added, "But I think we should—" I gestured. Most of the tables were empty. I meant *leave*.

I got up. The widow was eyeing Mark. "Come along, we'll say hello," she said. The Brazilian student, I remembered, told me once that the problem with Americans is that they don't know how to mourn. "Or is it grieve?" he asked me. "I never know." I told him either worked. I told him they can be different really only in the . . . transitive? Was that right? *It grieves me.* The Brazilian student nodded; *he* understood basic grammar. The brooched woman folded her napkin and explained that her husband had been very interested in politics; it was a passion for him. But that wasn't what he did; he was in business. At the end of his life, he *taught* business. Along with his nonprofit work. "And what do you do?" she asked me.

o O o

When I left I found Caroline.

"You'll have to excuse me," I said to the widow of the fellow who liked young people and politics and broadened horizons. The string quartet had swung into livelier music and waiters had moved several tables back to allow for dancing in the middle of the room, though no one was dancing yet, and at the back two long, narrow tables offered rows of dessert plates and white coffee cups, and I walked toward the nearest door and from the hallway stepped into a carpeted space beyond the elevator and when I opened the metal door with its thick handle and stepped into the stairwell there was a woman, below, smoking. She turned around. I said, "Oh!"

"Laura," Caroline said. "I thought you were here. Justin said so. Hey."

We exchanged exclamations. Yes, it was good to see each other; yes, it had been a long time.

"And you caught me like this." Caroline gestured with the cigarette in her hand. "It's awful, I know. I'm quitting at the New Year. I quit every New Year. This time, though."

"I don't mind."

She brightened. "You smoke?"

"No," I said. "No, not really."

"Not really." Caroline laughed as if we both knew this was a lie. "Come on down. Close the door anyway. I don't want to set something off. No one in there needs to know how awful I am."

"Can we get back in?" The door had already shut behind me.

Caroline shrugged. "I'm pretty sure."

I made my way down a flight of stairs to where she stood smoking. It was cooler here, and smelled vaguely earthen, beneath the cigarette smoke. Damp stone and cold metal—the combination was welcome after the hot, soft room of food and people.

"You're enjoying the benefit?" Caroline asked.

She was wearing a plain gray wool dress and heels. It looked like the kind of uniform a successful person wore every day to an office somewhere; there was a measure of power in wearing something this basic to an evening event. No jewelry except for small, thick gold hoop earrings. I could see a lot of makeup around her eyes. But this was the kind of makeup you were supposed to notice. "Am I enjoying—not really," I said.

Caroline laughed. "Yeah, that's not why you come to these things." Why do you come to these things. She added, "You okay?"

I was leaning against the concrete wall. "I'm okay. Tired. I'll sit down." I found the edge of a stair. "Do you mind?"

"Be my guest."

"Just for a second." I pushed my palms down on the step. Somewhere a door slammed. I asked, "How about you? You're . . . enjoying all this?"

"Oh, it's fine. About what I expected. Steak or chicken, red or white, speeches." She flicked her wrist. "The work I do, I've been to a lot of dinners."

"I forgot where you work."

"I work in development." She didn't seem to mind answering questions. Around the ends of the cigarette I could see her red-painted nails. She held a small silver portable ashtray. She was prepared.

"That was your degree," I said. "I mean at Oxford. Development."

"Well, development economics."

"Right." Caroline knew what she was doing. "Can I confess something," I said.

She gestured. "Be my guest," she said again.

"I never really knew what development was."

"Oh. Yeah." She exhaled. "You and everyone. It's not a thing, really." She was focusing on her cigarette. She had trained herself to be as efficient as possible about smoking, it seemed; she could enjoy herself anywhere, quickly and without fuss. "It's a bunch of people who wanted to do some good, and realized they couldn't, and kept going anyway. I think in, like, a few decades we'll look back on this time and wonder why we even had something called *development*. I mean, what was that? It seems very late twentieth century."

"Oh."

"And what could be less relevant than the late twentieth century. But I could be totally wrong."

"I doubt it."

"I'm not a big-picture person." She shrugged at that, too, unconcerned. "Everything comes around again, eventually."

"I guess that's true."

"Anyway I thought it was worth seeing who else would be here." She was talking about the benefit again. "Ten years on. That's how Mark sold it. And he got me a free ticket. I told him, 'I'm not paying for this.'"

"Mark?"

"Yeah, I saw him at Harvard, a little while ago. A conference. We had dinner together. Somehow Mark had the inside track on free tickets. I don't know how that happened."

How did that happen. What could be less relevant. Why do you keep going. Why do you come to these things. "Me neither," I said.

Another laugh. Caroline tapped her cigarette carefully.

"Did you know," I said, "that Mark and Heather were seeing each other the whole first year at Oxford?"

"Really."

"Yes."

"Huh. Sure, makes sense."

I kept going. "I thought you were together, back then. You and him." That was ungrammatical. "He."

"Mark and me. No, God." She shook her head and exhaled. "We worked together; I tried to teach him economics. Emphasize *tried*. We slept together a few times, sure. But I'm a behind-the-scenes person. The whole first lady thing—that's more Heather's deal."

"Everyone seems to—" I began, then stopped, then began again. "Somehow, everyone but me assumed from the start that Mark was going to run for office."

"Well, he has the right record."

"You mean war?"

"Among other things."

"He didn't always have war," I said. Caroline shrugged again; this was immaterial. I added, "And everyone hates the wars now." I wasn't sure what I was arguing.

"Everyone hates the wars now but they still need to vote for someone who fought in them," Caroline said. "You have to have done the thing before you're allowed to hate it. That's how it goes. It's what passes for expiation in this country. Hate it well, vote for the survivor, make the same mistakes over again in a few years."

"Yes." I felt sick with remorse suddenly; my stomach turned over. I put my head in my hands. "I shouldn't have said that."

"What?"

"Mark and Heather."

"It's a secret?"

"I don't know, actually."

"It was years ago. Don't worry about it."

"I'm sorry."

"You don't have to apologize to me."

"Right." I needed to stop. I kept going. "I didn't pay either." I explained—the benefit, a free ticket. "I couldn't pay. I shouldn't have come." I told her about the research. Ennis and Florence. The Weatherfield family. Sugar. "You know this history."

"Yeah, a little." She exhaled again.

"Do you think about it at all? Do you think about what it means?"

"What it means?" She stubbed out her cigarette.

I paused for a second, then said, "Forget it." I explained that the work had been canceled; I explained about the website. "I shouldn't have done that. I should have said no."

"Why?" She arranged herself on the step next to me now, unzipping her purse. "Better than nothing, right?"

"Maybe it wasn't." Caroline held out a pack of gum. I shook my head. I explained about Florence. "Apparently she was awful."

"Well, some people are," Caroline pointed out.

"Some people are," I repeated. "Is that all? Some people are."

"Does that matter?"

I leaned back against the wall again.

Caroline unwrapped some gum. "You did literature, yeah?"

I nodded.

"You know, I went to a poetry lecture once. At Oxford. I thought, I should try this. I should try something new. The lectures were open to everyone. You remember."

"Yes."

"It was maybe the first week we were there." She chewed her gum. "I was all eager. It seems so touching, looking back. It was one of those big rooms off High Street, I think? And the professor—could he have been wearing a robe? Was that a thing? And I didn't understand any of it. I thought, What the hell. I mean, I did the English requirement in college, and I liked reading books a lot. Still do."

"What do you like to read?"

"Oh, trash. I'd be embarrassed to tell you."

"No. Why?"

"Mysteries, mostly." She wasn't embarrassed. "I like your standard mysteries where a tough, damaged detective works within a corrupt system to punish wrongdoers and fix some small corner of the world." She shrugged. "Totally worthless stuff."

"Sounds very satisfying."

"Oh, it is."

"Did you go back to the poetry lecture?"

"Are you kidding? Never."

"I'm sorry about that."

"I should have asked you to come. You could have passed me notes with all the answers."

You didn't need to know answers, in lectures. You just listened. I had always liked lectures for that. "I might have been there, actually."

"Really?"

"I went to some lectures. But I don't know that I would have understood any better than you."

"I'm sure you did."

"You were probably just more honest about it."

"Ha. Well, there's that." Caroline chewed energetically.

I could hear the gum snapping in the back of her mouth. She was not worried. Her two feet in their square heels stood ready on the step. I looked at those feet and her small plump hands and realized that she had lived as much as I had. I stopped at the stupidly obvious fact I had hitherto overlooked, somehow, the plain empirical truth that every single day of 2001—every week of it, or hour, or minute; or every single day, or year, or week, or minute since—that all of it added not just to my knowing and being and feeling but also to the knowing and being and feeling of every other person I met, each of whom was sorting a different terrifyingly unique accumulation, all the time, while adding more to the task, knowingly, unknowingly, continuing somehow in this work that couldn't be recognized or shared, and the fact of human existence seemed miraculous and ridiculous, both. I had thought so little of others, I realized, while trying not to think of myself. I said, "Did you like Oxford?"

"Loved it." Caroline was quick, decisive.

"Can I ask you something?" Though I just had.

"Be my guest." It was her favorite phrase. Caroline blew a small bubble.

"What did you think of me, back then? I mean—if you

thought of me. I don't assume that you did, of course. And you don't have to say."

"Oh, I'll say, sure. Well—" Caroline considered. "You seemed very serious. I always thought there was a kind of dividing line, you know, between those who were serious and the ones who were not."

"Oh. I didn't think of it that way."

"That might not be the word. Intellectual. Justin, you know, he was very serious. Heather, too, but in a very different way. Or maybe—yeah, I think that's right. I think that's the best way to be, actually. Greta wasn't serious, but that wasn't a problem for her. Mark—I don't know. No, hang on, I do. Mark wasn't."

"Oh."

Caroline wasn't finished. "So I assumed you were—I don't know—judging, I guess."

"Me?"

"Not in a bad way. That you were sort of assessing everything all the time. That's why you weren't part of things. Mark and I talked about it once. He had this idea that if he passed muster with you, he would be okay. Or something like that. He was very interested in what you thought of him. It's not a bad thing," Caroline repeated.

"But I wasn't. Judging."

Caroline shrugged.

"What about you?" I asked. "Were you intellectual?"

"Oh, I didn't apply any of this to myself," Caroline said gaily. She unfolded the silver wrapper in her palm and carefully spit her used gum into it, then folded it again and dropped it in her purse. She zipped the top.

"I wasn't assessing everything," I said to her again. "I was—" I stopped. What was the word? *Yearning.* But I couldn't admit that.

And Caroline had already stood up. "I've got to go find Mark," she said. "We talked about catching a train together but I think he's going to ditch me."

"That sounds like him."

At the top of the stairs the door opened easily. "Are you coming back in?"

o O o

As I sat in the silence I thought about Renata.

I told Caroline I would be there in a minute, and after the slam behind her I waited in the echo and then quiet. I thought about other people and judging and seriousness and so I thought about Renata.

I had seen her two days earlier when I traveled to Harvard to empty my money-draining storage unit, after an email advertised discount rates for 2012 and I realized how stupid it was to hold on to the stuff any longer. Renata had written a third time, to the academic address that wasn't quite yet cut off: "I haven't heard from you. Let me know how you are and what you're working on, when you can." It was unlike her to write so often—to write at all. I chose Renata as my adviser because her specialty was vaguely applicable but also because she was known in the department to be uninvolved at best. I thought that was for me. I had been told that I should cultivate connections, that everything is about connection, and I believed this and chose Renata, who seemed to distrust connection as much as I did. She was not warm or close—not aloof or reclusive, either, but always carrying the impression of an unspoken and urgent agenda that precluded needless ingratiations. Her mere presence at a talk or reception produced a slight but perceptible bristling; she put everyone on guard. Short and solid, a round, bare face, close-cropped gray hair and rimless square glasses and a wardrobe of various soft black jackets and loose black pants and thick-soled sandals that she wore even in winter, with socks—I knew from others, from paragraphs at the back of her books, that she had been born to Holocaust survivors in Poland just after World War II and moved with her family to England at some point in her childhood, before attending college in Canada and graduate school in the United States, where she wrote a monograph on several American poets of the nineteenth century, a longer, more involved study on connections between pragmatism and naturalism, and a work in progress, now, about race and the novel and the pre-history of psychology. But I heard nothing of the project from her. Renata barely referred to her expertise; her comments on my work, like her questions after a public presentation, like her remarks at a department meeting, seemed to come from a disinterested place of general intelligence that drew on no specialization beyond commonly available perspicacity—this made them only more intimidating. I wrote back to her email, finally, the day I learned of the job at Royce; I was fine, I told her, but no longer working on James, no longer working.

"When can we talk?" came a line in reply. "We should meet in person if possible. Will you be in Cambridge?"

We met in her office; we always had. Renata saw no need for the pretense of a drink or lunch or cup of coffee. I was late because I had spent close to half an hour trying to maneuver Len's pickup, its truck bed full of boxes, into a parking space on Trowbridge Street. The English building was empty, already dusky in the 3:00 P.M. December light. Renata nodded when I remarked on this. "I do like this time of year around here. So quiet. But sit down. Tell me what's going on. You've changed

your research, apparently." A lifted eyebrow admired my duplic-
ity, as if I had been wily about this.

"No—I've stopped."

"You've abandoned your research?"

"I think it's more that my research abandoned me."

Renata folded her hands. "That sounds sophistic," she said.
She had one of the smaller offices, with just one window, and
the bookshelves shrank it further. I took one edge of the leather
love seat next to a stack of folders. She sat to one side of her
desk with her chair angled toward mine, both feet on the floor,
and her glasses pushed up into her hair. "You mean that you
haven't found the right job yet."

"Well, that too."

"But you had something. Didn't you? And you have been
applying. Till now. I see the report of recommendation requests.
This year you made none. Thus my email."

"I had no idea you checked."

"Of course."

"I appreciate your recommendation—" I began.

But she waved this away. "Understood."

I flushed. "My temporary position was canceled in August.
It felt like the end." It seemed so long ago, August. It seemed
so long ago that I had sat in a room across the quad and listened to experts explaining a decade of war. "The right end."
Yes, that was it.

Renata raised her eyebrow, dubious. "I don't see why."

I tried to put together another sentence.

"No position is satisfactory," she said. "Granted. But one's
work is not the job. The job is merely to enable one's work."
She frowned. "Yes? Perhaps I should have been explicit about
this. You were intelligent enough that one didn't point out the
obvious." Now she pulled down her glasses and looked at me

as if noticing something new. "Do you need some tea? There's a kettle at the end of the floor, I think."

I wonder what would have happened if I'd said yes. "No, I'm fine."

"The work of scholarship is essentially countercultural in a secular society," Renata went on. "There have been various more or less bothersome practical means for what we do. I mean historically. Most of them involve teaching. Alas." She stopped to look at me, someone she was meant to have taught. Advised, at least. "A medieval legacy. It's a mistake to fixate on that."

"I'll try not to," I said.

She nodded briskly. "Of course one does need to live. I'm not completely myopic about practicality." She peered at me through the gloom of a Harvard office. "Quite the contrary." Back to me. "So you were left with nothing, then, in August. And kept quiet about it."

Her tone pricked. "Well, I had another job. I have a job now."

"Ah. And it's endurable? Allows you to work?"

A job that allows me to work. "Yes. No. I don't know. I don't—I don't like it. I don't believe in it."

Renata didn't care about my likes or beliefs. "Do you have family on which to rely?"

"I—uh—"

"Tell me if these questions are unwelcome. My aim is information, not offense. I thought you were married."

"I was. He left me a long time ago."

"That's unfortunate," Renata said. It seemed mostly to be unfortunate for how it affected my ability to draw on his practical support for scholarship I had already abandoned. Then she added, "My husband also left me. That truly was a long time ago." She drummed her fingers on her upper lip for a moment. Then a question: "It was difficult?" An afterthought.

"It was. But I'm fine now."

Renata nodded. "We do know what it was like to have *been* married. A consolation."

A consolation? "Yes."

She was moving on. "Parents, or the like? Any other support?"

"Well, my father died."

Renata looked at me.

"When I was a child."

She nodded. That did not require an expression of sorrow, apparently. She did not say that at least I knew what it was like to have been fathered. Renata wheeled her chair back a few inches, toward her desk, considering. "Your record is good."

I started to say, No, or that I didn't want to use my record, or think about it, but I didn't want to sound truculent. "It hasn't come to much."

"That's not for you to judge."

"Who else?" It slipped out. I shouldn't have said that.

Renata looked at me. The sharpness registered, and required a response, but the response meant thought first. She said, "I see." Then: "I know the inevitable dissatisfaction, the continual dissatisfaction with one's subject." She paused. "The work, after all, is oneself, and the subject is that by which one proves—" She broke off. That was uncharacteristic. "I have only the obvious solution to offer, but it has the virtue of being true in my limited experience. Dissatisfaction with the task is part of the task."

"Which is oneself."

"Precisely." Renata gave a quick nod to indicate we understood each other. I had been trying to pose a question. "The practice answers the lack it makes plain." Another nod: She had just worked this out to an adequate standard. "But you may discover differently," she added amenably. "That, too, will be part of the work. Wherever it leads."

"You're saying to follow where it leads."

Renata smiled at this, as if I were being intentionally bathetic. "Humility, yes," she conceded, "may be an easier way to put it." Then she grew stern again. "But not a false humility." I didn't say anything; I didn't know what to say. She put her hands down on the desk. "Laura. I need to know, if possible, that you are all right."

It was such a plain expression of concern, uttered with so little feeling, that I blushed. I said, "I'm all right."

"You're certain." She was satisfied, barely.

"I'm certain." I almost mentioned my mother. I didn't. One didn't mention mothers to Renata.

"You know," she added, "there are many people around here"—she looked up and gestured with her eyes at the office around her, the building, maybe the institution, maybe the world—"who mistake their position, their professional position, their affiliation, for something significant. This always strikes me as tragic, in a minor way, when I see it. But you are not one of them, and you needn't pretend that you are." I didn't say anything. Renata waited, then added, "Life is not about belonging."

"Oh, I don't belong," I replied lightly, but I knew that wasn't the right answer, and so I said, "Or rather, I don't want to," and I knew that wasn't the true one. I blushed again.

Renata said nothing. Soon I would be driving back to my mother's house in my landlord's van with the boxes of books I had no place for. Soon I would be unloading those boxes into an attic, one corner of which was still covered in my father's files. "Thank you for the advice," I said to Renata.

But Renata wasn't listening, and wasn't done. "Where *has* it led?" she asked.

"My work."

"Yes."

I tried to think. "Oh—ah—I guess the last thing I did in my research was—well, Henry James and friendship. No, Henry James and war."

Renata said, "That sounds promising."

"It wasn't, really. His dates are all wrong. He died in the middle of World War I, and during the Civil War—he was alive, but he didn't enlist. Because of some injury he supposedly got while fighting a fire." I stopped. "He knew people who enlisted, I guess. His brothers."

"Not William."

"No, William went to Harvard instead of to war. That was his excuse."

Renata said, "You assume an excuse is necessary." She was matter-of-fact.

"William is worse," I continued. "William and his moral equivalents. I hate that speech."

"I believe," Renata said, "that the phrase first comes up in *The Varieties of Religious Experience*." She added, "That might be of interest. Though the *Varieties* is a series of lectures, of course, if you reject oratory outright."

"Oh." I stopped. "I didn't know."

"That was intended to be wry," Renata said. "The best of William James is the psychology. His absolute respect for individual experience as perceived and understood by the individuals themselves. I think that is what he shared with the novelist." She paused. "It helps to go back to the source."

"Yes. Sorry. Yes. I will."

Renata nodded a last time. I was dismissed. I drove home.

She was of course right. I looked it up later. William with the first mention of a "moral equivalent of war" was promoting "voluntarily accepted poverty": "It is certain," he wrote, "that the prevalent fear of poverty among the educated classes is the worst moral disease from which our civilization suffers." Voluntarily accepted poverty was difficult enough that it might replace the battlefield as a necessary "bulwark against effeminacy" without the need of "crushing weaker peoples." This was the end of 1901, beginning of 1902. "War" would have meant not whatever was begun in 1914 or 1861 but whatever was begun in 1898, with the U.S. blockade of Cuba—which drove William to anti-imperialist rallies in Boston and which he called "heart-sickening" in a letter to Henry, who was at this point in England, ready to compose another book about the marriage prospects of young women and trying to ignore the newspapers. Henry of the "obscure hurt," Henry of the "comprehensive ache"; Henry was not worried about manliness, about morals, about voluntary anything. "One must save one's life if one can," he wrote back.

After the Spanish-American War the United States annexed several islands useful for sugar growing and military operations. U.S. sugar companies expanded into Puerto Rico. The City Bank opened its first branch in San Juan. At some point, a socialist named Emilia who smoked glamorous cigarettes and wore high heels with buckles made a bad match in New York that led her to the disappointed house of a complaining heiress on Long Island and from there to the rest of a life that I would never, in all of its difficulty, all of its Jamesian and un-Jamesian difficulty, really know.

There was so much I would never really know.

I sat on the concrete stair now and thought about lives, how they are saved, and what came back to me was the feeling I didn't admit in front of a stack of books at my mother's house or a cart of boxes at the Dawes library or a page of questions on the train from the city or any of those anxious hours at Oxford. It was the feeling of taking things in; it was the feeling of needing more—information, words, understanding—and of having more and not enough and then again needing; it was the feeling not of wanting to work but of wanting to learn. It was not a moral feeling. Selfish, rather. But so utterly distant from myself at the same time. How badly I had served this desire, and yet how faithfully it continued nevertheless: That was something to trust. Yes. As I stood up to open the hall door I felt almost dizzy.

Because I had barely eaten all night. I would see about getting some cake.

○ ○ ○

But when I went back in I found others.

Justin saw me before I could fetch a plate from the back table. "Laura." He pulled me to one side of a curtained window. After the cool stairwell the room felt loud with sound and light. People were dancing now. The musicians had come to languid versions of Christmas carols that let various couples sway and stride without embarrassment in not exactly steps. No one could really dance. "I want to ask you something," Justin said.

He had a glass in his hand and I could see a faint stain of wine on his lower lip.

"It went well," I told him.

"What are you talking about?"

"The essay."

He made a scornful face—scornful of me. "No, it didn't."

"Well, it went fine."

"Yeah. Not even that."

"I'm serious."

He shook his head at my simplicity. "When I got back to the table, my dad said on the whole I should stick to the less personal stuff."

"Oh. Sorry. Your dad?"

"My dad was a fellow in the seventies. Had a great time. No way he was missing the party." He gestured with his chin to a couple standing in conversation with a few others at the edge of the dancers, a tall silver-haired man and an equally erect woman in velvet.

"That's your mom."

"Yeah, they've been married thirty-five years," Justin said. "So they're really thrilled with my choices so far."

"I'm sure they are, actually."

"Gee thanks. That's reassuring. Anyway. I wanted to ask you something."

"You said."

"Mark and Heather."

"Mark and Heather?" I looked back at him.

"Come on." Justin was impatient. "You know what I'm talking about. They're together, right?"

I refused to be impatient. "Aren't you friends with Mark?"

"No one's friends with Mark."

"Wow."

"Not like that anyway."

"Well, why would I know—"

"Okay, what are you two talking about?" It was Greta.

She grabbed Justin's elbow. She had a glass, too, in the other hand, tall and full of ice. Her cheeks were flushed. She said, "I'm trying to escape some woman telling me about the deserving poor."

"We're talking about Justin's essay," I told her. "Help me convince him the essay was good."

Greta nodded. "The essay was good!" she said to him. To me: "See. There you go."

Justin, angry now, said, "I don't really care?"

Greta looked at me. "He seems convinced."

"All right." Justin gave up. "I'm going to find another bottle of wine. I don't know why they took down the bar so early."

Greta said to him, helpful, "Mark's with that guy, chairman of the board, over there." Then, to me, when Justin had gone: "What's his problem? You haven't seen Judith, have you?"

"No. I haven't looked, though." I scanned the crowd.

"She's acting weird. I think she's just mad."

"I'm sorry."

"Don't be. She'll come around. She hates these things and takes it out on me. But I just go with it and everything is okay in the end."

"Let me know if I can help," I said.

"You can help. Come with me. I have to find the bathroom."

"Can we get some cake?"

"Yeah, the cake is so good," Greta said, ignoring the question. "I've had like three pieces!" She steered me toward the door, leaving her glass on the nearest table. "All of the food was really good. Though I'll eat anything; you know how I am."

The interior of the women's room was less elegant than I might have expected after the ballroom. I avoided my own reflection in the mirror as I waited for Greta. "Fuck zippers, by the way." She emerged, smoothing herself, and headed toward the sink. "I should never have worn a jumpsuit; I knew I would have to go constantly. Never fails."

I stared at her. "You're pregnant."

"Oh! Well—yeah, I am." She looked at me with surprise,

then approval, as if I had just made a lucky guess. "Don't tell anyone."

"Of course. Congratulations."

"It's too early. Complications, you know, blah blah blah."

"You were pregnant when I visited."

Greta thought that over. "I was, actually!" She looked at herself.

"That's great."

"You think so? Come on, tell me, am I nuts to go through this again?"

"Of course not," I said. "Does Judith know?"

It was an idiotic question, I realized as soon as I said it; somehow it had seemed the logical one. But the door opened before Greta could register her offense or amusement, and Greta said, "Heather!"

Heather paused in the doorway. "Oh, wow." Then she remembered to smile. "So this is where everyone is," she said brightly.

"All the important people," Greta replied, "now that you're here."

"Don't let me disturb you." She didn't look at me. "I just want to freshen up for a moment." She stepped in. "You two seem like you're deep in discussion."

I said, "We're talking about how good the cake is."

"I haven't tasted it," said Heather. "I know it sounds ridiculous but I haven't had the chance. Too much to do."

"Oh, yeah," Greta agreed. "I get that. Like a wedding. At the end you realize you're starving because you've been talking to people all night and haven't had time to eat. I mean your own wedding. But I'm in your way—"

"Oh, no, no," Heather said as she moved into the space by the mirror that Greta had left. She opened the bag she held in one hand, a thin fabric envelope, and took out a tube of lipstick. "I'm just trying to make sure everyone has a good time."

"We're having a great time!" Greta said.

"That makes me so glad." Her voice was calm even through the distortion of her mouth held taut and her eyebrows raised. She applied the lipstick. She capped the tube. "I worry that there's too much talk about the foundation."

"Isn't that the point?" Greta said.

"Yes, of course." Heather nodded. She pulled her eyebrows tight and pressed her lips together. "I hoped tonight would serve mostly as a kind of reunion, a chance for people to reconnect. Ultimately, though, we *do* want more people to take an interest in the foundation's initiatives." She frowned. It was hard to tell if the frown was an expression of her feelings or a test of her face.

"It's going great," Greta said definitively. "You'll get lots of interest."

"Thank you."

"Lots of money!"

Heather frowned again. There was a pause. I said, tentative, "I think this is the kind of event from which people can take whatever they want."

It sounded oddly formal out loud. Heather turned around. "That's a good way to put it, yes." She picked up her bag. "I should get back. I have to go rescue Mark."

Greta brightened at this. "Does Mark need rescuing?"

"He's deep in some sort of political discussion with an elderly donor," Heather told her. "Of course he's too kind to just leave. I imagine he'll have to get more practiced at that. He's exploring a run for Congress," she added patiently, "which of course involves engaging with a lot of people he wouldn't seek out otherwise."

"Oh yeah, sure," Greta said. "I got the memo. And you're

part of the—" She stopped suddenly and looked hard. "Oh my God. Heather!"

"What?" Heather turned.

"You and Mark."

"Oh, I—"

"It's true!" Greta crowed. "Oh my God, it's true." She didn't bother to hide how pleased she was to discover this—pleased with herself. "You two!" Her eyes were manic with it.

Or something else. I thought of the wet evening on an Oxford street, the shine of rain and cobblestones, when Greta was crying through heartbreak and I had only walked her home. And as Heather smiled at her in admission—yes, it was true—as Greta clutched Heather's arm in enthusiasm, and as I stepped back toward a stall door, I thought of the dark evening in the Oxford pub, the scent of mold and old bleach, when Heather was bleeding through the aftermath of her abortion and I could only offer her a tampon.

"Please don't say anything," Heather said. "We're taking it slow."

"I won't, I won't," Greta assured her. "Of course. I won't say a thing."

She would say a thing, I knew. Heather knew, too. Greta would tell Justin, at least, before the evening was out. Heather thanked her.

"And Laura," Greta continued, "Laura won't say anything. Though Laura probably knew the whole story all along."

"No," I said, watching the strange tableau we made in the mirror, the three of us. My face a little behind the others. Heather and Greta would be good friends for each other, better than I had been to either. "No, but I'm glad."

And Heather glanced at me then for the first time since she

had entered the bathroom; I couldn't tell what was in her eyes, but it wasn't meant for anyone else.

"We'll all go rescue Mark," she said after a moment.

So the three of us pushed out of the swinging bathroom door together, where we met Caroline, a coat over one arm, and when Greta screeched that no one could leave, not yet, Caroline said she had to, sorry, "But what have you three been plotting together in the women's room?" I answered quickly with the word *people*, which didn't quite make sense, but Caroline nodded, approving. "Speaking of," she said. "I'm due uptown. But I told Mark I was heading back early and I couldn't share a cab with him so if he asks don't blow my cover, okay?"

She was blithe. We all agreed. Greta told her to have fun, and Caroline shook her head, shrugging on the black wool of her coat. "Oh, I definitely will. That's exactly why I shouldn't go. Remind me," she said, pulling a glove from her bag, "to write a little anonymous book sometime about men who weren't loved by their mothers."

Heather nodded. "Or those who were."

Caroline laughed at that; we all did, though we didn't know—at least I didn't—what we agreed to with the laughter, and Caroline said, "Fair," then added, "So, yeah, great to see all of you, keep in touch, all that," and strode in the opposite direction down the hall. The ease of her dismissal, leaving for her night of inadvisable pleasure, lying about it, confiding about it, uttering the obviously superficial phrases of parting that no one was meant to believe, the ease of all the unconcerned competence with which she went about her life—it seemed to buoy us, Greta and Heather and me, as we made our way back to the ballroom, where the lights were higher and the quartet had stopped playing and small sociable clumps of people congealed, all over, fellows from the same or adjacent years; this was late-stage party, when optimism or determination had worn off and people came back to those they already knew. We drifted our way to where Mark was standing with Justin, also Lindsay, and Jay, and there was Zac, along with a fellow from one year later whose name I couldn't remember. Lindsay was saying something to Mark, or rather, about Mark, which she explained to us as we came up: "All the stories we could leak, once *this* one is a public figure." I didn't remember Lindsay and Mark having been friends, but now, in this conversation, they always had been. "Then we were reminding ourselves," Lindsay added, smiling, "that Mark is a specialist in unconventional warfare." Mark didn't say anything. He smiled, looking slightly down and away, embarrassed and pleased at the stories, the warfare. Justin made a small gesture with his hands that was meant to quiet the group so he could add something, but another voice had begun a different topic—it was Zac, who looked fit and satisfied, in a dark suit, saying in apparent earnestness how quickly time passed, confessing his jealousy, so often now, of interns in his office, though he was the one giving them jobs. "I'm thinking," Zac said, in a sort of wonder at his thought and the ability to articulate it, "I'm thinking, No, no, I want *your* life."

Others agreed. Others added their findings about the passage of time. I thought about what was still to come, the good work Mark would do in Congress, the good work Heather would do in nonprofits and for women's empowerment, the good books Justin would write, the stories he would tell, the good work Greta would do for her students, her friends. These goods were not mine. I had been jealous of their work—I knew that now—deeply jealous. I had been jealous of their having work. But I did not want their work, their lives; I did not want to live them, to go on living them; till now I had not, mostly, even wanted my own life, the one I hadn't lived and yet still needed to atone for.

I needed to leave.

On my way toward the coat check I saw Judith, who was waiting by the empty dessert table. "Greta is up there," I told her—uselessly, since she could see Greta herself, at the front of the room.

She knew, she said. "I'm waiting for her to get sick of this."

I was startled, a little, at her tone. "I don't know that she will."

"She will." Judith's voice was tired; her face, too, when she turned to look at me. "You forget that I met her just after she had been a long time with these people. She barely escaped." She made a sound in her throat and turned away. "I won't let that happen again."

"Oh, I didn't know," I started to say, "or, um, I didn't mean—"

"I don't think we've met!" The smiling white-haired man was at our elbow. He had been moving among the remaining groups. "I'm trying to say hello to as many guests as possible." He stood too close to us. The board chairman, I remembered. He said, "I hope you enjoyed the evening."

Judith had already moved off, murmuring something, so I replied, "Very much so," and added, "Thank you."

"That's wonderful. You're a fellow?" And he asked my year, my subject of study, and I told him, and I heard his. "It remains the most deeply valuable time of my life," he told me.

"Oh mine, too," I agreed.

"And what came after that?" he prompted, cheerful still. "What do you do?"

Judith was nowhere to be seen; I looked back to the group of fellows I knew, where no one had noticed I'd left. "I work in a library," I told him. "And I live with my mother."

I had decided, for now, that it would be the truth.

○ ○ ○

But someone had noticed I'd left after all; Mark found me. "Laura."

I turned around in the hallway. I was holding my puffy down jacket.

"I'm glad you aren't gone yet," he said.

"I'm just going."

"Come out to a drink with us? Justin and Heather and me. Greta, if her wife agrees. Some others maybe."

"I have to catch a train home."

"Heather said you can stay at her place."

"Yes, thank her for me. Not tonight."

"It would be good to talk," he said. "I haven't heard how you're doing."

"Oh, I'm doing well," I said. "I'm fine. I'm good."

"Heather and Greta and Justin were saying that you're working for students who need—"

"Not anymore." I cut him off.

"Ah—right." He nodded to hide his embarrassment. My embarrassment. "Got it."

Then I remembered: "I did want to ask you something, though."

"Oh. Sure—" Composed again.

"There are visas, right, for people who helped U.S. armed forces in Iraq? There's a program?"

"Yeah. Not quite as simple as that, but—"

"I know of someone who might qualify," I said. "I mean she should. A woman and her son. Visas. College. Would you see what you can do? I mean, I'll work on this; I just need help. You have influence, I'm assuming."

"Um, I don't know, I guess I—"

"I'm not asking for a guarantee."

"Sure," he said. "No guarantees."

"College or a visa might not be much of a recompense." He looked ready to object. "But I think people should have everything."

"Uh—"

"I think people should have everything and they can decide."

"Uh, sure. Yeah." He rallied now. "That visa program is very important."

"Agreed."

"You've got to take care of your people."

"Exactly."

He seemed to be waiting for more. The closer one is to military action the less likely one is to question it. I thought I remembered this fact from somewhere in my reading about war, years ago. Also the most durable reason for fighting is a sense of responsibility and fellowship for other soldiers. "Congratulations on the campaign," I said.

"Oh, that. That's not a thing yet."

"It will be. It will be great. Public service. It's what you want to do?"

He looked puzzled. "Well, yeah, I mean—"

"I was remembering what you said at that conference."

"In August? The Mitchell Center?"

"No, no, in 2001. The recruitment. Training. Whatever. Right before September eleventh."

"Right."

"The most important thing, you said then, is not to do anything you don't want to do."

"I said that?"

"Approximately. It was a long time ago."

"It sounds dumb enough to be something I said." Mark shook his head. "I don't know how you put up with me then."

"Oh, I didn't really."

He smiled more genuinely at that. "No," he said. Then: "I've been meaning to get back there."

"Puerto Rico?"

"Yeah, as far as I remember, we didn't see any of it on that— whatever that weekend was."

"We didn't," I agreed. "We saw nothing." I started to say something more, something about the list of books I would assemble on the ride back to my mother's house, in the margins of my benefit program, books that might help me understand better what could have been part of Emilia's life, something more about what was, already, part of my own—but it was all so tenuous, and so unnecessary, and so private, and Mark was turning in the opposite direction. *Wherever it leads.* That's what Renata had said.

Mark asked, "You sure you won't come out for a drink?"

"No," I said. I meant, no, I won't come. I was pretty sure.

He smiled. "They thought I could convince you. The others."

"And what did you think?"

"I hoped I could convince you."

"Don't feel bad," I said. "You're very convincing."

"Thank you." He put on a voice then, deeper, more pompous, the voice of someone playing at being grown-up. "Your support means a lot to me."

I smiled. "*That* wasn't convincing."

"Oh, well, I meant it."

I remembered the other, more basic fact of my reading about war, which is how absolutely, totally, completely horrific it is.

Also the most basic impression, which is that reading about it gave me absolutely no idea, no idea at all, not the ghost of an idea, about what it was like. To have fought. That absence was also part of my life.

"I mean it, too," I said. "The support."

"See you."

"Take care."

I left, not looking back; I went down the hall to what I thought was the staircase we were supposed to use, but I didn't look; I pushed instead through a different set of doors, and when I kept going I saw ahead of me an unfamiliar exit sign and when I turned to that, another door, a short hallway, a room of blank white lights and stainless-steel tables. The kitchen.

The room was almost empty. Two servers rolled a huge skein of plastic wrap around a metal cart. In the back some water was running.

"Can I help you?"

"Sorry—" I stopped.

"You all right?"

The woman who spoke stood in front of a large cake on a raised tray with just one slice cut from it. But she was ignoring the cake, figuring something on a sheet of paper, biting her lip. She wore drawstring pants and a chef's coat and a large white apron, with her blond hair pulled back into the small bump of a bun. Everything was gray and white except for her shoes, which were orange-and-black sneakers, cushioned and high. They made her feet look dainty.

"I'm fine," I said. "I made a wrong turn."

She didn't seem bothered. "You must be one of the guests."

"Yes. I guess I am."

"I love that dress, by the way."

"Thank you." I shrugged out of the half of a coat I had on and stood for a moment. "Yes. I like this dress."

The woman was about my age. Maybe a little younger. She gestured at the tray. "Can I interest you in a slice of chocolate peppermint torte?"

"That's okay."

"You're sure."

"Well, actually. I would love some." I was breathing better now. "Did you make it?"

"Nah." She picked up the trowel of a serving utensil and slid a piece onto a napkin. "I don't do cakes. We don't do cakes. The client picks something from a bakery and we just serve it. Do you need a fork?"

"I can eat with my fingers, if you don't mind."

"Not at all. Saves us washing."

"Good." I broke off a piece. I was so hungry.

She turned back to her paper, companionably. "Let me know what you think."

"About the cake?" I swallowed.

"Of course."

"Honestly." She waited. "I don't think it's very good."

The woman nodded. "Yeah, it's not."

"I don't mean to be ungrateful."

She shook her head, unbothered. "These are just leftovers."

"What happens to the leftovers?"

"Servers, dishwashers, assistants. Everyone takes some home if they want. My kids have come to expect leftover cake. Actually they've come to expect better than this." She smiled. "Cake snobs."

"That's great."

"It sets them up for a lot of disappointment."

"There are worse things."

"I should tell them this is smart-people cake. Helps them get good grades."

"Smart-people cake?"

"Isn't that right?" She pushed her pencil back into her bun. "Some sort of foundation for smart people?"

"Oh! Yes. I mean, no. No no no." I had eaten all of the slice on the napkin. I wanted more. I crumpled up the paper and tossed it in the big gray trash barrel nearby. "Thank you."

"You feeling better?" She folded her sheet of paper.

"Yes," I said. I put on my coat again. I felt steadier. I said again, "Yes. Thank you."

"No problem."

"Is there a back way out of here?"

She nodded, as if this were a perfectly reasonable request. "Always, from the kitchen." She pointed to a door. "Down a long ramp, then a service elevator. It takes you to a door that leads to the street."

"Got it," I said.

She had moved away on her cushioned feet.

The room was empty. Time to go.

And it was exactly as she'd said. A door, then a ramp lined with black rubber matting, a large elevator walled in gray felt pads. I pressed a button and descended. I came out into the winter air near a sloped driveway. No one was around. For a moment I couldn't tell what street I was on, where I needed to turn, and I paused to look up at the clouds shifting companionably around in the fathomless dark.

Sources

1.

BBC coverage of the events of 9/11/2001; Andrew Bacevich, ed., *The Short American Century: A Postmortem*; Andy Beckett, "PPE: The Oxford Degree That Runs Britain"; Nathaniel Fick, *One Bullet Away: The Making of a Marine Officer*; Dexter Filkins, *The Forever War*; David Finkel, *The Good Soldiers* and *Thank You for Your Service*; Joshua S. Goldstein, *War and Gender: How Gender Shapes the War System and Vice Versa*; Eric Greitens, *The Heart and the Fist: The Education of a Humanitarian, the Making of a Navy SEAL*; Hazel Hutchison, "The Forgotten Story of American Writers on the Frontline of World War I"; Sebastian Junger, *War*; Phil Klay, "The Citizen-Soldier: Moral Risk and the Modern Military"; Margaret MacMillan, *War: How Conflict Shaped Us*; Scott Malcomson, "A Free-for-All on a Decade of War"; John Nagl, *Knife Fights: A Memoir of Modern War in Theory and Practice*; George Packer, *The Assassins' Gate: America in Iraq*. The quotations on page 42 are from William James, "The Moral Equivalent of War," and Henry James, "The American Volunteer Motor-Ambulance Corps in France." I am grateful to Eric Gardiner and Christopher Sovich for information about military service and to Logan Cort for information about swimming.

2.

Joyce Appleby, *The Relentless Revolution: A History of Capitalism*; César J. Ayala, *American Sugar Kingdom: The Plantation Economy of the Spanish Caribbean 1898–1934*; Daniel Catlin, Jr., *Good Work Well Done: The Sugar Business Career of Horace Havemeyer, 1903–1956*; Mark Dowie, *American Foundations: An Investigative History*; Bartow J. Elmore, *Citizen Coke: The Making of Coca-Cola Capitalism*; Joseph C. Goulden, *The Money Givers*; David C. Hammack and Stanton Wheeler, *A History of the Russell Sage Foundation*; David C. Hammack and Helmut K. Anheier, *A Versatile American Institution: The Changing Ideals and Realities of Philanthropic Foundations*; David Harvey, *A Companion to Marx's Capital*; Harry W. Havemeyer, *Henry Osborne Havemeyer: The Most Independent Mind* and *Merchants of Williamsburgh: Frederick C. Havemeyer, Jr., William Dick, John Mollenhauer, Henry O. Havemeyer*; Peter James Hudson, *Bankers and Empire: How Wall Street Colonized the Caribbean*; Henry James, *The Golden Bowl*; Karl Marx, *Capital*, volume 1; Scott Reynolds Nelson, *A Nation of Deadbeats: An Uncommon History of America's Financial Disasters*; Waldemar A. Nielsen, *The Big Foundations*; David O. Whitten and Bessie E. Whitten, *The Birth of Big Business in the United States, 1860–1914: Commercial, Extractive, and Industrial Enterprise*. The cartoon described on page 67 is by Randall Munroe, xkcd.com. The quotation on page 79 is from *Industrial Relations: Final Report and Testimony*, 64th Cong., 1st sess., Sen. Doc. 415. I am grateful to Michael Burstein for information about consulting and Jennifer Schaefer for information about math.

3.

Elizabeth Abbott, *Sugar: A Bittersweet History*; Matthew Bigg, "Imperial Sugar Plant Explosion Was 'Preventable'"; Stephanie

Black, *H-2 Worker*; Julia Blakely, "Joe Froggers: The Weight of the Past in a Cookie"; Marie Brenner, "In the Kingdom of Big Sugar"; Stephen Greenhouse, "Hard Feelings Outlast a 20-Month Strike at Domino"; Rachel Kushner, *Telex From Cuba*; Patricia A. Matthew, "Serving Tea for a Cause: The Kitchenware That Helped British Women Fight Against 'Blood Sugar' on the Home Front"; Sidney W. Mintz, *Sweetness and Power: The Place of Sugar in Modern History*; Leigh Raiford and Robin J. Hayes, "Remembering the Workers of the Domino Sugar Factory"; Rachel Kushner, *Telex From Cuba*; Daniel Rasmussen, *American Uprising: The Untold Story of America's Largest Slave Revolt*; Andrew F. Smith, *Sugar: A Global History*; Robin Shulman, *Eat the City: A Tale of the Fishers, Foragers, Butchers, Farmers, Poultry Minders, Sugar Refiners, Cane Cutters, Beekeepers, Winemakers, and Brewers Who Built New York*; Richard Tucker, *Insatiable Appetite: The United States and the Degradation of the Tropical World*; Craig Steven Wilder, *A Covenant with Color: Race and Social Power in Brooklyn*. The quotation on page 102 is from Henry James, *Daisy Miller*; the quotation on page 103 is from C. L. R. James, *The Black Jacobins: Toussaint L'Ouverture and the San Domingo Revolution*. The sources for descriptions of sugar work are Human Rights Watch, "Turning a Blind Eye: Hazardous Labor in El Salvador's Sugarcane Cultivation"; Sidney Mintz, *Worker in the Cane: A Puerto Rican Life History*; Alec Wilkinson, *Big Sugar: Seasons in the Cane Fields of Florida*. The format of this chapter borrows from Heidi Julavits, *The Folded Clock: A Diary*.

4.

Annual Reports of the Alumnae Association of Bryn Mawr College, 1899–1901; Annual Reports of the President of Bryn Mawr, 1894–1899; Bryn Mawr College Calendar, 1908; Craig

Robertson, *The Passport in America: The History of a Document*; Kathryn Schulz, "Final Forms"; World Health Organization, "ICD-11: Classifying disease to map the way we live and die."

6.

David M. Kennedy, *Over Here: The First World War and American Society*; Jeff Kisseloff, *You Must Remember This: An Oral History of Manhattan from the 1890s to World War II*. The quotation on page 188 is from the Catechism of the Council of Trent; the one on page 189 is from *The Life of Saint Teresa of Avila by Herself*. I am grateful to Marcus Key for information about fossils.

7.

Henry James, "The Art of Fiction"; Kirk W. Johnson, *To Be a Friend Is Fatal: The Fight to Save the Iraqis America Left Behind*; Sarah Stillman, "The Invisible Army."

9.

Daniel Immerwahr, *How To Hide An Empire: A History of the Greater United States*; Robert D. Richardson, *William James: In the Maelstrom of American Modernism*. The quotations on page 296 are from Henry James, *Notes of a Son and Brother*; William James, *The Varieties of Religious Experience: A Study in Human Nature*; and letters between William and Henry James in Ignas K. Skrupskelis and Elizabeth M. Berkeley, eds., *William and Henry James: Selected Letters*.

Acknowledgments

In addition to the people and works listed in the Sources section, I am grateful to many for their help and support during the writing of this book. A much earlier version of one section was published in *The Missouri Review*; thanks to Evelyn Rogers and everyone at that journal. Thank you also to the librarians at the Waidner-Spahr Library of Dickinson College and the UCLA Library; to Erica Rothschild and Suite 8; to Joe Gannon, Laura Hart, Molly Mikolowski, Elana Rosenthal, and everyone who worked on this book at Bellevue Literary Press; to the Research and Development Committee of Dickinson College; to the Faculty Personnel Committee of Dickinson College; to everyone in the English and Creative Writing departments at Dickinson; to Sameen Gauhar, Erika Goldman, and Sam Stoloff; to Franky Abbott, Maria Bruno, Alyssa DeBlasio, Margaret Frohlich, Alix Hawley, Idara Hippolyte, Sarah Kersh, Evan Kindley, Michelle Kuo, Emily Ryan Lerner, Aida Levy-Hussen, Sarah McGaughey, Erin McGee, Robert McGill, Wendy Moffat, Sharon O'Brien, Emily Pawley, Susan Perabo, Claire Seiler, Nirvana Tanoukhi, Jessica Winter, and Kelly Winters-Fazio; to everyone in my Phillips, Peiffer, Fulford, Sovich, and Brophy family, including Caleb, Chris, Prudence, Sheila, and Steven Peiffer; and to Brian Phillips.

Bellevue Literary Press is devoted to publishing literary fiction and nonfiction at the intersection of the arts and sciences because we believe that science and the humanities are natural companions for understanding the human experience. We feature exceptional literature that explores the nature of perception and the underpinnings of the social contract. With each book we publish, our goal is to foster a rich, interdisciplinary dialogue that will forge new tools for thinking and engaging with the world.

To support our press and its mission, and for our full catalogue of published titles, please visit us at blpress.org.

Bellevue Literary Press
New York